Eight Days at
The New Grand

Eight Days at The New Grand

Patricia Fawcett

ROBERT HALE · LONDON

ISBN 0 7090 7424 7

Robert Hale Limited
Clerkenwell House
Clerkenwell Green
London EC1R 0HT

2 4 6 8 10 9 7 5 3

Typeset in 11/13 pt Palatino
Derek Doyle & Associates, Liverpool.
Printed in Great Britain by
St Edmundsbury Press, Bury St Edmunds, Suffolk.
Bound by Woolnough Bookbinding Ltd.

Prologue

> *Mr Toby Morrell, owner and managing director*
> *of The New Grand Hotel, Devisham*
> *requests the pleasure of the company of* ————
> *at the grand reopening, following the extensive refurbishment.*
> *Surprise celebrity to perform the opening ceremony.*
> *Champagne reception in The Clovelly Conference Room*
> *with dancing and fireworks at midnight.*

TOBY Morrell walked quickly across the neatly swept gravel towards the hotel entrance, admiring, as always, the vast expanse of the creamy exterior. He wore a personally tailored, up-to-the-minute pale-grey suit, a pink rose in his lapel to complement his tie and a sparkling white shirt with discreet gold cuff-links. At forty-three, after several failed relationships – the bitches – he was desperately seeking Miss Right. He had read somewhere that women were attracted by a successful man and that looks were of secondary importance and he firmly believed that philosophy. Somewhere out there, there was a beautiful, dutiful woman meant just for him.

Entering the foyer, he was once more taken aback by the minimalist appearance, but there was no point in refurbishing, as the decorator Louis had almost screamed at him, if you were going to get cold feet. After all, with the onset of the Millennium and its facelift, the hotel was now renamed The *New* Grand and that had to mean something.

It was the dawn of the twenty-first century and Louis had said it was time to ditch all traces of the Edwardian splendour of The Grand that used to be. Toby had doubts about Louis's sanity but he put it down to his artistic leanings. Frankly, he was glad to say goodbye to him, for his fees had shot the budget through the sky. Still, as Louis had said, what price perfection?

Toby shot a glance towards the chrome and mirrored sweep of the reception desk, noticing the pretty little brunette with the bust, Fiona Jennings, was on duty. He had taken a cursory interest in the hiring of the reception staff and knew them to be lookers all but it was a sexual minefield out there in the workplace and it would be most unwise to mix business with pleasure.

'Alice. . . ?' He caught the eye of the duty manager. 'A word in my office, please.'

'Yes, Mr Morrell.' She was an ash-blonde, far too tall for him, whose manner straddled an odd line between chilling efficiency and hapless confusion.

'Time's getting on,' he reminded her, as they hurried down the corridor towards his office. 'Everything going to plan?'

'Absolutely, sir. At least . . .'

'What?' He motioned her to a seat opposite him at the imposing desk. 'The celebrity has confirmed, hasn't she?'

'Not exactly . . .' Alice flushed, dipping swiftly towards confusion. 'She's full of apologies, being very sweet about it, but she's just discovered she's pregnant, Mr Morrell, and she's having a horrible time. She doesn't think she'll make it. In fact, she definitely won't. She can't walk ten paces without throwing up.'

'She's an actress, isn't she? I thought the show always goes on, no matter what.' Toby cursed under his breath. 'So – only a week to go and you're telling me we haven't got a surprise celebrity?'

'Yes. Well, no.'

'Get one,' he said firmly. 'I don't care who the hell it is so long as it's somebody we recognize. Somebody on television. We need a face, Alice. We've got the entire town council coming along and the Press. Local television have promised to try to fit us in the schedules. I shall be giving an interview, hopefully taking them on a little guided tour.' He looked hard at her. 'Everything else OK? Chef settling in?'

'Oh yes.' She managed a smile. 'At least, he's stopped threatening the staff with a knife.'

'Good. Let me see the nibbles menu as soon as possible.'

He picked up the calendar when she was gone, used a red felt pen to cross through yesterday's date, feeling an uncomfortable anxiety in his chest. A lot was hanging on this grand reopening.

Champagne corks popping followed by spectacular fireworks.

A night to remember.

Seven days to go and counting . . .

Chapter One

Up in Leeds, the view from Amanda Lester's fifth-floor office was of roof-tops. A plane droned across the sky disappearing into the clouds. For a moment, Amanda wished she was on it. It didn't matter much where it was going. She hadn't had a decent long break in ages, but Frank and Jean, the senior partners, never took them either. In this office, taking a holiday of longer than two days was deemed to be an admission of failure. Sooner or later though, someone had to give – and she had a feeling it might be her.

The woman opposite, pale-faced with tightly dragged back hair and dangly ear-rings, looked close to tears but that was nothing new. She had obviously worked herself into a frenzy for this meeting and Amanda, though putting her at her ease, kept it all strictly professional. From past experience, she knew any hint of cosiness was best avoided. A cup of tea certainly but not too much sympathy.

'Leave it with me, Mrs Barr. I'll be in touch with your husband's solicitor Mr Arnold at Webster, Kneale & Hirst directly,' Amanda said, clicking the file shut, prior to winding up the interview. These first meetings with a client were always the trickiest when they were getting to know each other, and she liked to exude an air of confidence, even if, as on this occasion, things did not look good. This one was going to backfire, she felt sure. It was going to be a messy divorce, a fight to the death, with both participants in bitter mood. Amanda recognized the tell-tale signs. The woman was hiding something and that was a worry. Ridiculous, too, because Amanda would find out sooner or later and Amanda was supposed to be on her side, for heaven's sake. There just had to be trust between solicitor and client or it was hopeless. After reiterating that a venomous letter to her husband via Mr Arnold was simply a waste of time and would probably only be read by Arnold himself, time for which he would charge, Amanda stretched out her hand in goodbye.

'Thank you, Miss Lester.' The woman fussed with her things. She was in a sorry state, had rather let herself go. Her nail polish was chipped, her ring finger conspicuously bare. 'It's such a weight off my mind to get things moving. I just want rid of him, as soon as possible. And I want my fair share too. I worked hard to make that house a home and what thanks do I get?'

Amanda showed her very firmly to the door before the flood-gates opened. Thank heavens there were no children of the marriage for them to fight over.

Mrs Barr had to get a final word in though, accompanied by a sad shake of her head.

'You have no idea what a strain I've been under these past months . . .'

Ah, but she had.

Although unmarried at thirty-three, Amanda felt she knew all there was to know about marriage, or rather its failings. As a lawyer specializing now in family law, there were few surprises left. It was so sad that there were so many problems and so many couples unwilling or unable to confront them. When – if – she got married, she reckoned she would have a head-start when it came to problem time. Sometimes, she felt like an agony aunt and just sometimes, she took the problems home with her, especially if they involved children and love-tugging.

Her 4.30 appointment had cancelled, so Amanda, due time off anyway, took the opportunity to finish early and do some shopping. She might as well have a new outfit for this evening. Something other than her black trouser suit. Something glam. She should make some sort of effort with James, even though it felt like a waste of time, whilst he still lived in a little world of his own. A year on now and it was time he snapped out of it, although she wouldn't dream of being so brutal as to tell him. Although, perhaps it's what he needed, a shot in the arm.

'Are you two an item yet?' Henry, her brother, had asked recently. 'You and James. You'd be good for each other, Amanda, and financially he won't let you down. He's doing very nicely.'

She smiled at that. Henry was very keen to keep her on the straight and narrow regarding money matters. Here she was a competent lawyer and he still thought he had to look after her, his little sister. Rather sweet.

'I'm well aware he's financially sound and that's really not an issue.'

He ignored her. A tall gangly man with only a smattering of dark hair left on his head, her brother was such a nice man. 'The company's taking off, you know,' he went on. 'We're on the shortlist for a contract for a very big outfit. Complete new packaging design. They've been losing their market share and are very anxious to upgrade the products.'

'Who?'

'Can't say yet.' He grinned his little boy grin. 'I'll let you know soonest. Anyway, we're going to have to take on temporary staff to cope if we corner it. As I say, James is doing very nicely and *he* doesn't have a family spending all his money for him. That's why he can afford to drive that super car and wear that expensive gear.' He spread his arms wide, showing off checked shirt and baggy cords, his habitual uniform.

There was no earthly point in trying to fool Henry. She made a big play of saying how fulfilled she was with her blossoming career but Henry was never fooled. Amanda wanted the lot, husband, children and career. She had to make sure though that there were no misunderstandings about James.

'I don't care if he is the catch of the season,' she had said. 'We are not an item. He simply uses me as a convenient shoulder to cry on. We are just good friends.'

'You mean he's never. . . ?'

'Henry,' she warned with a slight smile.

'Patience,' he said. 'Give him time. After all, he was married to Victoria for a long time. A perfect marriage at that.'

Amanda said nothing.

'I can't think of many of those off-hand, can you?' Henry went on, shaking his head in bewilderment. 'There's me and Ellie, of course.'

'You two are not married,' she reminded him.

'That's right, neither we are,' he said in some surprise. 'It's

10

Ellie's fault,' he added with a grimace. 'She won't consider it. Relishes her freedom.'

There was no point arguing that one either.

As Henry worked with James, it was easy enough to concoct these dinner parties, without it looking like he was trying too much. Tonight, it would be eight people for dinner. Eight people sitting on an odd selection of chairs round the big oval table Ellie had rescued from a house sale. Ellie excelled in discovering treasures in old houses or salvage tips. They would dine in the immense morning-room of their shambling, rambling house. Despite a few minor discomforts from the seating arrangements, Henry and Ellie knew how to entertain. Masses of good simple food and excellent wine.

Tonight there would be Henry and Ellie, Henry's darling and mother of his two children, a couple of doctors and a dreary couple who were doing up a cottage and talked of nothing else. Making up the numbers, herself and James.

Amanda checked her watch as she hurried into Harvey Nichols. This was a rare treat but she felt like splashing out. She would spend a bit more than usual on tonight's dream frock. Maybe get James to look at her for once.

Moments later, snuggled into a long, slinky, dark-red creation, whose price tag she had not yet dared to consider, she contemplated her reflection in the mirror of the spacious fitting-room. She ought to have had her hair done too, but she had given up on the sleek smooth style she craved, letting her brown hair bounce about at will these days. As for make-up, she kept that natural. A touch of lipstick. A dash of blusher perhaps. Perfume was the only item she could not do without and she was extravagant with it, different scents according to her mood.

A knock on the changing-room door: a polite enquiry if madam was all right or did she need to try on the next size after all.

Are you kidding?

'This is fine, thank you,' Amanda said, breathing in.

She smoothed down the dress, admiring the way the quality material showed her figure off to best effect.

Wow!

If this didn't make James Kendall's eyes stick out on stalks, nothing would.

11

Henry and Ellie lived in a lovely leafy avenue of grand houses, bang in the catchment area of an excellent school, houses snapped up eagerly by the middle classes in this pleasant suburb of the city.

'You're hours early,' Ellie complained with a smile, leading Amanda through to the living-room, light and airy with child-unfriendly, off-white sofas and shelves crammed with books. 'What is it with you?'

'Hardly hours. I thought you might appreciate some help. Isn't there usually some large-scale panic at this stage?'

'Never.' Ellie laughed, slumping down on her chair, from which she could stretch to warm her toes on the open hearth in winter. There was no fire tonight but a lovely display of dried flowers in a pewter pot graced the chimney opening. 'I am too organized for my own good tonight,' she said. 'Glad you're here anyway. We can talk.'

'Where's Henry? And the children?' Amanda looked round, missing them, particularly her adorable four-year-old niece.

'The children are at my mum's,' Ellie said. 'And Henry is not back yet. I shall kill him of course. He promised faithfully he would be home early.' She seemed to notice Amanda's disappointment. 'I'm sorry. I know you like to read to them but children are best out of the way at dinner parties and my mother spoils them rotten. They love it there.'

'I know.' Amanda reached for a few nuts, hungry now after a very light lunch. 'It's just as well *your* mum spoils them; it makes up for Enid.'

'That woman. Don't let's start on that. It makes Henry's blood boil.' She took a careful look at Amanda. 'You look fantastic. Where did you get that dress?'

'Harvey Nichols,' Amanda smiled hugely at the question in Ellie's eyes. 'Don't ask. Terribly extravagant.'

'I don't blame you,' Ellie said cheerfully. 'There comes a time when you have to go all out. You had James in mind, did you?'

'What do you mean?'

Ellie laughed. 'Don't pretend. You just light up when he comes into the room. Even Henry notices and you know how useless he is about such things. I'm afraid it's very obvious, love.'

'Is it? Oh goodness.' She reached for more nuts, a whole handful, nibbled earnestly at them. 'Not to him though. James never notices me. Short of striding naked into his office . . .'

They exchanged a broad smile.

'It's early days,' Ellie said. 'Only just over a year since Victoria died. He will get over it but give him time.' She smoothed strands of the reddish-gold hair that framed her pale freckled face and leaned forward to look at the mantel clock. 'Five minutes and I have to check things in the kitchen.'

'I'll give you a hand,' Amanda said automatically, thinking about Victoria.

Ellie was doing the same. 'The trouble with Victoria,' she began, fiddling with the belt of the blue flowery-print dress she was fond of wearing for entertaining. 'The trouble with Victoria was that she was a total shambles emotionally. You never knew where you were with her. Did you know anybody who actually liked her?'

Trying to be generous, Amanda considered the question. 'No,' she admitted at last. 'I admired her,' she added quickly. 'She was damned good at her job. So talented, according to Henry.'

'Oh yes, there was that,' Ellie said, not impressed. 'But she was a complete pain in the neck, wasn't she?' She paused, before producing a passable imitation of Victoria's breathless, little-girl-lost voice. 'Oh Ellie, I do wish you and Henry would get married. I can so recommend it. James and I are blissfully happy.'

Uncomfortable suddenly, Amanda could only manage a tight smile. After all, Victoria was not here to defend herself.

'Sorry.' Ellie pulled an apologetic face, stood up. 'Must look in the oven. No, sit there, it won't take two of us. Have a drink if you like. Help yourself.'

Amanda decided to wait for the dinner wine. Relaxing, as well as she could in the enormously expensive dress, she took in the lovely calm of Ellie's living-room and thought about James.

She had met James for the first time some years ago, shortly after he and Henry set up in business together. They were both graphic designers, previously colleagues at MacMillan Associates, a prosperous, long established if rather ungainly outfit, according to Henry.

Victoria was also a colleague. Hailing from a wealthy Yorkshire family, she found her way into MacMillan's via a leg up from an uncle who knew the big chief, her appointment immediately getting everybody's back up. She was only partly qualified but infuriatingly possessed a natural flair that made something of a mockery of paper qualifications. Her ideas might be of the sweetly naïve variety but they did cause others to ponder on why they hadn't thought of that themselves. Within months of her arriving on the scene, she and James were together and, a year on, they married.

It didn't take long, according to Henry – everything was according to Henry – before James became totally fed up with working with his wife, as she rapidly shot up the company ladder, ending up with a big office, a secretary, a car and, worse, her own parking space. Typical man that he should mind that when he had to make do with a particularly awkward staff car-park. Amanda scoffed at that and felt a moment's sympathy for Victoria who seemed to be short on the congratulations she deserved.

But that was before she met her.

She was not proud of the way she took an instant dislike to her, to the blonde, blue-eyed fluffiness, a throwback to those fifties Hollywood film stars, but it might have been something to do with the way she felt about James. Meeting *him* for the first time was ingrained in her soul. She was snatching a lunch-break and she popped into Henry's office to pass on one of Enid's terse messages.

'I'm fed up acting as go-between,' she told him, after delivering it. 'It's ridiculous. It's high time you and Mother made it up.'

'I will speak to her when she apologizes to Ellie,' Henry said firmly. 'And not before.'

'Oh, you two!' Amanda said, with neither the time nor the inclination to carry on trying to persuade. Enid, their mother, was just as bad. Turning abruptly, in order to make a huffy exit, she bumped into somebody just coming in and there followed

14

one of those daft moments when they each did a little dance before smiling and muttering apologies.

'You haven't met James Kendall, have you?' Henry said, his annoyance quickly forgotten as he introduced them.

'Hi . . .'

It was a combination of things that did it, any of which on its own would not constitute such a big deal, but together it seemed that James Kendall was simply the whole lot rolled into one and it took just a single glance, a very firm handshake and a few moments' closeness to realize it. Afterwards, she could not recall what she said, what he said, what Henry said.

If that was what being hit by Cupid's arrow meant, then she did indeed experience a quite physical sting, followed by a rosy numbness. Of course, she would never in a million years own up to that, for it was just too ridiculous for words. In her line of work, she was dealing constantly with romances that had long fizzled out, leaving bitter dregs.

Rushing back to her own office, Amanda spent the rest of the afternoon operating on professional autopilot, when all she could think about was James.

It didn't take long to discover he was, of course, happily married to Victoria, a tall, beautiful, willowy blonde – everything she was not.

But now he was widowed, and brutal though it was, it was time he shook himself free of her.

From the grave, Victoria still held on to him.

One of the dinner guests that evening was a psychiatrist, a woman with a round face and spectacles to match. She was squeezed into a baby-pink top, one or maybe two sizes too small, powdered breasts provocatively peeping out every time she leaned forward. After the usual innocuous dinner-party chat, she turned her attention to James and with just a couple of well-aimed questions succeeded where others had failed in prising a spectacular torrent of information out of him.

Amanda and Ellie exchanged a worried look, for James was unpredictable when Victoria was mentioned but Ellie's attempt at a diversion failed, as the psychiatrist, despite a well-meaning nudge from her partner, continued to probe. She apologized for this, saying she had a problem about leaving work at the office and that, if it annoyed them, they were just to say and she would tell them about her hobby, which happened to be quilting. Seeing James gamely trying to express his feelings as if he were lying on her consulting-room couch, Amanda felt a sudden sharp irritation.

If he wouldn't tell this woman to get lost, she would.

'Leave it, Jennifer . . .' she interrupted. 'I really don't think James wants to talk about it.'

'Oh, I'm so sorry. Although perhaps you should let James decide that for himself,' the psychiatrist said, her sympathetic look directed squarely at him.

'I don't mind,' he said, shooting Amanda a glance that said all too plainly she should mind her own business. 'In fact, I'm willing to consider your idea, Jennifer. Maybe it is time I confronted the past.'

'Baloney!' Amanda said, before she could stop herself. Henry was instantly on his feet, refilling glasses, as the others stared at her resentfully.

'I beg your pardon,' Jennifer asked chillingly.

'If I could just explain?' Amanda went on, her smile begging forgiveness. 'If you ask me—'

'Nobody was asking you,' Jennifer said, her own smile now tight, choosing to ignore the warning glance of her partner.

'Oh come on, let's lighten up,' Henry said, putting on his best host voice. 'I'm going to open another bottle. Red again?'

Amanda watched as he disappeared. She was not going to let this go, not yet, not until she had made her point.

'Let's take giving up smoking,' she began again. 'When you decide to quit, you find yourself confronted with all these cures: nicotine patches, hypnotism, substitute gums. Whatever. All this when all you really need is willpower.'

James laughed, seeming in an odd way almost to be enjoying this.

'How can you compare giving up smoking, Amanda, to what happened to me?'

'Why not? No matter what your problem is, trivial or monumental, you have to look at what it's doing to you and decide to do something about it. In my case, smoking was addictive, smelly and my fingers were starting to stain. I was also beginning to be treated like a leper in the office. So, I stopped.'

'Good for you,' the psychiatrist's partner said warmly. 'That's what I keep telling Jennifer. She really ought to know better, but she insists it calms her nerves.'

Jennifer gave him a look that clearly said there would be nothing doing when *they* got home tonight.

'I agree with Amanda,' the woman doing up the cottage said. 'Look at us. Everyone said we were fools to take on such an enormous project but we were determined.'

Amanda smiled at her, grateful for the support, although she did not quite see the point of that but, sensing she was gaining ground, she decided she now had nothing to lose.

'Forget all about going back to your honeymoon hotel,' she pleaded, turning back to James. 'It's a year since Victoria died and you now have to make a big effort to forget her, or at least to stop remembering her so vividly. You have to get on with your life.'

'Amanda!' Ellie was clearly shocked. 'What a terrible thing to say! She doesn't mean it, James.'

'Yes I do. I wouldn't say it if I didn't mean it. Going back to the honeymoon hotel is crazy. It will only stir everything up again.'

'With respect . . .' Jennifer's breasts heaved. 'Perhaps I am just a tad more qualified than you, Amanda, to dispense this sort of advice and I am seriously recommending that he gives it a try. It is not the advice I would give to everybody but it is what James needs to do.'

'And there speaks the expert,' Henry said, passing Amanda the cheese with a big-brother look that told her to stop it at once. 'I should book a room tomorrow, James, if I were you.'

'I might do that,' he said, glancing mischievously at Amanda. 'Why don't you come with me?'

'Come with you?' she said faintly, feeling herself blush. 'What for?'

'To keep me company of course. What else?' He was relaxed, smiling in fact. 'I'll book two rooms.'

She wished he had not said that, the implication clear, because it produced a snigger from the couple with the cottage and she was grateful for Ellie's intervention with the coffee tray. Recovering herself, Amanda thanked him for the offer but it was out of the question. She had far too much work to do, clients to consider and she couldn't just rush off on a whim.

'Neither can he.' Henry said drily. 'But I can see that's just what he's going to do.'

Chapter Two

JAMES, stuck in standing traffic beyond Bristol, switched off his
engine and contemplated a long wait.

With nothing else to do, other than catch the eye of a burly,
white-vested lorry driver smoking and fuming beside him,
James thought about last week's dinner party.

If he hadn't gone to that, he wouldn't be here now.

If that soothing voiced woman doctor hadn't sounded so
convincing, he would not be stuck here, *en route* for Devon.
However, if you were at a party with a fully-blown psychiatrist,
you might as well take advantage of the free advice offered and
he told himself he needed a break anyway. He was jaded after a
long, busy winter.

Even so, as the miles rolled by, the idea seemed ever more
stupid. That dinner party had been quite an eye-opener and it
worried him that his friends were becoming crushingly fed up
with his moods, losing patience with him.

Henry had insisted they could manage without him and,
although not quite believing it, James had taken him at his word.
After all, hadn't his New Year resolution been to 'go for it'?

As the traffic started moving at last, James found himself
relaxing. The secret of Devon was to pace yourself properly.
Slow down. He could hear Victoria as if she was here beside him
and somehow he felt it was she who eventually pointed out the
old signpost with its selection of village names. Take your pick,
all idyllic sounding. The signpost was still leaning after all these
years and why was that no real surprise? The place he wanted
was on the upward slant, heavenwards, and James indicated left
and headed on.

Memories began to kick in as he squeezed the car over as far as it would go, brushing against high grassy banks when other vehicles edged by in the narrow lanes. At last, a slightly wider road and he pushed on, anxious to be done with it.

'Not far now,' he muttered, as if she were here beside him.

He knew he had to get out of the habit of talking aloud to her but people coped with death in different ways and this was his. He could not quite let her go, not yet, not even after a whole year, twelve long months, fifty-two weeks.

It did not seem like a year. It was as if the clock had stopped after it happened but now, with the first anniversary out of the way, time was back to spinning out of control. He was only thirty-nine, he reminded himself, and he refused to believe it was all over, but before it could go on, he had somehow to click the door on the past. And that was why he was here for, fourteen years ago, he and Victoria had been here too.

On their honeymoon.

At what was then simply The Grand. The Grand Hotel, Devisham.

Despite what that psychiatrist had said, he still worried that this idea was seriously defective, smacking as it did of pure indulgence. Maybe Amanda was right after all.

Very up front, Amanda. He smiled a bit, recalling her unapologetic stare from those sometimes serious brown eyes, as murmurs of dissent had started up all around at her blunt words. She was wearing a cracker of a red dress, ankle length but slit to the thigh as he had been quick to notice. She could be quite sexy if she put her mind to it and sometimes, just sometimes, a little hankering for her started up, but it always stopped. Victoria's image prevented it going further, for Victoria had not liked her.

He pulled into the car-park of the hotel at last – The New Grand now – stepping out into a pleasant warmth. He stretched, then stood and stared, the view from here of the tumbling gardens and the pretty harbour long forgotten but instantly remembered. Turning from it reluctantly, he heaved his bags out of the boot and strode in.

Never mind what Amanda said, it was time to bite the bullet.

*

From the hotel veranda, Sophie Willis had spent most of the afternoon idly watching the comings and goings in reception. It had been a glorious day, one of those great early summer days that produce a rare optimism in English hearts.

She had taken the baby for a walk in the morning but, after lunch, Sophie took the opportunity of catching up on some reading and some people-watching too whilst Lily slept.

Saturday was very busy and there had been a steady stream of arrivals and departures. After three days, she felt like an old hand already and she and Lily had quickly settled into a routine. Routine was important for babies and Lily's had been disrupted but she was such a good baby and she had adjusted.

All they needed, the two of them, was a rest. Sophie looked on this time away as a retreat, a time for contemplation, for reflection about the future and where it was leading.

If it was leading anywhere . . . she stopped that thought in its tracks.

Think positive. Positive thoughts, positive deeds. And, in the end, it would all resolve itself. Life had a habit of doing that.

Something had happened recently – something she could not quite remember – but she had needed the anonymity of a seaside hotel and when she thought of seaside, she thought of Devisham where she had spent one of her happiest childhood holidays.

She could remember this hotel quite clearly, sprawling amongst its close-cropped lawns, a sparkle of four stardom. At the edge of the lawns, paths led steeply down through the terraced gardens to the shingly beach and harbour. It had recently, according to the owner Mr Morrell, been given a facelift to go with the name change. Not just a nip and tuck, he had explained earnestly, but a positive transformation. No expense spared. Mr Toby Morrell, whose face with its swept-back hair beamed out of the top of the staff pyramid on display in reception, made a point of having a few words with each guest in turn. Sophie found him polite but hard work and Lily had been deeply unimpressed by his blatant attempt to win her over, howling and forcing a hasty departure.

Sophie mostly ignored the other lounges Mr Morrell recommended, preferring to sit on this comfortable veranda that she suspected to be the one place to escape the refurbishment. It had a colonial feel with its cool, tiled floor, potted palms, flowery sofas and cane chairs and she and Lily spent much of the day here.

It was a fifteen-minute trek to the town, a bustling little place with some specialist shops and even a couple of designer boutiques amongst the chandleries around the quay. In the height of the season, Devisham with its single entry road was incredibly difficult to get in and out of, impossible to park in and, as a result, visitors with cars tended to become entrenched, opting for a hassle-free car-less existence.

After three days, Sophie felt she had explored anew every nook and cranny, the quaint little rows of fishermen's cottages clustered round the harbour, the bigger houses on the hilltop. All this activity was wrapped around Lily's daily schedule of feeds, changes and whatnots. When she thought of how her life had been before Lily, she marvelled at what on earth she had done with her time. Had there been life before?

Lily, stirring, half awake, was making her funny windy face and Sophie shifted her position, rubbing the baby's back, until the wind released in a burp and dribble. At four months and thirteen pounds and a bit, she was beginning to feel rather solid.

'Is that better, you little sack of potatoes?' she said soothingly, her attention caught by a new arrival at reception.

He was casually leaning against the desk and, without doubt, her body language giving it away, the receptionist, the full-lipped voluptuous brunette, was making eyes at him. Sophie smiled gently in womanly agreement.

He was some distance away, but that did not matter because there was just something about him, something nice, that she liked at once. It was a failing of hers in a way, this snap judgement. She did it with places, houses and, more worryingly, people. It could lead to major errors of judgement and her marriage to Roger was proof of that.

The man had completed his checking in and was being handed keys and so forth. He was just over middle height, slim but not thin, dark-haired and handsome enough, although he did not possess the peacock demeanour of Roger. Modestly unassuming then which was nice, wearing expensive casuals and here for a while judging by the bags.

22

*

'If you need anything else, sir, just ask . . .'

Fiona Jennings, in her uniform of short, flared black skirt and smart, fitted red top, flashed him a smile, willing him to notice her. She would be sacked for cavorting with a guest but who cared about that? She had long since decided that her career was going nowhere, so the alternative in her quest for a life of idle luxury was to hook a man. A man of means.

She was dating someone just now but he was not shaping up – not in monetary terms – and she would ditch him soon. So, she was prowling again and trying to insinuate herself into the yachting set. Easier said than done for they were cliquey beyond belief and, frankly, boring.

She sized up the man opposite immediately. Very all right. Sexy credit card too, one of those super ones that meant you earned quite enough, thank you. He lived in Leeds, which was a shame, for it sounded very northern and was therefore sure to be grim. She could help him use that credit card with some flair and, more to the point, it would not be exactly disastrous to wake up with him beside her. Even so, on a purely practical level, her heart sank at the thought of Leeds. Cloth caps and whippets, or was that Manchester? Or Newcastle? They were all the same to her. Grim.

There had to be somebody else.

For some time past, she had been considering making a play for Toby Morrell but it had to be done carefully and she had decided not to tell the other girls. He could sack her if he took offence, but what had she got to lose? A crummy job that starved her of serious funds. Setting aside Toby's looks which left a lot to be desired and his lack of inches, he had quite a bit going for him. He was unattached and beginning to look desperate. He lived in one of those up-market apartments down by the harbour, he drove a fabulous car and he treated women with a certain old-fashioned courtesy that the other girls laughed at but that she found appealing. After all, she could always shut her eyes and pretend he was Robson Green. Now, he was a north-erner she could definitely fancy.

Fiona watched as James Kendall, having declined the assistance of a porter, effortlessly lifted his bags and made his way up the stairs.

Sophie watched too, hugging the baby to her. She thought soberly that it was a pity she had nothing better to do because her love life was on hold just now, until she got things sorted out.

As if reading her mind, the man glanced her way, returning the social smile she felt obliged to give. Using Lily as a shield, in case he looked her way again, Sophie watched him fairly bounding up the steps.

To her surprise, the glance had caused a flutter of excitement and she looked after him thoughtfully. She normally took dinner in her room so that she could be with Lily, but perhaps she might take advantage of the baby-sitting service tonight and dine in the restaurant.

Get her glad rags on. Why not? she deserved a break.

Beatrice Bell, an octogenarian and long-term resident of The New Grand, had spent a most enjoyable morning relaxing under a parasol in the gardens. Quite warm enough. Surprisingly so for England even in summer. People were splashing in the outdoor pool but Bea thought that most unwise.

She never swam. Even when she and her husband Oscar had their own pool at the plantation house in Virginia, she never swam. In her opinion, chlorinated water chilled the bones and there was no telling what swallowing it did for your insides.

She was now taking tea on the veranda terrace. She spooned strawberry jam on to her scone, applied a dollop of clotted cream and observed Sophie watching the latest arrival at the reception desk. Following her gaze, screwing up her own aged eyes and concentrating, Bea, even allowing for her wobbly vision, could make out that he struck a handsome figure.

What fun!

Bea regarded all the guests as fair game, acquainting herself with as many as possible over the short time they strayed into her own life. Snatches of their lives, caught in a freeze-frame almost, were so very interesting and it was amazing what one found out when people were off-guard and relaxed. All you had to do was display a sympathetic manner and you were in grave danger, thank the Lord, of being told innermost secrets.

Women guests, pointedly alone with a baby, were rare.

As were lone handsome men.

Unless Bea was much mistaken, after months of sheer boredom when it came to roses and romance, the sparkling start of a love affair was on the cards.

Chapter Three

JAMES was settling in his room, a superior sea-view with balcony. Number thirteen, the very same room and he could not quite believe the coincidence. Still, in for a penny, in for a pound as Amanda would say. It would amuse her no end.

He took stock of the room, different after all these years, the floor now sanded and polished, a selection of rose-pink rugs lying on it, heavy, shot-silk drapes and cream, sheer inners. The bathroom, Italian marble, sparkled and James was relieved that standards were still high. It had shaken off all suspicion of faded grandeur and was all it was cracked up to be in the shamelessly boastful brochure.

Toby Morrell beamed up from the information folder on the table. James picked it up and glanced at it, noting that the rules – for the comfort of our guests – extended to a full page.

Tossing aside his bags, he made himself a coffee before stretching out on the bed. Victoria's mother had been sniffy about Devon. There was to be an announcement and photo-graph of the happy couple in *Yorkshire Life* and it simply would not look good enough when most of the bridal couples honey-mooned abroad.

However, because Victoria refused to fly and they could only spare a week away, Devon and Devisham it was. And, even though her mother thought otherwise, the honeymoon idea was a sham for they had been sleeping together – discreetly – for the past six months. James adored his brand new wife, her blonde good looks, her gentleness, her shyness.

Although, there was the problem of the teddy bear.

Lying on the bed now, James glanced over, absurdly expecting to see it there in the position it normally occupied. He had thought it weird but teddy was non-negotiable. Three in a bed had taken on a whole new meaning and his suggestion that she put it away now she was grown-up had met with an astonished refusal.

Before he got too maudlin, James jumped up and went over to the window that opened on to the balcony. The south-westerly sky was perfect and a week of mostly fine dry weather was promised. He flexed his shoulders, feeling the tension already draining away.

He wished Amanda had come with him and perhaps she would have if he had tried harder and not sprung it on her like that. Holidays, he remembered her once yelling, what on earth are they?

It was becoming uncomfortably comfortable being with Amanda and he could think of several reasons why getting in any deeper was just not on. For one, it was too soon. Two, there was Henry and he could not imagine the quirkiness of being Henry's brother-in-law. Three, he liked blondes. Oh, and four . . . for unfathomable reasons, he did not fancy being married to a woman in the legal profession.

Over the past year, Amanda had acted as his unofficial personal counsellor. She was a link back to Victoria, for she had been a friend to both of them more or less, less in Victoria's case. No two ways about it, Amanda had been a lifesaver, kept him sane, and for that he was eternally grateful.

Thank God for work, and thank God for Henry, too. He was aware that, submerged in grief as he had been, he must have been a liability but Henry had never once complained. The original decision to go it alone, just the two of them, was largely forced on them by Victoria, who metamorphosed from his nervous bride into a challenging, powerful career woman. James was aware she was not liked, too distant with the men and downright snotty with the women. So, when Henry approached him with the idea of branching out together, he jumped at the chance.

His coffee was cold.

James roused himself and went to telephone home. He tried Henry's home number and his mobile but neither came to anything so he rang Amanda and, after a few rings, her answering machine switched on.

'It's me,' he said, after the beep. 'Can you get a message to Henry? I think one of the kids must have been messing about with the phone. Can you remind him about the Pattley contract? The papers must go out Monday. Thanks. I'll be in touch.'

Showering the journey away, he found himself whistling, guilty as always when he did something like that. Surely Victoria would have understood. She would not want him to shrivel up and die too. She would have wanted him to get a new life, a new wife, although, if he was honest, he wouldn't bank on that. They had not discussed things like that, in fact at the last they had found it difficult to discuss anything.

The phone rang as he was towelling himself dry and, wrapping the big towel round his waist, he went to answer it.

'Only me,' she said.

'Amanda! You needn't have bothered to ring back,' he said at once.

'I had to,' she said coolly. 'I lost the last bit of your message. When have the papers to be out? You're right incidentally about Henry's phone: it's dead.'

With a sigh, he repeated the message.

'OK. Got it. I will let him know, but I suspect he will know already. Stop fussing, James, for goodness' sake. Forget work.'

'Like you can,' he reminded her, for she was the world's worst at switching off.

They met up occasionally for lunch, both stressed out, grumbling together over a pizza. But that was about it, as far as it went. If he ever made a lunge for Amanda, he just knew that somewhere up there Victoria would be watching and disapproving. And how did he explain that to somebody as down to earth as Amanda?

'Have you eaten yet?' she enquired.

'Not yet.' He glanced at the clock. 'Shortly.'

'Lucky you. Jacket and tie?'

'You bet.'

'Did you have a good journey down?' she went on, obviously yawning heavily into the phone.

'Could have been better, thanks.'

She clicked her tongue. 'I thought as much. I did warn you about that stretch near Birmingham. You were due to hit it at the wrong time of day.'

He smiled. She took her route planning very seriously.

'That was fine. The problem was further down.'

'Oh. Well, you're there now.'

'You think I'm mad, don't you?' he said. 'Mad to be here.'

'Absolutely bonkers. You'd be better listening to me than a psychiatrist. I thought she was shifty-looking and she had no business talking shop at a dinner party. She should jolly well be defrocked or whatever . . .'

He laughed. 'And I don't think she took too much of a shine to you either.'

'If you'd asked me, I'd have recommended a few days in New York. Some glitzy hotel.'

'This is glitzy enough. In fact it lives up to its name. Very grand,' James said, amused by her indignation. 'It's had money spent on it. You should see the bathroom, shower practically big enough for a rugby team.'

'I'm impressed. But Devon, James . . .' She sighed. 'It's so old hat. Have you had your cream tea yet?'

'Don't knock it,' he said lightly, even though he found her remark irritating. 'I suppose there's no chance of you managing a few days off later in the week?'

'Not a hope in hell,' she said. 'I am practically submerged in my clients' affairs. Why do you ask? You're just bored, aren't you, on your own. Give it a chance. After all, you might meet somebody interesting.'

'No chance. I'm not planning a holiday romance, Amanda.'

'Are these things planned?'

He was smiling a little later as he replaced the receiver. Despite the sometimes coldly bright exterior she exuded, there was a warmth about Amanda that always got through to him.

Bearing in mind the dining regulations, he reached for a tie. Victoria had loved dressing up for dinner. A quick look on the way in had confirmed that the dining-room was very smart with a profusion of pink and white and more than its share of sparkling chandeliers.

Picking up the room key, he exited into the calm of the

29

corridor and, bypassing the lift, found his way to the stairs.

Amanda rented a first floor flat in Headingley. With her reasonable salary and because she was on her own, content to drive a Fiat Punto and buy most of her clothes from stores other than Harvey Nichols, it fell well within her means. Henry was on at her to buy. Get your foot in the housing market, he kept saying, and she knew he was right but she was biding her time, waiting for that special relationship to come along when the two of them could choose a house together. Two problems challenged that happy scenario: she was too damned picky and there was James.

James still lived in the large three-storey terraced house, the house he had shared with the blessed Victoria. It reeked of her still, its interior oyster silk and dark polished antiques, lace mats and little bowls of long defunct pot-pourri. James's home was very upmarket and in a much sought after area, like Henry's. Annoyingly, James seemed content to stay put and had not changed things much. Amanda had made a few tentative suggestions but, although he had not rebuffed her, he hadn't done anything she suggested either.

Poor James. Nothing would ever change until he accepted that Victoria had not been perfect. After her death, he had put her on this pedestal and there she would stay.

It was good to hear his voice, even though he had contacted her only in passing. Brushing a slightly gloomy feeling aside, she decided to cheer herself up by making an effort with her meal tonight, but it was only as she was assembling the ingredients for a recipe by Delia Smith that it dawned she was short of a fairly essential item. Although it was tempting to settle for yet another baked potato shoved into the microwave, she thought otherwise and grabbing her car keys scuttled off to the supermarket.

Returning, armed with three carrier bags, she struggled a moment with her key before almost exploding into the hall at the entrance to her flat. Kicking the door shut, she was taken aback by the presence, far too close, of a heavy breather, although as the man in the ground-floor flat frequently lurked and waylaid her, she ought not to have been surprised.

'You scared me to death,' she accused, managing a nervous

smile, holding on to her bags. 'I've been shopping,' she explained unnecessarily, attempting to bring some normality on to the scene for this was one odd character and she did not want to upset him.

'Amanda – how lucky I bumped into you,' he said, his smile not a pretty sight. As well as bad teeth, his hair was lank and greasy and he shaved badly, nicks and cuts everywhere. A tiny scrap of pink toilet paper still clung to today's blood. 'We're having a party tonight. Just a few friends. Sorry, but it's going to be noisy and you're right above. Why don't you join us? Any time after nine.'

'Thanks but no thanks,' she said firmly. 'I'm up to my eyes in work.'

'All work and no play. You know what they say?'

She could hardly say that she would rather go to a party with Hannibal Lecter than with him. Ellie had said she ought to tell him where to get off but Amanda had no wish to cause trouble with the neighbours, although he was becoming a nuisance.

Up in the safety of her own flat, the meal she eventually produced was actually rather good although it needed somebody sitting opposite to gush about it and tell her what a clever girl she was. Congratulating herself was a bit hollow.

Finishing off her glass of wine, it all seemed suddenly so pathetic. Was this how it was going to be forever? For a mad moment, she even considered getting dressed up for the party downstairs but she wasn't that desperate.

She wondered what James was up to. On the bright side, she had to remain hopeful. After all, she loved him so much that, sooner or later, it would surely dawn on him.

Chapter Four

SOPHIE decided against eating in the dining-room after all and ordered room service as usual. Lily was a bit unsettled after her last feed, letting off little baby bursts of wind and her discomfort was making her cry, so it was not fair to leave her.

She opened the window wide and let in some fresh air. The man who had checked in earlier had moved his car round the back and parked it quite close to her own. She had no intention of driving anywhere whilst she was here. At home, she sometimes felt as if they lived in the car and it was so novel to walk or take the bus and even the ferry across the estuary.

Sophie wondered about the man. On holiday alone.

'I must be mad to be thinking about men, Lily,' she told her, lifting her out of the cot and sniffing her rear end suspiciously. 'Heavens, you pong, little madam.'

Expertly, she attended to the baby's needs. She did not object to being changed and offered assorted gurgles and other new sounds as well as little smiles.

'Right, you horror. Clean again,' Sophie said, laying her on the playmat and talking to her. All this was registering in the little brain. Colours. Shapes. Touch and feel. Sounds. Sophie's voice.

Turning away from Lily, the world revolved a minute as the panic flooded her. What was it? What was it she could not bring to mind?

A polite knock at the door brought her swiftly back to her senses. Her meal had arrived – chicken salad, crusty bread and a bottle of sparkling mineral water – and she smiled at the woman who had brought it up. Mary Parker according to the name tag on the uniform; they had met several times over the last few days. She was in her mid-forties, Sophie guessed, and a faded red-head. A tiny creature, a little round-shouldered with deeply disappointed grey eyes. She was yet another of the hard workers doubling up on an extra shift, she explained to Sophie, as she laid the meal with more enthusiasm than expertise on a little side table. She was covering for another member of staff who had called in sick. Extra money anyway and she could always do with it.

Sophie, reminded, dug in her purse for a tip.

'Thank you.' Mary seemed reluctant to leave, smiling at the baby. 'What a picture she is! Do you just have the one, Mrs Willis?'

Sophie nodded, asking if the dining-room was going to be full this evening.

'You can't get a table for love or money,' Mary told her. 'A party of yachting folk are booked in. Sixty of them. Celebrating something or other. They're eating out on the terrace, so the dining-room's crowded. I shouldn't be saying this but the kitchen staff are at full stretch. He's ranting and raving, that new chef. You should see him with those knives, Mrs Willis. There'll be an accident before long, mark my word, and I know all there is to know about accidents.'

Sensing it might be a long story, Sophie chose not to take her up on it. 'I might go down to dinner tomorrow,' she said. 'Lily's very good so she won't be any trouble.'

'Let reception know by ten-thirty, Mrs Willis,' Mary said with a smile. 'The girls on baby-sitting duty check every ten minutes so you needn't worry.'

Sophie, the familiar knot of anxiety picking at her, ate her meal without enthusiasm when Mary was gone. She would have to make an effort if she went down to dinner tomorrow and it would be no bad thing. She had let herself go a bit lately and she must do something before she retreated into a perpetual decline. It happened to women of her age. Forty next month and she dreaded it as she had once, yesterday it seemed, dreaded being thirty.

She shuddered, looking anxiously at her reflection, checking for wrinkles. This past year with one thing and another had been difficult but, under the circumstances, she did not look too bad.

She had clear hazel eyes, had been having wispy golden tints in her hair for years and she supposed on a good day, when she hadn't been up all night, she would still pass for an attractive woman.

Tomorrow was Sunday but Mary said the shops were mostly open, so perhaps she might go shopping, see if she could get the baby one or two new little dresses. There was a baby boutique that looked promising and she so liked Lily to look feminine with smocked or embroidered dresses.

'Tired, sweetheart?'

She picked her up, cuddled her close, breathing in that special delicious baby smell. On top of the little skull, the pulse beat, reminding her of the child's vulnerability. All the responsibility for this tiny scrap of life was hers. Hers alone. Her love for Lily almost frightened her. If anything happened to Lily, she did not know what she would do. She had let Roger out of her life without regret but Lily was quite different.

On the terrace, partially covered over in case of rain but pleasantly open to the evening air just now, there was what the hotel referred to as a live pianist, singing his heart out to minimum applause from a load of indifferent locals.

'Special party this evening, sir . . . yachtsmen,' the head waiter explained apologetically with the slightest of sniffs. 'We would be very happy to reserve a table on the terrace tomorrow evening if you wish. The good weather is set to continue until the weekend so I understand. In the meantime, we can accommodate you tonight in the dining-room, if that is all right.'

'That will be just fine,' James said, following him to a table in the corner, where he could observe without being too much under scrutiny himself.

The dining-room had changed considerably, but again there was still something of what it had been years ago. Then, he and Victoria had opted for a table in the centre of the room, very much an on-show position, Victoria's confidence on a high now that she was a married woman. He recalled she had looked wonderful in a cornflower-blue dress.

He had told her so. 'It matches your eyes,' he had said.

'I know. And I knew you would notice, darling. Do you know,

you look pretty good yourself? I saw one or two women looking your way as we came in.'

'Did you?' He had grinned. 'That's a wonder. I'm knackered. And I dare say I'll still be knackered in the morning.'

'James . . .' she had frowned, blushed, shushing him as the waiter arrived with their champagne.

No champagne for him tonight, alone at a table meant for two. James studied the menu intently, more intently than he needed to but it was little things like this that did it. He went for a long time now without thinking about her but it was still capable of striking at any damned time. He could see her so clearly, that accusatory blue-eyed stare.

Looking up, he caught the sympathetic gaze of an old lady also dining alone at a nearby table. My God, she firmly believed in dressing for dinner. Grey shimmery dress. A lot of jingly jewellery and the *pièce de résistance,* a helmet of a hat with silver threaded beads, the sort of thing synchronized swimmers wear. A cloche!

They exchanged a nod and a smile.

Beatrice Bell dined precisely at a quarter to eight each evening. Any later, and she was plagued with indigestion and could not sleep.

For the privilege of allowing the hotel to be charmed by her continued presence, she had negotiated a special rate seven years ago and had taken great pleasure in so doing, although money matters were vulgar. She was born into money and married money. Oscar's Virginian family had made their fortune from a mixture of cotton, rice and real estate. Bea's own family tree was aristocratically well documented and she had inherited the lot because her two dear brothers – and her lip trembled at the thought – had been sadly killed in action.

At her table in the dining-room of The New Grand, Bea waited for the emotion to pass. She had looked after the fortune and met with her accountant once a year to discuss how it was bearing up. Unless she lived beyond 102 when there might be a need to cut back, there was no problem. So, she fully intended to live out the rest of her life here.

Bea Bell might be very old but she still cared greatly for her appearance. The more or less complete loss of hair was a nuisance and wigs were far too hot to wear all the time so she chose to wear a hat, even in bed. She wore silk or cashmere garments and possessed no casual clothes whatsoever.

She was thin but then she always had been. Thin then but with shapely hands that she took great pride in. She had them manicured weekly at the beauty salon in Fore Street, attended to by a sweet little girl called Lucy. She had tried the beauty parlour here in the hotel but the girl who had attended her had been silent and unresponsive and one needed an audience for gossip. This evening, Bea's perfectly shaped nails were painted a silvery pink. In addition to the pearl choker with diamond centrepiece around her neck, on her fingers gleamed an array of rings including the impressive rock Oscar had bought her just before his death.

She smiled at the young man, one of the new guests, the same young man who had caused quite a stir when he checked in. There was a sadness about him, just now a faraway look in his eyes. Very alone, poor darling. Bea wished the young woman with the baby, Mrs Sophie Willis, had come down to dinner. Pity about the child. A baby was an encumbrance when it came to beginning a love affair. To conduct an affair successfully, one had to be clutter free.

'Dessert, Ms Bell?'

She waved the waiter aside disdainfully. He ought to know by now. She never took dessert, simply a pot of peppermint tea.

The young man was not strictly at ease. Bea put it down to the fact that it was his first night and he knew nobody. She therefore saw it as her Christian duty to engage him in conversation, not now for she was exhausted but, if she were to see him tomorrow, she might.

She had no qualms about meddling.

Bea poured herself another cup of tea but, with her attention caught by the antics of a novice waiter, she slopped the tea on to the snowy white linen dinner cloth.

Not quite under her breath, she swore.

Oscar had taught her. If you are going to swear, Bea honey, he told her, for the love of the Lord, do it with flair.

*

Concentrating like merry hell on not dropping anything on this his first duty proper, the waiter could have sworn he heard the old bag mutter something as he squeezed past her table to avoid a wandering guest. It made him very nearly let the top plate slip.

Never in a month of Sundays, he decided, proudly presenting the desserts intact to his table although he did spare a quick glance at the old prune as he swivelled back. Money to burn, they said, a figure like a coat hanger and a face, pale and rouged like a china doll, hair never to be seen under those barmy hats.

Tight-arsed as a tipper, he was informed, so he wasn't going to waste much time on her.

Although, you never could tell with some of these oldies.

By half past ten, following a stroll by the harbour in distinctly chillier air, the water choppy now and not so inviting, James was back in his room. He switched channels on the television lazily, but nothing interested him and he switched off. Amanda, via Henry, had thoughtfully dropped off some paperbacks but he was in no mood for reading.

His intention was that this holiday would finally get Victoria out of his system. Unpleasant as that sounded, it was the only way. He was rotten company these days and women were put off by it. Oh sure, you got the sympathy vote at first and they were always madly curious but, after a few dates, they did expect that your interest would have transferred to them.

The trouble was, not wanting to dwell on the bad bits, she came over as practically perfect and women, women like Amanda, could not compete with perfection. He did not want a quickie either, he wanted another wife, but someone completely different from Victoria.

With a sigh, James reached for a book. A couple of thrillers, a heavyweight biography and one of the runners-up in last year's Booker Prize.

He opted for that, opened the book but could not concentrate.

Victoria's presence was suddenly very strong.

She had refused a stroll that first evening after dinner and James was happy to go along with that, for he had suggested it only because he thought it might relax her. She looked tense, but he put it down to the excitement of the day.

She wanted to talk. She wanted of all things to discuss future plans. Her earnest look as she stood there, still fully dressed, ought to have been a warning and when she picked up the worse-for-wear teddy bear, who was wearing a blue bow this evening, it ought to have been a double warning.

Determined not to upset her, not tonight of all nights, he ran a bath and climbed into it, letting her talk from the safety of the open door, for she was uncomfortable with nakedness, hers and his. With a sinking heart, he listened to what she had to say. She wanted a baby straightaway.

It took him by surprise for, discussing it briefly before, they had decided to wait a few years and this change of mind was completely mad. He told her as much. Financially, it would be crazy. With the big chief practically under her thumb, the office promotion they all craved was hers for the taking.

She peeped in, explaining that the promotion was no problem. She would have a discreet word and MacMillan would surely give James the promotion instead. He would do it for her.

No bloody way! He exited the bath in a wet, slippery, soapy flurry, furiously towelling himself dry. He had never sucked up to the likes of MacMillan and he was not starting now. He would resign first.

With them both suffering an attack of huffiness, the love-making that followed came about more because it was felt to be obligatory on what was after all their wedding night, rather than spontaneous.

And the teddy observed it all silently from the pillow.

Looking back, James supposed, that as honeymoons go, the start could have been better.

He realized he had read the first page of the book several times and was none the wiser. He put it aside, switched off the lamp and let his eyes adjust to the gloom. There were distant cheerful voices from the shore but they passed by and the silence that followed was night-time heavy.

The empty side of the bed was very empty.

Just before he fell asleep, James wondered if Amanda had got that message through to Henry.

Amanda was in bed, too, surrounded by paperwork and crumbs from the bedtime toast she had consumed. From down below, music thudded and laughter, but she had no regrets. The incident downstairs though with that fate-worse-than-death character had formed up the resolution that she had to look for somewhere else to live.

She returned her attention to the matter in hand, some preliminary notes on current cases that she would pass on to the office secretary next week. She loved her work. She knew she grumbled like hell about it but she could not imagine life without it. She was not cut out for the domestic thing and when she got married, if she got married, it would be on that understanding.

Although ... she sighed and dumped everything on the bedside table before switching off the light. She had this funny feeling that, for James, she would compromise all ends up and throw all her grand ideals out of the window.

Just like Ellie.

Down below, the music turned up a notch.

Outside, two streets away, the church clock chimed a stately one o'clock.

Tense and infuriated, she thought determinedly about fields of fragrant lavender and tried to compose herself for sleep.

Chapter Five

Sunday

TOBY Morrell was awake at six after a restless night. In his dream or rather nightmare, the new chef had got the culinary hump and shot himself, bleeding all over the iced cake – a replica of the hotel – that was to form the centrepiece of the celebratory buffet on Saturday evening.

Toby was only half amused at the anxiety that had fuelled the dream. He simply could not relax, he would not relax until the grand reopening was successfully concluded. He had a lot to prove. He had to prove to his father, who thought he could do nothing right, that he in fact could. He had waited a long time for the reins to pass to him and this would be the first big event he had organized without his father breathing down his neck and trying to cut costs.

His father had grown stale and increasingly tight in the last few years, had just accumulated profits and let things slide. The chef, that old one, had been complacent and dull. There had been too many pieces of furniture in odd spots covering worn bits in the carpet, the faded artwork hanging on embossed-walls was horrendous and there was a limit to the life of pink velvet curtains.

A new broom, Toby had not only swept clean, he had annihilated all traces of the past, one of the reasons for the name change, which had been costly in its own right with new stationery, brochures, linen and so on. In the process, he had come to the notice of the big boys in the hotel trade, dangling golden carrots, but no way was he going under to a hotel chain. The New Grand was a one-off, privately managed and run, and it would remain so as long as he had breath in his body. One day, the next generation – he felt a lump in his throat when he thought of the son he might have – one day, he would take over.

Unfortunately, there was a price to pay for the renovation and the quotation from the building firm had proved to be a joke. They blamed the Millennium which had apparently put up the price of their basics – paint, sand and cement – like nobody's business. Cornish cowboys! Toby had very nearly delayed delivery of his new midnight-blue luxury limousine but he consoled himself by deciding that the £35,000 was a mere drop in the ocean and image was tremendously important. If he drove a Ford Ka, what would that tell the guests?

Over breakfast though – orange juice and a banana because he was watching his weight – he gloomily considered the loose cannons he was working with: a new, as yet unproved, chef; a celebrity yet to be confirmed; a duty manager in Alice who could go either way.

Christ! The potential cock-up factor was enormous.

And already, in a lot of people's diaries in Devisham and district, days were being crossed off. Dinner suits were at the cleaners. Posh frocks were being bought. Reporters' pencils were being sharpened. The mayor was polishing his chain of office. The sweet little girl who was presenting the bouquet to the celebrity was in full rehearsal.

Nothing must go wrong.

Six days to go and counting . . .

It rained during the night and, up at half past two and then at five with the baby, Sophie found it difficult to go back to sleep. Peering out of the window, she could see rain slanting across the partially lit courtyard. Letting the curtain drop, she quietly made herself a cup of tea, creeping past Lily's cot although, having gobbled her bottle, she was now out for the count.

Sophie sipped her tea, catching a glimpse of her sleepy tousled self in the mirror. On Monday, she had an appointment with the hotel hairdresser and she and Lily would spend a lovely pampered morning there. A complete restyle and colour. She needed a new look. Sharper. Sexier.

They were down in the hotel dining-room at 8.30, first in. Sophie was wearing a dress, tights and heels because it was Sunday. Stupid really, for who cared a fig these days. However, it was ingrained in her, courtesy of her parents, and hard to shake off. She felt guilty that she would not attend church, but she could not bring herself to do so. Hadn't she been to church recently on a very sad occasion? She could not remember why or when and it was so infuriating that her memory should play these tricks.

In her pram, Lily, in a beautiful hand-smocked little dress and matching bloomer pants slept the sleep of the innocent.

Someone came into the dining-room, track-suited, a fresh-faced girl who selected a large green apple and a glass of juice for her breakfast. On her way past them, she stopped and smiled down at Lily.

'What a lovely baby!'

Sophie smiled. 'Have you been out jogging? Or to the gym?'

'Jogging. The rain's cleared,' the girl replied, munching on her apple. 'I've been round the harbour and up through the town.'

'You look very fit. Scarcely puffing,' Sophie commented in a friendly fashion, gently drawing the conversation along, for she had nothing better to do.

'I have to keep up with my training,' the girl said shyly. 'I'm in a cross-country event next week back home.'

'I used to run,' Sophie said, unable to stop herself. 'Quite a lot of junior events.'

'My goodness!' The girl seemed astonished, rather to Sophie's chagrin. 'What was your race?'

'Sprint and relay. Long time ago, of course. My coach had high hopes for me, but I gave it up. Let him down I suppose.'

'Why did you give up?' The girl sat down opposite. 'Were you injured?'

Easy to say she was but no, she would be honest. 'I got fed up,' she said simply. 'And if you lose your enthusiasm, you might as well pack it in.'

'It can be awful sometimes,' the girl agreed, although there was a certain smugness in her voice.

Sophie sighed as it all thundered back. That pounding in her heart as she pushed herself. Concentration such as she had never known before or since. 'I started to think about what I was missing,' she went on, desperate to explain. 'It had become a chore, all those punishing sessions. They play havoc with your social life, don't they?'

'Don't I know it?' the girl said.

'Don't let your school work slide,' Sophie said, hardly believing she had uttered such mumsy words. 'Sorry, I'm sure you know that.'

'I do. I want to go to medical school but I don't see why I can't do both.'

'Oh, good. Then you'll be terribly busy, won't you?'

'Incredibly. But you have to make sacrifices in life if what you want is important enough to you.'

'Quite.' Sophie looked at her thoughtfully, not sure if that was her coach talking.

She wished her well in the cross-country event, finished her breakfast in silence when the girl was gone. She admired her determination and the way she talked glibly of sacrifice. She was young though and the young were apt to have a very rosy view of life.

Life was full of 'if onlys'.

If only she had pressed on with her own running career, gritted her teeth and shrugged off the pain barrier, she might well have earned that Olympic medal. As it was, at seventeen and suddenly free of what she had come to regard as wearisome training schedules she broke free with a vengeance. Coming a little late to the social scene her contemporaries had been part of for a year at least, she dived wholeheartedly into it. Boys of her own age she dismissed, setting her sights on someone older and wiser.

Roger Willis was all of that.

'Sophie? That is a beautiful name. Where have you been all my life?' was his opening smiling gambit.

He was tall and dark and had a smile that melted your insides.

He cut an heroic figure and could have easily graced the pages of all those silly romances the girls were passing around.

She really ought to have known better.

*

James woke early and, wouldn't you just know it, with an idea buzzing in his mind. Too good to forget and, within minutes of waking, he was downing his first coffee of the day, sketching at the desk in the corner. He worked best full to the brim with caffeine which at the end had infuriated Victoria who was very health conscious.

'I'm sorry, James,' she said to him once, tidying up after a dinner party, 'but you will have to tell Henry's sister that she can't smoke in this house.' She sniffed the air. 'It will lie around for days.'

'I'm not telling Amanda that,' he said, not thrilled with the smell either but unhappy at the thought of making guests unwelcome. 'Open some windows if it bothers you that much.'

'Why won't you tell her? Scared of upsetting her?' She smiled a little. 'She is a bit fierce, isn't she? I've always thought there's something a little funny about girls who study law. So intense. Never mind, I shall tell her myself. I'm not afraid of her.'

'There may be no need. She's trying to give up, Henry says.'

And within the month, Amanda had done just that.

Concentrating hard, James worked on, taking a break at last when he was satisfied with the rough. He and Henry had had the initial meeting with Simmons Supermarket Group. The management team wanted to upgrade their own brand label, getting away from the 'cheap' connotation and concentrating on the value aspect. Tricky but challenging and the design had to be suitable for a wide range of materials, paper, plastic, card, bottles and so on.

And today, he thought he might have cracked it. Bold, eye-catching yet simple.

Deciding he could go no further without technical checks and Henry's go-ahead, he pushed the design aside, going out on to the balcony. The view had not changed and the tubs were still filled with pink flowers. He took it all in, the sparkle of the morning sea, the moist green of the lawns after the heavy overnight rain. The clouds had passed over and it was bright already with the paths below drying out fast.

There was a woman walking along one of them, with a baby,

44

a pretty woman with longish, sun-streaked hair. She did not see him, bending to fiddle with the mechanism of the pushchair. In it, a baby lay, legs kicking. A baby girl, he assumed, from the pink cover.

Unobserved, he took the opportunity to examine the woman quite closely as she bent over the baby. A shapely bum, he decided admiringly.

She did not, thank God, remind him in the least of Victoria.

Sophie took a stroll in the grounds after breakfast, found herself catching up fast with the old lady walking ahead of her.

She stood to one side, smiling, as Sophie passed.

'Good morning,' she said, causing her to slow. 'The rain has cleared the air, hasn't it?'

Sophie agreed. 'It's Mrs Bell, isn't it?'

'Ms if you don't mind.' she said. 'I must be the only person of my generation who approves of the title. So very modern. I approve of all things modern.' She glanced back towards the hotel. 'Well, almost all . . . I guess that makes me feel slightly less ancient.'

Sophie contemplated a polite denial but decided against it, as she caught the woman's bemused expression. Introducing herself as Mrs Willis, she shook the hand proffered.

'You have such a good baby,' Ms Bell went on, as they proceeded on their leisurely way. 'I have always regarded babies as essentially amenable creatures but some mothers make such a fuss. You set the standard you require of them and they surely follow.' She touched the long silver chain that nestled between the folds of her sage-green cardigan. 'Not that I know a thing about it. I never had any of my own.'

Sophie guessed as much. She had a very pristine look, unhampered by the tribulations of child-bearing and rearing. She also rejoiced in a quite heavy make-up at this hour and today's outfit was beautifully draped, softly expensive. And the jewellery! Sophie had never seen her wearing the same jewellery. The old eyes under a haze of blue and lilac eye-shadow and mascara'd lids were darting and almost black. The turban closely fitting around her head was chic and flattering.

'Do you have help with the baby?' she asked.

'Oh no, I prefer to look after Lily myself.'

'How commendable.' The plucked eyebrows rose in astonishment. 'I should never have coped. But then she is very good,
isn't she?'

'Not always. She was awake twice during the night.'

'Oh my. I'm afraid if I lose my beauty sleep, I am quite
peevish.' A brief smile flashed showing an old lady's faded
teeth. 'Oscar, my late husband, knew better than to speak to me
before ten o'clock in the morning. He was an attorney at law,
travelled a lot on business, but when he was home, we liked to
breakfast together. Such amazing breakfasts, but then we had an
excellent staff.'

'Where was home?' Sophie queried, against her will but
curious.

'I lived for many years in Virginia, my dear. Near Lexington,
Rockbridge County.'

'Sounds lovely.'

'It was. Indeed it was.' Disconcertingly, she stopped dead,
looking at but perhaps not seeing the purples and ice-whites of
the alpine garden that tumbled on either side. 'We took breakfast
on the terrace at ten. Often, we lunched out there, even dinner
parties, although the insects were a nuisance. It's one of the
things I miss most, the outdoor dining. Here, in this climate, you
get everything ready and as likely as not, it pisses down.'

Startled, Sophie glanced up, not sure she had heard right but
Ms Bell, unperturbed, just carried on.

'I never did get used to the time difference. I had two clocks,
one set at English time, which I kept in my dressing-room for my
eyes only. As a result of constantly checking that clock, I was
permanently exhausted. The heat drains you. Stifling. Do you
know Virginia?'

'No. But I would like to visit someday.'

'You must.'

By common consent, they turned back at the end of the alpine
walk, began to drift back towards the hotel. In the pushchair,
Lily dozed on. . . .

'I came back to England but I left my Oscar Lee there,' Ms Bell
said quietly. 'It is what he would have wanted. Go home, honey
bee, he would have said. He is buried beside the plantation

46

house under the shade of a mulberrry tree. Such a romantic soul, you see.' She smiled brightly. 'So nice to talk to you, Mrs Willis. Now, if you don't mind, I will take my leave. I must have a little rest before I attend church.'

Sophie steered Lily indoors.

She noticed one of her little socks was missing.

The dining-room was nearly empty by the time James arrived.

'Sorry,' he said to the waitress. 'Any chance of some breakfast? Kick me out if I'm keeping you.'

The waitress forgave him at once, thought he was a very nice man to say that and he did have a smashing smile.

She hesitated though. It was past the official end of breakfast and she had been just about to lock the dining-room door and she knew that the breakfast chef had a lunch-date and was trying to get away early. He would go nuts if this guy wanted anything cooked.

However, it was more than her job was worth to upset a guest.

'We do close the dining-room at ten,' she said, using her initiative and making one of those corporate decisions Mr Morrell was always on about. 'But I think we can make an exception, Mr. . . ?'

'Kendall. Room Thirteen.' He waved his room key at her. 'Thanks. Could you rustle up some scrambled eggs, please? With a few mushrooms and tomatoes.'

She hid a sigh, scribbled it down. 'I'll catch the chef, sir.'

James contemplated a rare lazy Sunday. A drive into the country, stop off at a pub for lunch, drive back and dissect the Sunday papers in the lounge.

The door opened and he thought it was breakfast quick off the mark but no. It was the woman with the baby. She was wearing a short cream dress, fitted and flared, and he noted she had good legs, too.

'Sorry to bother you.' She approached his table, a faint flush on her cheeks. 'We were sitting here earlier, me and Lily, and we've managed to lose one of our socks. Would you mind if I had a quick look for it?'

'Not at all.'

She rummaged below the tablecloth before triumphantly

47

emerging with a tiny frilly sock.

'She kicks them off and these are her best Sunday ones.'

'I see.'

James found he was smiling as she disappeared. Sunday socks, eh? He was lucky these days if he found a matching pair, never mind what day it was. As for the woman, it confirmed what he had imagined. She was nice and dotty about the baby. He wondered about the absence of a partner but it was none of his damned business.

The waitress, hurrying back with his breakfast, was a lovely little thing but, sensing she was flirting, James put the stops on that, abruptly cutting out the charm. He was nearly old enough to be her father.

And with that sobering thought, he peppered his perfectly prepared eggs and enjoyed his breakfast.

Up in Leeds, Amanda's breakfast consisted of a glass of still water with a slice of lemon. On Sundays, she tried to make up for the excesses of the week and ate sparingly. She refused to pander to diets, but she did have a weight-check dress and when that pinched, it was time to forget puddings for a while.

At the moment, it was pinching.

She had slept badly, finally getting off after umpteen heavy-footed treks around lavender fields, heard the church clock strike four and then the alarm, which should have been switched off, rattled off at seven.

This flat was getting on her nerves. Henry was right, she needed to buy her own place, put down some roots, start going into DIY shops and being frog-marched on a rainy Sunday around Ikea. With a sigh, she carried her glass of water into the sitting-room, tossing aside the supplements to the paper. Sometimes it was Wednesday before she got round to reading them. Always adrift.

This room was not much bigger than a rabbit hutch and a bit bare apart from her shelves of books. Most people had framed photos of loved ones somewhere, but she had no wish to look at pictures of herself and the only ones she had of her parents were stuffed away. It wasn't that they made her weepy, rather that they meant so little to her.

Losing them at such a young age, a mere baby as she had been, meant that the memories were deep, hidden, and had slipped away easily. It was harder for Henry who was five years older and retained most of his memories. She and Henry rarely discussed it, that far back, but it made them particularly close. They niggled at each other, of course, but they were close. She was delighted for her brother that he had found such a wonderful partner in Ellie and she knew nothing would please him more than her finding someone too.

She wondered what James was up to. She didn't understand why he had felt the need to do this. Stuffing the past in a bottle and stoppering it up tight was a much better option. So far as she was concerned, her mother was Aunt Enid, who had made the best of what she had considered to be a bad job in bringing up the two of them. They, she and Henry, had been left on that fateful day with their grandmother, the only grandparent left, and after the accident, she was left so shocked and unhappy, she was unable to cope so Aunt Enid did the decent thing and stepped in.

The telephone rang as Amanda was debating what to do with the remainder of her lazy day.

It was Ellie.

Amanda settled down to a long session.

'Why are you here and not down in Devon with James?' Ellie began aggressively. 'I've heard of playing hard to get but honestly, Amanda.'

'He wasn't exactly forthcoming with the invitation,' Amanda said. 'You heard him. You were there. I thought it was a bit off-hand. Surely he never expected me to say yes?'

'Who knows? But he did ask and you said no,' Ellie said in exasperation. 'You just don't try. Victoria's dead and she's been dead for a year now. Do you know if there's anybody else?'

'No, I do not.'

'Well, it's time he got himself fixed up. He's hopeless on his own.'

'Yes, we all know that but how's my chasing him round the country going to help?'

The sigh was obvious. 'You have to work to make things happen. When I met Henry, at an auction you may recall, I decided there and then that he was the man for me. It's the eyes, Amanda, they are just like a spaniel's. But you know Henry; if I'd done nothing about it, he'd still be working up to asking me out. So I organized things.'

'And that's what you expect me to do?'

'Too true, and stop sounding so defeatist. Get yourself down there. Now.'

She wavered. Ellie was very difficult when she was in this mood.

'How can I? I've got shopping to do. Some milk—'

'Amanda!' Ellie yelled at her. 'Forget the milk. Ring the hotel and book a room.'

'Stop interfering.' The protest was half-hearted for she knew, deep down, it was what she wanted to do herself. 'I've got wall-to-wall appointments next week. I can't let people down.'

'Yes you can. Plead a domestic emergency. Use your initiative. I'll see you in about half an hour,' Ellie went on, unperturbed. 'We have packing to do.'

Chapter Six

MARY Parker, part-time general chambermaid, the tired little redhead, whom Sophie rather liked, had a day off from her duties, although, as she had so much to do at home, it was hardly a day of rest. Lucy, her daughter, did not help much, but she knew that was her own fault for running around after her. She had run around in much the same way after her husband Geoff.

Geoff had never done a sausage around the house, but she had let him off because, working on the lorries and doing all that driving up to the Midlands, staying away from home in rotten digs, he had had enough on his plate without being expected to help out at home. Little had she known, when she married him, that it would turn out to be quite so tough. Her mother had warned her, but since when do girls listen to their mothers? Marrying him had meant leaving home – Lancashire – and coming down here, his home, and that had been that. Her mother never forgave her that.

Mary was past forty, just, but, for all it mattered, she could be past fifty and sometimes she felt like it. It didn't help that Lucy, at seventeen, was getting to be a real handful and now Geoff was gone, she had to cope with it all herself.

It was Lucy's day off too, but she was still in bed, young madam, at ten o'clock in the morning.

Taking a cup of tea into the living-room, ducking at the silly point where the ceiling lowered and the floor raised, Mary sat down in the old armchair by the window. There wasn't room to swing a cat but she liked this room. The window looked directly on to the street with The Porthole Inn down on the corner and you could see people passing, hidden as you were by the nets.

Church today for those who bothered and that meant hardly anybody in this street. Mary used to go regularly because she enjoyed a good sing-song but, after Geoff disappeared, she let it lapse. What was the use? If God had heard her, he was not coming up with a proper answer. Nine months on and she was still none the wiser. Christmas come and gone, summer now, and she was no wiser.

It fascinated Mary, people watching, but as she watched, her one real hope was that one day Geoff would walk by, give that quick tap on the window and just walk on in. Large as life and twice as daft and, by all the gulls in the harbour, he'd have some explaining to do.

Feet pattered down the steep stairs and Lucy wandered in, yawning. For bed, she wore a long T-shirt, not long enough in Mary's opinion, and nothing else. She flopped on the settee opposite and curled up her legs, showing the lot.

Mary tutted. 'Why don't you put your dressing-gown on?'

Lucy grumbled, did not budge. She was a lovely girl, who worked in the beauty salon in town, a trainee beautician, and Mary had to admit, she looked a treat with her coppery hair and huge grey-green eyes.

'Do you want breakfast?' she asked, already putting her cup down, half finished, ready to jump up and get out the frying pan. She knew she was a fool to herself, just like her mother before her, but she couldn't help it.

'I don't want breakfast,' Lucy said. 'Just a coffee. Did you get decaffeinated?'

Mary nodded. All these fancy ideas!

'Just a coffee is no breakfast for a growing girl.'

'Growing? I'm seventeen, Mum,' she said indignantly.

'You weren't out with that new lad of yours last night on his bike, were you?' Mary asked, picking up her tea.

'Is that a rhetorical question?'

Mary sniffed. Clever young miss. She had no idea what she meant but she was not going to ask.

'I don't know what your dad would say,' she went on firmly. 'He never liked motor bikes. Death traps he called them.'

'Pity he didn't have the same reservations about boats,' Lucy remarked, stretching out long, very smooth legs. She used a special tanning cream from the shop and they were always this lovely sunkissed colour. 'If he had, he might have thought twice about what he did.'

'That's enough,' Mary said. 'If he walked in this minute, he wouldn't let you talk to your mother like that.'

'He won't.' Lucy was suddenly subdued, self-consciously tugging at her shirt. 'Can't you get it into your head, Mum, that he's dead? Drowned. He's at the bottom of the sea.'

'Lucy!'

'Sorry. But you have to face facts. Wasn't that what the counsellor told you to do?'

'Not necessarily dead,' Mary said, ignoring the bit about the counsellor. 'If there's no body, how can that be dead? He could have been washed up somewhere. Lost his memory. Or been picked up by a foreign ship and not be able to make himself understood. Those cargo ships go all over. He could be anywhere,' she finished desperately.

Lucy giggled. 'And I'm Cleopatra.'

'Right. That's enough.'

'I give up.' Lucy rose in one graceful movement. 'Don't wait up for me tonight, Mum. I might be late in.'

Mary sighed when she was gone. It was hard to credit that she and Geoff, both such sobersides, could have produced a girl like Lucy. She had not done well at school, disappointed them, but she was streetwise and Mary knew she had to trust her, to some extent anyway.

Mind you, Geoff only had a meagre share of brains himself, the crackpot. Otherwise, why would he have set off in that boat, late at night, half sozzled, and rowed out to the open sea? Off to America, he told the folks peering at him from the quay, folks who ought to be ashamed of themselves for not stopping him. Would you let a drunken man get into the driving seat of a car? And yet they let him go off, heard the splashing of the oars, let him drift off in search of the Atlantic shipping lane. Seeing as there were no actual roadsigns in the water, what chance did he have? Cold too, very likely freezing out at sea.

'When you get back, Geoff Parker, I'll give you what for,' she said aloud, glancing towards the street.

They never found the boat.

And they never found the body.

The job at the hotel was not Mary's only one. She juggled several, doing a spot of light cleaning at the craft centre and helping out with a little tea-stall there. The hours she worked at The Whistling Kettle just about made things add up. She managed all right and there was no sense in feeling envy for, working at The New Grand, she saw people who had real money.

Some of them looked pretty miserable at that.

They usually came for a couple of weeks, sailing folk some of them, and this was the holiday they threw in, doing their bit for the local economy, flashing their money and their designer gear and so on. Lucy had some tales to tell about the women who came to the salon. They tipped her handsomely and Mary wished they were as free with the tips at the hotel.

All she got as chambermaid was loose change, if that. For skivvying after them, tidying up the mess – and you should see it sometimes, turned your stomach it did – all she got was coppers. Once she had been given two twenty pence coins by somebody who was supposed to be a millionaire. She'd stuck them in the charity box at the craft centre in disgust. Now and then, they left tiddly foreign coins she hadn't a clue about, but, more often than not, nothing.

To hell with them.

So, she did the only thing she could do: she had a bit of a rummage. When she was doing the rooms, she looked through their drawers and their suitcases and read their letters, if they left anything lying around. It was amazing what she found out.

Over the time she'd been doing the job, she had developed a sixth sense. Just as, sometimes, she felt that Geoff was still out there somewhere, she knew that some of the guests were not always what they were cracked up to be.

Older men with young women for instance. She could always tell. The cheek of the devil and the women bold as you like. Comical lot, men. Most of them didn't have the brains they were born with, although Mary had to admit that her friend Dennis, who dabbled in antiques, had more than his share. Dennis could duck and dive. Fly, Geoff would have called him. She had known Dennis for a while now and he often came in the café for a cuppa. He lived out at Shabley Sands, a bit of a dead spot, but quite pretty. He had a shop in Devisham and a couple more up in North Devon.

It was all above board. They were just friends, never mind what Lucy thought. It was Dennis who had suggested she have a dig through people's belongings. One of the perks, he reckoned. Serve them right for treating you so bad.

Geoff would have been horrified. Honest as the day is long. Honest to the point of daftness. He'd once found a ten-pound note lying in the gutter on a wet day. What sort of person would take it round to the police station, getting soaked in the process because it was at the far end of Harbour Walk, instead of just pocketing it?

Geoff would and did.

Mary knew she was playing with fire and her heart beat like a drum when she was doing it but somehow, with Geoff gone, it did not really matter.

It added a bit of spice to life.

Lucy reappeared, all dolled up, tossing her a fiver in passing.

'Thanks. Sure you can afford it?' Mary tucked it away in her bra, a very safe place because nobody looked there, not even Dennis until she gave him a bit of encouragement. 'You off out then?'

Lucy nodded. Her lovely little face was done to perfection, but then she knew all the tricks. She had a shapely figure, emphasized by a tight-fitting top that showed off a tanned midriff and she wore bum-hugging pants that showed too much as usual.

'You've never had your tummy button pierced?'

Lucy smiled. 'Everybody's doing it. Do you like it?'

'I do not. It's vulgar.'

'Oh Mum, relax.' Lucy's smile was even broader.

'Enjoy yourself then,' Mary said, unable to take her eyes off the sight of that tummy button adorned as it was with a silver ring. She remembered when Lucy was born, when the cord had been a stumpy bloody piece of skin. She was beautiful then. Beautiful now.

'I've been thinking,' Lucy said, in no rush to go now, 'about you, Mum. You want to get yourself a holiday. Abroad.'

'Don't be daft. People come here for their holidays. What would I want to go abroad for on my own?'

'Go with Dennis.'

She felt herself flush. 'Why would I do that?'

'Because . . .' – Lucy raised her eyebrows, looking a lot older than her years – 'he's lively and not bad-looking. He's good for you, Mum. You brighten up when you're with him. I bet he'd marry you tomorrow if you wanted.'

'Now you are talking daft. How can I get married when your father might walk in any minute? I'm not free to marry for a long time yet.'

'It'll be a year soon,' Lucy said, sticking a packet of cigarettes in her bag. 'He's not coming back. Remember there was a whole lot of people who saw him rowing off in that crappy boat, roaring drunk. He wasn't fit to row in the boating lake, let alone the sea. He was washed over. Don't you see?'

'That's enough. And don't say crappy. Anyway, they weren't that reliable, if you ask me. He was the best husband ever, even if he did like his bit of drink,' she said, incensed at the way Lucy had given up. 'Good and thoughtful and he thought the world of you. He'd be dead proud to know you work in a beauty salon. I tell you something, Lucy, you'll be all right if you get a man as good as him.'

Lucy sighed. 'God, get out the violins,' she said.

Chapter Seven

TOBY liked to surprise the staff occasionally on a Sunday morning. Catch them out if possible. This morning, on his way to the golf course, he suddenly decided on a detour to see how things were doing.

The girl on duty at the reception desk smiled as he came through. Toby smiled back broadly. If Fiona Jennings was to be recommended for employee of the month, he would not object. In fact, the way she smiled at him made him wonder if he might relax his own rule about business and pleasure. The trouble was she would talk about him if they were to engage in an affair, however short-lived, and he did not fancy the other girls hanging on to her every revelation. And, although he had no reason to believe he was anything other than superb in the sexual department, it was wise to maintain an aura of mystery so far as his staff were concerned. In any case, on a purely practical level, a sexual harassment charge would clean him out completely. You had to keep your hands pinned to your side and zips firmly closed or all hell could break loose.

'Good morning,' he said, popping into the duty manager's office, where Alice was already there, winding up a telephone call quickly and efficiently when she saw him.

'Good morning, Mr Morrell,' she said, covering her surprise with a welcoming smile. 'You weren't expected this morning.'

'Just passing,' he said. 'Everything OK? Any luck with the celebrity?'

'I'm working on it,' she told him, evasively he thought. 'It's awfully short notice. We may have to increase the fee.'

'Pay whatever it takes,' he said. 'Throw in the best suite,

champagne and flowers. Whatever. Just get somebody, Alice.'

He gave her an encouraging smile, his executive smile that he imagined must be pretty near devastating to mere employees. One of his lady friends from way back had once said he had a nice smile and he had spent the following week smiling at himself in the bathroom mirror trying to understand what she meant.

He was not trying to seduce Alice; she was not his type. He noticed she was wearing high heels and wondered why, when she was verging on six feet tall, and towered over him. Professionally, she was well qualified, having served an apprenticeship in one of the hotel chains, three-star, and she was fully acquainted with what everyone did from the lowliest upwards and that made the minions respect her judgement. It mattered. A team player, Alice, and he had high hopes of her, if only she could rid herself of the occasional dithers and self-doubt that overcame her.

'The weather forecast's not good,' she said, out of nowhere.

'For what?'

'The party on Saturday, sir,' she said. 'We want the guests to mill about outside on the terrace, don't we? And then there's the fireworks. If it rains. . . .'

'It won't,' he said confidently, remembering for an instant the eclipse of '99 and the wash-out that had proved to be. They had, he reflected vividly, seen bugger all of the star attractions, the sun and moon, although it had gone two shades darker.

'I hope you're right, Mr Morrell,' she said, with a worried shake of her pale hair.

'How are you settling in?' he enquired silkily, looking up at her. She had been quiet at last week's in-house meeting, but he had allowed her that, as she was the comparative new girl. 'Come up with any ideas yet?' he asked, the question mischievous at this early hour.

'As a matter of fact, yes,' she said, surprising him. 'Have you a moment to discuss it?'

He glanced at his watch, making sure she noticed it as it was a splendid affair purchased from a renowned jeweller's in Lugano and had set him back a vast amount of Swiss francs.

To his irritation, it seemed to pass her by, so he slipped the sleeve of his golfing sweater back over it and smiled that he was giving her the moment she desired.

'I don't know if you are aware, sir, but the new edition of the *Harlequin Recommended Hotel Guide* is on the boil. I'm told they will be making sweeping changes to accommodate the new hotels they wish to include.'

'I know that,' he said impatiently. 'A few slip out each year.'

'If we are to hold our place . . .'

'I beg your pardon,' he said coldly. Just who did this woman think she was, daring to insinuate that they were in any danger of losing their very long established position.

'We must not be complacent,' she said. 'Some excellent hotels floundered last year. There are no guarantees for inclusion.'

'Oh yes there are,' he said at once. 'Tip-top quality and the very highest standards. I admit the time it took to refurbish has been unfortunate.'

'Exactly,' she said triumphantly. 'We will have slipped a little simply because of that. Not our fault, but some of these inspectors can't see beyond the scaffolding and the workmen. They see chaos. And that is why I believe it is vital that we adopt a more aggressive marketing policy. The success of the Millennium celebrations should teach us something about that. We really pulled the stops out.'

'Yes indeed, Alice. We featured in the *South Hams Holiday Times*, front page no less.'

A slight smile, pitying surely, appeared on her face and he was not sure he liked it.

'For what it's worth. . . .' she said.

'You must not underestimate the power of the local Press,' he said, gentle but firm. 'Many of our bookings are from a radius of fifty miles. When people are thinking wedding receptions and other celebratory occasions, they will think of us.'

'Oh yes, but we must try to do more nationally. We should go all out to keep up the Millennium momentum.'

'It's all died a death,' he said. 'Here we are. It's the year 2000 and we're just toddling along as usual. A bit of a let-down all round.'

'Oh come on, Mr Morrell,' she said sharply.

Taken aback, he managed a slightly condescending smile.

'Let's have your ideas then, Alice.'

'There's no harm at pinching ideas from other people,' she said. 'For instance, we don't go in much for themed weekends. We should do some special ones, murder mystery that sort of thing. I always found them extremely popular at the other hotels I worked at.'

'Really?' he frowned, not liking the sound of it. A touch down-market.

'Anniversary breaks then,' she went on. 'For example, we could plan an entire month of romantic celebration next February to link in with Valentine's Day. And the four-poster bedrooms are so beautiful. We should capitalize on them a bit more. Advertise in *Brides Magazine*.'

'Nothing new. We've been doing romantic breaks for ages,' he said, smiling because she was genuinely trying. 'They are advertised in one of the short-break holiday brochures we are linked to.'

'We ought also to consider producing a little newspaper to hand out to guests and to send to previous guests. More a newsletter but glossy, if possible, with lots of pictures. Four pages max. Colour, of course. Staff profiles. With links to some of the local attractions, complimentary tickets, discounts. Even if people can afford our prices, they still like the idea of a bargain.'

She was right. He liked this.

'How often?'

'Quarterly, Mr Morrell. Get people to think about their breaks in advance. We need them to be pencilling in dates.'

'OK. You can bring that up at the next meeting,' he said. 'Well done.'

Keen sort, he decided, leaving her to it as she threatened to draw him into an entire morning's discussion.

On the way out, he smiled again at the little brunette receptionist, who surely blushed, before catching up with Ms Bell on her way to church.

'May I say how delightful you look this morning, madam?' he said.

'You may.' She inclined her head graciously. 'Thank you. I've been meaning to enquire about your dear father. How is he? Enjoying his retirement?'

'Yes. Enjoying himself immensely,' he said. 'Gardening and so on.'

'I always thought him charming,' she said, sugar sweet, glancing sideways at Toby. 'And he treated the hotel with such loving care.'

'Absolutely,' he said, feeling she was getting at him. 'You do approve of the refurbishment, Ms Bell?'

'Normally I approve of all things new,' she said. 'But I saw no need for changing the name. In my opinion, some things are best left as they are. I am entirely comfortable with faded grandeur.'

Too true.

Toby gushed a farewell, walking neatly over to his car. He would have to work doubly hard to restore her faith in him. He could not risk upsetting her and having her move on, taking her fortune with her. His father had always maintained that there was a hefty chunk coming their way. So, some flowers were called for, a big bunch, a small thank you for her continued most welcome presence.

He had a golf date now with Dave Price, a local businessman of some flair. One of those thirtysomethings who had struck it rich too soon. A very naff approach to money. He lived in considerable splendour in a house overlooking Salcombe. Nasty character, having made his money from computer games, and his success stuck in Toby's throat, but you could not ignore people like that. Together, they dished out a fair amount of charitable contributions, more because it was good for their public image rather than because it was their generous nature. Tax deductible at that.

He knew that Dave did not like him either, but that was not necessarily a bad thing. When you got too chummy, it usually came to grief.

Toby, with Ms Bell's ticking-off ringing in his ears, felt his competitive urge rising.

The way he was feeling, he would sweep Dave Price off the course.

Churchgoing was an unfortunate habit Bea could not break. Oscar Lee had been fervent about religion, praying on his knees at the side of the bed without embarrassment every day of his

61

life and, every Sunday, she and Oscar attended the little white-boarded church in the quaint nearby town with the smoky Blue Mountains shimmering in the distance.

Suddenly, coming out of church here, she felt homesick for Virginia and its sweet summer heat.

'Mrs Bell . . .' The vicar, young and earnest, took her hand, gave her a very direct look. 'How are you?'

She smiled. He refused to comply with her wish to be Ms and she did not press it for fear of offending him. Never offend the clergy, or you offend the Lord himself, Oscar said.

'Interesting sermon,' she murmured, although she could not recall a word of it. She never listened in church except to her own thoughts. She attended church simply because it was her Christian duty and, waiting for her up there, Oscar would never forgive non-attendance.

Joining the throng exiting, she paused here and there for a few polite words before beginning the walk back. She took her time, mindful of the slope, taking neat high-heeled steps. Oscar, in his middle years, had swelled out and started to waddle and, on his death, it took six strong men to carry his beautiful ivory-coloured coffin.

Brushing aside a sadness, Bea bustled on, pausing a moment at the bottom of the hotel gardens.

She saw that the veranda was filling up. People with Sunday papers and endless pots of coffee and, as she drew nearer, she saw that Mrs Willis and her baby were there. She would refresh herself in the ladies' powder room and then she might join them.

She had the funniest feeling about Mrs Willis.

On his drive out, James got lost. It didn't matter for he wasn't going anywhere in particular but it irritated because he prided himself on his sense of direction. Arriving unexpectedly, there-fore, at an oak-timbered inn at the edge of a village that appeared to have no name, he decided to stop off for lunch.

It was only as he ducked under the porch door that the sense of déjà-vu pounded in his head. It was the same inn, the one he and Victoria had dined in on the Sunday.

'Hello there, on your own today, sir?' the barman enquired, for all the world as if he remembered him.

Quite shaken at the thought, James ordered a beer and asked for a menu.

He looked around.

Like the hotel, it was the same but different.

By the Sunday of their honeymoon, Victoria had been a little more relaxed, apologizing for trying to discuss serious matters the night before. They would have lots of time to talk about things when they got home. Even so, it managed to produce a doubt in his mind and, married one day only, it was too early for doubts.

Today the inn was nearly full and the waitress had to squeeze past tables to deliver his lunch, a magnificent roast dinner.

'There you go,' she said. 'Pickles? Sauces?'

'This is fine. Thanks.'

James tucked in. Last night, eating alone, had been a bit awkward but he was determined not to retreat to his room and it would be easier tonight. As he reached for his wallet to pay the bill, a piece of paper fell out, the one with Dave Price's number on. Oh yes, he had promised to give him a call, fix a meeting. He knew Henry would go daft if he knew he was thinking of conducting a business meeting without him and that was why he was keeping it dark. Dave was an old university acquaintance, hardly a friend, who lived down here and there was a standing invitation to come and see him, one of those casually tossed invites you were never sure of. Rather surprisingly, they had kept in touch and there had been a condolence card when Victoria had died and then a Christmas card with the invitation renewed, plus a cryptic message suggesting that Dave might have some work for him.

He would give him a ring. He knew Dave was big time and it was a shame to pass up the chance. As well as the computer business, he was now into yacht charters, as well as other tourist-iinked ventures. He did not like Dave, too single-minded, too confident and arrogant, but that was hardly the point. When he got back to the hotel, he would give him a ring, arrange a meeting.

He stepped out blinking into sunshine amidst the scent of flowers from the tubs and troughs, strong in the midday heat.

Retracing his footsteps, he came to a T-junction with no sign-post. Interesting. He took a moment to consider which way, opting for left which almost at once brought him to a road he remembered.

Who knows?

Perhaps if, all those years ago, he and Victoria had taken the right-hand bend, things might have been different.

Ellie, true to her word, came round to help with the packing.

Amanda smiled wryly as she let her in.

'That guy downstairs . . .' Ellie shuddered. 'He is something else. Now, tell me you're booked in. Please.'

'All right. You win, you big bully. I am booked in from tomorrow.' She held up both hands in mock anguish. 'It's caused mayhem at work. Great inconvenience to everybody.'

'So what? Do them good. Now, where is everything? Have you done your list?' In jeans and tight T–shirt, feet stuffed into trainers, Ellie looked about sixteen.

'List?'

Ellie clicked her tongue. 'Sometimes I cannot believe you are a lawyer. When it comes to the simple things in life, you are clue-less.'

'My things are in drawers,' Amanda said, not minding the rebuke. Ellie talked to everybody as if she was talking to a child. 'You really needn't have bothered,' she continued, watching helplessly as Ellie rolled and folded and put things in corners. 'I can do it on my own.'

'I know, but I like packing. And I always think you need somebody else to confirm what to take. Such as this.' She held up a grey skimpy top. 'This is great. You do have some nice stuff.'

'You sound surprised.' Amanda perched on the bed and let her get on with it. 'I'm under instructions to stay strictly sober for work, so that we don't distract clients. Daft and a bit insulting, don't you think? As if I would turn up to court in slinky satin?' She pointed to a pretty pale-pink camisole and cover-up. 'Most of this has hardly been worn. Impulse buys.'

'I wish I could afford impulse buys,' Ellie said, but not too

64

unhappily. 'The children cost so much and I'd rather buy things for them.'

'You're a good mum, Ellie.'

She laughed. 'Nice of you to say so. Sometimes I seem to spend my time yelling at them, the little monsters. And it really is so tempting to stick them in front of the television with a video when you know you ought to be broadening their little horizons.' Busying about, Amanda could not see her face. 'Henry's brilliant with them,' she went on. 'Incredible patience. I suppose he's trying to make up for having no parents himself. I wish he would talk about it a bit more.'

Amanda felt herself tighten up. 'Mother did her best for us.'

'Oh God. That sounds awful. I only met Enid the once and she told me straight that she could not condone our relationship until we were married. Henry was furious. He hasn't spoken to her since.'

'I'm not surprised. She thinks I don't make the best of myself.'

'Well . . .' Ellie held up a short black dress. 'Have I ever seen you wearing this gorgeous number?'

Amanda was not listening. 'She had her life all mapped out and we messed it up. We ended up being the children she was not going to have herself.'

'Poor her. It was very inconsiderate of your parents to get themselves killed.'

Amanda smiled. 'Mother's proud of us really. She pushed us to go to university. She just finds it difficult to show her emotions.'

'You see the best in everybody.' Ellie looked unconvinced. 'If she can't forgive me, then she shouldn't take it out on the kids. They'd like another granny.'

'Yes, well . . .' Amanda was not going to get involved in this. They had to sort it out themselves.

'Have you told James you are about to descend on him?'

'No. Should I have?'

Ellie shrugged. 'You know him better than me, I suppose. I feel like shaking that man sometimes. We all know Victoria was as awkward as you can get. Henry couldn't stand her and she drove the whole office mad.'

'I hope I'm doing the right thing,' Amanda suddenly blurted

65

out. 'It feels like I'm running after him and I hate that.'

'In this day and age? Can you do that?'

'You can in my book,' Amanda said quietly. 'He might not approve of my chasing off down there.'

'For crying out loud, don't be such a dimpled daisy. Get after him.' Seeing Amanda's face, she came across and sat beside her. 'Look, you two are just made for each other. James has to be made to realize it and when he does, knowing him, you'll be beating us to the altar. Henry's very slow about commitment.'

'Is he? I thought . . .' Amanda stopped. It really was nothing to do with her.

'Right, underwear. Where do you keep it?'

'If I'd have known I was going away, I'd have bought something new,' Amanda said, feeling ashamed as she surveyed it. 'You tend to forget, don't you, how long you've had some of it.'

'Can I give you some advice?' Ellie said. 'It's now or never with James. You've got him on his own, on holiday, relaxed. Perfect. You've got to seduce him. Think of those wonderful sunsets, walks along the beach, all that stuff.'

'We'll be in Devisham, remember, not the Bahamas. And I don't see myself as a *femme fatale*.'

'Why ever not? There's nothing to it. I bet you anything that Victoria was pretty cold when it came to sex. No, I'm sorry but I have to say it. I know you don't like me to say nasty things but honestly . . .' She gave a deep sigh. 'As for James, he has a very sexy air about him. Surely you've noticed?'

'I have, you idiot,' Amanda murmured.

'Of course you have. Goodness me, I even find myself flirting with him sometimes and don't you dare tell Henry that.'

When Ellie was gone, she found her words echoing in her mind. Maybe Ellie was right and they just needed a little push. If only she could stop seeing Victoria as the enemy then there might be a chance.

Last thing before she went to bed, she painted her nails for the first time in a long time. Coppery bronze.

It made her feel a different woman.

Spending a few moments in the quieter lounge, Sophie, out of politeness, asked Ms Bell if she would like to hold Lily. To her surprise, the invitation was equally politely refused.

Be like that, Sophie thought, bouncing the baby on her knee. Lily was awake but happy, practising her repertoire of sounds and holding on to one of Sophie's fingers tightly. She was wearing a new lemon, frilled dress with white lacy tights and a little bobbed cap over her sparse hair and, looking so adorable, she had attracted quite a few admiring glances.

Sophie wondered when they could decently leave for she had not bargained on entertaining Ms Bell all afternoon. She was, however, interesting to listen to and Sophie was charmed by descriptions of Oscar Lee, the husband whom Bea had obviously adored. Hiding a little sigh as she held Lily, she wondered if it were as obvious to others that when she mentioned Roger, she had almost come to hate him.

'My husband and I are separated,' she told Ms Bell, who had been quizzing her for ages.

'Oh my Lord.' She seemed genuinely shocked. 'How boorish of me to enquire. Do forgive me.'

'It's all right,' Sophie said quickly. 'It's been a time now.'

'You are still very young, my dear.'

'Not that young. Very nearly forty,' she admitted.

'A mere babe,' Bea said. 'I am sure you will find somebody else someday.'

'Perhaps.' Enough was enough and Sophie gathered up the baby things. 'If you'll excuse me, she needs changing.'

Going upstairs, she fed and changed Lily and laid her down on the playmat with some toys. As she sang to her, she conceded that she had been a little economical with the truth there, making Roger out to be worse than he was, giving the impression he had left when she was pregnant.

Why did she tell these lies?

Not quite fair to him.

As Lily dozed, she found herself thinking about the man at breakfast and the episode with the sock. He had been friendly, but she grew hot at the thought of making a fool of herself. If she had wanted to create a favourable impression, she had gone about it the wrong way for desirable females do not spend their time bent double hunting for socks.

However, as she picked Lily up and smiled into the sleepy

baby eyes, she decided she would put on some make-up and go back downstairs. With a bit of luck, Bea would have retired for her afternoon nap and, if she did happen to run into that man again, a few words would not be inappropriate.

Chapter Eight

MARY could not eat her lunch. She had a fit of conscience sometimes and today, it being Sunday and all, with all the church
bells ringing out, it was worse than usual.

She kept thinking about the ear-rings she had taken the other
day from Ms Bell.

Ms Bell had a proper dressing-table in her bedroom with lots
of pretty bottles and pots arranged on top, standing on little
mats. Mary always helped herself to a splash of perfume when
she did her room.

Truth to tell, she always helped herself to the guests' perfume.
A dash here, a dab there.

Mrs Willis had nice scent, flowery, not like the sort Lucy used,
hot and spicy in a red bottle. That smelled cheap when it was
not.

Mrs Willis was more careful than most of the guests. She kept
her suitcases locked and took the keys out with her and she
rarely left anything of interest lying about. The collection of
clothes in the wardrobe was tidily arranged and the baby's
things occupied almost a complete chest of drawers. Short of
nothing, that baby.

Mrs Willis excited her curiosity, but it was too risky, Dennis
said, to take something from people like her. Old vague folks
were the best because they never trusted their own memories.

For instance, she remembered two elderly sisters who had left
the hotel for home after their holiday, never realizing that one of
their gold lockets was gone. They had been toffee-nosed and
once told her off when she had accidentally barged in. Returning
to the room after they'd gone, she found an envelope addressed

to 'the chambermaid' containing a ten-pound note. And worse, beside it, a box of After Eights. It was a bit awkward that, being nice to her at the last, and she would have run after them, if she still had the locket, but it was gone, passed to Dennis. So she pocketed the money and ate the chocolates, although she wondered later if the resulting tummy ache was caused by indigestion or guilty conscience.

It wasn't her fault if Ms Bell chose not to use the safe in her room. Hardly anybody did. None of the other cleaning staff liked doing her rooms because they were so fiddly with all the ornaments and knickknacks and, if you left a spot of dust, she complained. Beside her bed, there were photographs of her and her late husband. He was a bit on the fat side, Mary thought, but she must have loved him a lot because she never stopped talking about him. The whole hotel knew all there was to know about Oscar Lee Bell.

She kept the jewellery, tossed anyhow, in a drawer. At first, Mary had not been able to believe her luck, although she had thought it was just costume stuff. You had to look at the settings, Dennis told her, for they told you a lot. The rings were stuffed in a couple of red velvet drawstring bags and then there were the necklaces and pendants and cameos and ear-rings. Lots and lots of ear-rings.

Over the last few months, she had stolen three items. Not much because she had to be extra careful with Ms Bell living here permanently. Not surprisingly, nothing had been missed.

Last time, Dennis was delighted and he had given her fifty pounds out of the takings and splashed out on a fish and chip supper. He kept the lion's share because he took the bigger risk. Mary could have argued that she was taking a risk herself, but she liked him and didn't want to fall out with him for the sake of a few pounds. She supposed she did entertain the notion that, given time, they might make a go of it together, if that daft husband of hers didn't turn up. She could not wait for ever although it would be years before she would be properly free.

She did not like the idea of just living with Dennis, not with Lucy knowing, but happiness was an elusive thing and she was still a young woman – well, youngish – and she had needs of a sort.

Making sure Lucy was not around, she took the ear-rings out of the pocket of her skirt and examined them. They had turquoise centres set in gold with pearls and diamond clusters. They looked not unlike some of the ear-rings you could get in the craft centre and she hoped she had not slipped up and they were just cheap. Dennis would make her smuggle them back then which was risky because the housekeeper did spot checks sometimes and she couldn't keep being lucky.

They felt heavy which was good. Dennis would be pleased then and she liked to see his face light up.

She knew Dennis did not love her, not yet, but he was lively and not at all bad-looking. The other evening, when they'd been talking about her getting the ear-rings, he'd told her she had lovely eyes and, true or not, it was a long time since a man had told her that.

Taking a deep breath, she slipped them back into her pocket and went to phone him.

Bea Bell waylaid James in the lounge where he had retired with a pot of coffee and the Sunday supplements. Big read time.

'I see you have the *Times*,' she said, sitting in the comfortable chair beside him. 'Would you mind terribly if I swapped my magazine for yours? I have read every single item in mine and I have nothing to read.'

With a smile, he made the suggested swap but Bea was in no hurry to begin reading. Putting the magazine aside, she dived into the business in hand.

'How do you do. My name is Beatrice Bell, but I prefer to be called Bea,' she said, extending her hand and being told that he was James Kendall.

'And do people call you James? Or Jimmy?'

'James.'

She nodded. 'Quite right. James is one of those names that is quite dreadful when abbreviated. Take Jimmy Carter for example – I had great difficulty in taking him seriously. He hailed from Georgia and we knew him from way back, my husband and I, long before he became President. A charming man but . . .' She let it slide, having long discovered that politics were best avoided with anyone, friend or foe. Instead, seeing she

71

had succeeded as intended in grabbing his attention – everyone was impressed that she should have a passing acquaintance with an ex-US President – she gave him the potted version of life in Virginia.

'You must go there,' she told him. 'I grew to love it in a way although the summer heat is so oppressive. It's often over a hundred degrees and in my view that is a temperature at which the brain starts to deteriorate. As I was telling Mrs Willis earlier, even though I lived there for years, I was always the stranger.'

James laughed. 'It's just the same in Yorkshire. I wasn't born there so I might as well be from another planet. I was just about forgiven because my late wife was from Ilkley. The Ilkley of the song that is.'

'Really?' Bea smiled politely, having never heard of Ilkley or the song. However, she had established that his wife was dead. Interesting. 'My own dear husband, Oscar, was an attorney-at-law. You have the look of a lawyer, if I may say so.'

'I'm flattered,' he said a touch wryly. 'But I'm in graphic design.'

'Oh. Creative then?'

'I like to think so. We work with computer graphics but essentially we are creative.' His smile widened. 'Not everybody holds that view especially with our speciality which is commercial packaging. I suppose it is hard to assign creativity to designing a new baked beans package for example.'

'Is that what you do?' Out of the corner of her eye, she saw Mrs Willis approaching with the baby. She waved and it had the required effect of drawing the woman to them.

'This is Mrs Willis, Sophie, with her baby Lily,' she whispered, before they were in earshot. 'She's very charming. Sadly separated from her husband.'

To Bea's irritation, James rose and very quickly made his departure after the introductions were made.

'Shy, poor soul,' she said. 'A graphic designer.'

'That sounds interesting.'

'It is,' Bea said, deciding not to mention baked beans which struck her as singularly dull. She had never, in her entire life, shopped for food. Sophie seemed impressed though and that's what counted.

'Won't you join me for afternoon tea?' she asked. 'I'm just about to order.'

'No thank you. Lily and I need some fresh air. I'll leave you in peace.'

Bea watched her go. To her joy, James Kendall was a man of principle like Oscar. A respectable sort but with too much of a winning smile to be boring. Mrs Willis was a little weary of men so, all in all, their relationship needed a kick start.

The lounge had emptied. Covering her mouth with her hand to hide a yawn, Bea wondered what to do next. With spectacularly thrilling ideas in short supply, she ordered a Devon strawberry cream tea instead.

Chapter Nine

'Perhaps you might like to join me for coffee. I've asked them to serve it in the lounge,' James said, as he passed Mrs Willis's table. She looked odd without the baby in tow and, during the course of the meal, they had on a number of occasions exchanged quick, slightly embarrassed glances.

He was getting past this sort of thing, working up to asking a woman out. Still, they were both here for the rest of the week so who knows? He hardly expected her to end up in his bed, but she might prove to be good company and he needed that. He also needed to talk to somebody, somebody roughly his age, somebody other than Amanda.

Sophie joined him in the small coffee lounge off the dining-room, the waiter bringing them a big pot of coffee and some mints. She was wearing a dark-blue dress with a scooped neck-line and she looked pretty and feminine and also worried.

'This is nice,' she said, fidgeting in her chair. 'Look, would you mind if I checked on Lily.' She was already standing up, jingling her room key. 'Back in a minute.'

She was true to her word.

He noticed, with some amusement, that she had put on fresh lipstick, a plum shade, and more perfume.

'Everything all right?'

She nodded, happy now, and James poured them both a coffee.

'What do you make of Bea Bell?' she asked, relaxing at last in the chair, crossing one shapely leg over the other.

'I've only spoken to her briefly,' James said. 'She approves of the fact that I'm called James not Jimmy. Oh, and she was at pains to tell me that she knew Jimmy Carter.'

Her eyes widened. '*The* Jimmy Carter?'

'Right.'

'She's certainly had an interesting life.' Sophie was sipping her coffee, looking at him and he suddenly reckoned they had said quite enough about Bea.

'I'm in graphic design,' he told her. 'We, my colleague and myself, run a small company up in Leeds. What do you do?'

She laughed. 'Was there life before the baby? Is that what you mean? I was a secretary, since you ask.'

'I see. So you're on maternity leave then?'

She reached for a mint, unwrapped it.

'I'm not working for a while,' she said. 'It's difficult being on my own.'

'Of course. I'm sorry, I didn't mean to pry. Victoria and me . . .' he paused, wishing he had not started on this. 'We didn't have children. She wanted them, but we didn't have them. She resigned herself to it or rather she seemed to,' he added swiftly.

'You didn't think of adopting?'

'No. We were neither of us happy with that.' He smiled slightly, knowing he had simply fallen in with Victoria's wishes. 'After we made the decision, she threw herself into her work and became very successful.'

'And what about you, James? Did it matter to you that you couldn't have a family?'

Right to the jugular.

'I didn't think so at the time. Now ... well . . .' He shrugged. 'Seeing you with Lily, for instance. You look so nice together. You're so patient with her.'

'You think so?'

'I do. She's a beautiful baby.' He reached for his coffee. 'I could be quite converted.'

The smile beamed. 'What a nice thing to say.' She glanced towards the window where the mild evening air pressed against it. 'Fancy a walk? Lily is fine and I've arranged for the sitter to stay up there with her.' She reached for the wrap she had brought downstairs with her and looked at him questioningly.

'You're on,' he said.

*

75

'I came here as a child,' Sophie told him, as they set off. It was light but fading fast and the water sparkled in a low-key manner below the evening sky. 'Not to this hotel because my father was always counting the pennies, but to a guest house up in town. A very happy holiday. I love boats but Mother worried and wouldn't let me set foot in one. She didn't like planes either.'

'Just like my wife. Victoria would never fly.'

'Wouldn't she? Isn't it extraordinary!' She smiled sympathetically. 'It must have stuck in my mind, this place, and that's why I've come back. Have you been before?'

'We came here on honeymoon,' he said, hearing her intake of surprised breath. 'I know, glutton for punishment and all that. But it was something I felt I should do. I'm trying to lay the ghost.'

'That's a brave thing to do,' she said, moving a fraction closer. 'She must have been so young. Awful for you.'

'Yes, it was. But I was lucky I had her for the time I did,' he said, wondering why he was always making Victoria sound as if she was a gift from heaven. 'She was a wonderful woman,' he added, just to underline the fact.

They took the shallow steps down to the promenade, brushing past a bank of flowers. There were a few couples out strolling and they exchanged a few 'good evenings' as they passed by. It occurred to James, wallowing in the evening stillness, that this place beat the hell out of anywhere else when the weather was kind.

'And what did your wife do? Very successful you said.'

'She was a designer like me.'

'And did she. . . ? I mean, was it sudden?'

They always wanted to know. Women always wanted to know.

'Unexpected,' he said shortly and she took the hint.

'How long were you married?'

He hid a sigh. That was another thing. Once women got it in their mind, they constantly worried a chain of thought.

'Fourteen years.'

'A long time. I married at eighteen.'

'That's very young.'

'Too young. Absolutely too young.' She cast a glance his way.

76

'Can I tell you a something?'

'Go ahead.'

'It sounds awful, but Roger was never the right man and the awful thing is that I knew it almost as soon as we got married. I persevered because you have to but it was never going to work out. I expect Bea has told you already that we are now separated?'

'Yes. I'm sorry,' he said.

She managed a smile. 'There were always other women with Roger. He expected me to be more cosmopolitan about it. After all, he said, don't I always come back to you?'

'Difficult to understand,' James murmured, a little out of his depth. If he'd been married to this very attractive woman, he didn't think he would have felt the need to stray. 'Didn't having Lily help?' he asked, seeing that they were getting down to the nitty-gritty.

She gave a short, sharp laugh.

'Goodness me, Lily doesn't belong to Roger,' she said, the words bleak and angry in the salty gloom.

'Oh, I see . . .' he said, even though he did not. It was hardly his business and as she made no move to elaborate on it, he did not press it. It had the strange effect though of him wanting to take a step back. He did not want more complications in his life and hers sounded hellishly involved. He knew nothing about Roger, but this woman was spitting venom. It was there, in her eyes, her voice. He wouldn't give a lot for Roger's chances if he came in scratching-out-eyes distance.

'Whereabouts do you live?' he asked, steering the conversation into safer waters.

'The north,' she said, and from the tight reply he knew that was all he would get.

'I sometimes fancy a change of scene,' he said lightly. 'We could set up shop anywhere I suppose, me and Henry. I might even persuade him to move down here. A great place to live I would think.'

'But do you want to move?'

'It's tempting.' He looked at the darkening water, sniffed the sea salts, saw the lights of the yachts as they bobbed and creaked, their masts tinkling and it was indeed tempting. 'A long way from anywhere though,' he added, almost to himself.

'That entirely depends on where you want to be,' she said with a laugh, a nice friendly one this time. 'I haven't a clue where I want to be. Other than with Lily of course.'

James looked across to the row of little shops clustered round the harbour. They were still open and people were crowding into them and the nearby restaurants.

'How old is she?' he asked.

'Four months,' Sophie replied, with that familiar motherly pride. 'She'll be starting on solids soon.'

'Great,' he said, deciding he was on dangerous ground here. He shouldn't have mentioned Lily. Once mothers got talking about their babies . . . 'Fancy a night-cap in the bar? A brandy maybe.'

'No, thank you. I might have to get up during the night and I need a clear head.' She smiled. 'Thanks anyway. Ordinarily . . .' she shrugged, making it clear that she would have liked a night-cap very much. 'I'm having my hair done in the morning,' she said briskly. 'But we'll be around in the afternoon if you're doing nothing.'

'I thought I might drive over to Totnes.'

'That would be lovely,' she said. 'Lily's never been to Totnes.'

Hey, wait a minute . . . but it was too late.

They arranged to meet in the foyer at two and then they parted and he drifted into the bar for that night-cap.

'Cheer up,' the barman said in that age-old refrain. 'It might never happen, sir.'

It just had.

He had somehow managed to ask a woman *and* baby out for a date.

Amanda set the alarm for an early start in the morning. Thank heavens for all-day Sunday shopping. Taking Ellie's advice, she had ditched the shamefully untrendy undies and bought several new sets. And, just on the off-chance that James might end up in her room, she had gone to town on a pale-blue nightgown with shoestring straps, elegant and sexy. You couldn't go in for the *femme fatale* role in red cotton pyjamas.

She smiled at the very idea. Was she completely off her head?

EIGHT DAYS AT THE NEW GRAND

Lying in bed, unable to sleep, she seriously contemplated calling the whole thing off and never mind what Ellie would say. She could in all honestly say she had changed her mind because of her heavy workload.

On the other hand . . .

This thing she had for James for so many years was close to pathetic.

And one of the worse things was that Victoria had guessed.

Sociable souls as they were, Henry and Ellie started up what was to become a dinner party circuit, in which they always included Amanda and – Ellie being ever hopeful – a mystery male. Amanda, never taking it too seriously, happily played her part, although the male guests Ellie dredged up became increasingly odd. But it was when Victoria joined in the matchmaking efforts that it all became a bit uncomfortable.

And on one of those occasions, it dawned on her that Victoria knew how she felt about James.

It was late November and bitterly cold and, standing stamping her feet on the steps of Victoria's house waiting for her to answer the door, Amanda felt herself growing snuffly.

'Goodness. You're early!' Victoria said, opening the door.

It was a failing of hers. Over-zealous punctuality.

'Am I? The taxi driver came on time for once,' she said, wondering why Victoria always managed to do this, make her apologize.

'It's supposed to be eight for eight thirty.' Victoria continued, with a very bright smile, glancing at the grandfather clock that dominated the hall.

'Do you want me to go away and come back?' Amanda asked, annoyed at herself because everything always came out wrong when she talked to this woman.

'Don't be silly. You're here now.'

'So I am.' Amanda unwound her scarf and slipped it off, ruffled her hair, sneezing without warning and sending millions of germs in the direction of Victoria's severe black dress. 'Sorry, it's cold out.'

It was and she had very nearly come a cropper on the path in the new intensely uncomfortable high heels.

79

'Now, if I can just get a few things straight about this evening...' Victoria took Amanda's coat, held it away in a distinctly sniffy manner before hanging it up. When Victoria attended dinner parties, she had a gorgeous green velvet cape that draped beautifully and looked fantastic, the sort of item only tall, elegant blondes can get away with. 'I've searched high and low,' Victoria went on, 'and managed to find this wonderful man for you and he's coming along. So, you will be nice to him, won't you? He works in the coroner's office.'

'Oh goodness me, does he?' She glanced at her hostess, unsure. 'You are joking, I hope?'

'He'll be along shortly,' Victoria said, ignoring the comment, taking hold of her arm and escorting her through to the sitting-room where a log fire blazed in the hearth. 'Sherry?'

'Thank you,' Amanda said, even though she hated sherry.

It was compulsory, followed by a good wine at dinner, followed by a liqueur. Although Victoria rarely touched alcohol herself, she knew how to dispense it with flair and that's why Amanda had come by taxi.

'James will be down in a minute,' Victoria said. 'He takes such an age to have his bath and shave and so on, and now he's fussing about what to wear. You know what men are like. ...'

The table Amanda had glimpsed in the dining-room was already low lit, casting a pink glow over the white cloth and gleaming silver. Flowers in great abundance. Yes, Victoria knew how to entertain, providing an entirely different experience from Ellie's more informal hospitality.

She also knew how to make the best of herself and the dress she was wearing was extremely flattering with its crossover top and slim skirt. Her hair was shiny and deceptively simple, her make-up perfect.

As she said, everything under control. And yet ... there was an edginess about her in the constant hand movements, in the way she kept looking this way and that. She was not relaxed and never had been. Henry said she was as brittle as a stalagmite and had never explained why.

'How is James?' Amanda ventured, sipping the sherry. 'I haven't seen him for ages.' She kept the enquiry cool enough, for she had long decided she was big enough to deal with this.

There was no reason for Victoria or James to know her feelings, and she would never in a million years upset either of them. Their marriage seemed sound enough, although to Amanda's mind they never seemed quite the same peas-in-a-pod couple as Henry and Ellie. With them, it was difficult to imagine one without the other.

'James is fine,' Victoria said with a knowing smile. 'It's the best thing he's ever done going into partnership with Henry. Although I was upset at the time, I realize that our working together was not a good idea.'

'I should think it must be a problem,' Amanda agreed. 'They say you can see too much of each other.'

'It wasn't that. We didn't actually work side by side. The problem, Amanda, was he couldn't take my being senior to him. Men are such babies, aren't they, in some respects? And my having my own parking space really riled him. Can you believe anything so petty?'

She could.

'I know this will come as a shock,' she continued, 'but James and I are thinking of moving.'

'Moving?' She knew her voice echoed her dismay. 'Where on earth to?'

'Oh, not far . . . heavens, did you think we were emigrating?' Victoria asked, with another of her trilling laughs. 'Did you imagine you might not see us ever again?'

'To a bigger property then?' Amanda asked, calmer now, for she had, for a fleeting moment, imagined exactly that.

'Yes, with a large garden. Out towards Boston Spa.' She sighed. 'I haven't exactly discussed it with James but he'll go along with it. He always does anything I want him to do,' she added firmly. 'Men are such darlings, aren't they? Especially James.'

And James is all mine, the look confirmed, so if you have any ideas you can forget them.

Victoria knew.

Refusing to acknowledge it, Amanda changed the subject. There was no future in her feelings, and she could deny it until she was blue in the face but the fact was that he was the only man for her. She had tried others, a select few, but nobody

matched up. She could easily find herself a nice man, unattached, and it ought to be enough.

But, of course, it was not.

James was married and it was just tough luck. Married to
Victoria at that. What the hell had possessed him?

Hurried footsteps down the stairs.

'There he is at last.' Victoria rose to her feet, smoothed down
her skirt. 'In here, darling. Amanda got here early.'

'Not that early,' Amanda protested, as James came through.

'Hello,' he said, smiling at her. 'We'll have to put some salt
down on the path, Victoria, or we'll have everyone flat out. I've
just peeped out. It's freezing out there.'

'I nearly slipped.'

Victoria glared at her, the gaze as cold as the night air.

Oblivious, as he so often was, James carried on cheerfully,
'Sorry about this but my wife's trying to matchmake again,
Amanda. She's raked up this guy for you, who works in the
coroner's office, so we can't promise a bundle of laughs.'

He proved to be dead right and, as dinner parties go, it was
not one of the most memorable. Across the table, Amanda found
her gaze constantly brought back to Victoria. She was a very
bright presence, such a golden beauty, a butterfly with a halo of
light around her, her blue eyes quite startling and James clearly
adored her. It was hard to take but a fact of life.

Amanda watched closely. The fidgeting continued more or
less unabated throughout the evening, the laughs loud and too
often, and Amanda, good at this, picked it up and filed away the
signs, to remember them much later.

She was not glad it happened. Of course she was not glad,
only a cretin would be glad, for it nearly destroyed James.

It would, she knew, take time.

But, when he finally came out of it, she wanted to be the one
who just happened to be there.

Bea Bell had spent most of the evening in the smaller lounge,
where there was a bridge match in progress. A well-chosen seat
giving views through to the reception area and, from the
window, she watched with interest as the two young people,
James and Sophie, came in from their walk. So far, so good then.

They were together but not touching, chatting quite freely though, faces animated.

All she desired was that this week would be the first week of their love affair. The beginning. There was always a beginning.

The little waitress, a bubbly blonde with half-moon glasses and purple nails, appeared, asking if she could get her something from the bar.

Bea considered. 'Thank you. I'll have a double bourbon on the rocks. I'll take it in the bar.'

The waitress watched with concern as the old lady teetered off on very high heels, trailing a beautiful fringed stole in her wake. Scurrying off herself, she managed to get there first, to warn the bar staff in advance that Ms Bell was on her way, about to start on another of her binges.

Some considerable time later, James escorted Bea to the lift.

She had had one drink too many and, stepping in ahead of him, she somehow managed to press the button and take-off took place before he could scramble in behind her.

God knows where it would take her, he thought anxiously, half expecting that when it returned she would still be there, but no, it was empty, and assuming she had found her way safely to her room, James pressed the key and went up to his.

Bea had been a touch maudlin this evening, full of harrowing Virginian tales, some of which had left her captive audience open-mouthed. He had listened, declining to comment on his own tragedy, which frankly beat the tin hat out of most of them. Bea's language had been hilariously appalling and the barman had finally cautioned her, saying with a wink that gentlemen were present, if she wouldn't mind moderating it.

James smiled, deciding he would sleep late tomorrow, maybe do a bit of work, have lunch and then meet Sophie. Selfishly, he wished she was not bringing the baby with her for he would much prefer her on her own.

Sophie . . .

It was a long time since he had gone off to sleep dreaming about a woman, a particular one. He thought of those lovely hazel eyes, the enquiring way she looked at him, her softly alluring body.

It was just as he drifted off that Victoria nudged into his mind. And this time it was an irritation.

A few months before Lily was born, Sophie moved house. Incredibly busy as she was with other things, it was bad timing, but just the way it worked out. The stone cottage, Grade II listed, on the fringe of a small village was all she ever hoped for.

Roger, in a fit of conscience perhaps, had done well by her, even allowing for the fact that, as a result of a personal financial inheritance, she was hardly destitute. She almost wished he had not been quite so agreeable. A hostile Roger to the bitter end would have been easier.

'A clean break,' he said. 'A one-off payment so long as you don't bother me again.'

'Suits me,' she said, pleased with the financial arrangements that had enabled her to hang on to the big house.

She remembered him looking at her then, momentarily a little abashed. 'No hard feelings?' he asked quietly. 'It just didn't work out, did it?'

'Oh, for pity's sake . . .'

She turned her back on him.

The house in Harrogate, the one she had shared with him, the one they had painstakingly and at great expense renovated into a single home rather than flats, was returned, again at some expense, to its former use and she was now beginning to profit from the rents she collected from the three apartments.

After years of living in huge, high-ceilinged draughty houses, Sophie was ready at last for something cosier and the cottage she found in what the estate agent glowingly described as an elevated rural location was on the edge of a village. Her relief at not having him around any more meant she could relax and start to map out the rest of her life. She ought to have known that careful plans are certain to go awry and, in the event, Lily's unexpected arrival meant a rearrangement of those plans. It was best she stayed home and she could manage without the money her secretarial job delivered.

Lying in bed at The New Grand, Sophie found she was missing home. The estate agent had not exaggerated the splendour of the views from every single cottage window and, just drawing the curtains in the morning and looking out gave her so much pleasure. The views here were equally splendid but seaside was different.

She sighed, pounding the pillows and glancing across at the sleeping babe in her cot. She was always like this on holiday.

Roger had been impatient with her. 'For Christ's sake, we're supposed to be on holiday. Enjoy it. Stop crossing the days off like you're in prison.'

Now, after only a few days, she was beginning to feel itchy for home.

But this time, for some reason she could not quite recall, something nasty had happened at home, and she knew she could not go back yet.

Chapter Ten

Monday

TOBY was a little concerned. Alice had hinted that there was a potentially serious problem in the offing and he had scheduled a meeting with her for ten. He hoped it was not another financial fiasco. Those cowboys who had done the refurbishment would have to wait a while for their money. He had made various complaints about finishing touches, even suggesting that the cream exterior was taking on a faint browny-orangey tinge, as if dusted with cinnamon and that would have to be rectified. He anticipated that payment could be delayed considerably and the cash-flow problem temporarily ebbed. There was some fine tuning to be done to their current financial state and now was not the time to lose his nerve. However churned up and panicked he might be, he must never show it.

Added to his staff worries, one of the guests had created a bit of a scene last night in the bar and there had been a few high-handed complaints from other guests. Beatrice Bell had to be handled with kid gloves and next time she turned up in the bar, it might be advisable to provide a discreet escort, someone to listen to those interminable tales, help cool the language, and take her mind off the bourbon.

'Right then . . .' He checked his watch and looked across the desk where Mavis, his secretary, was going through the mail with him. He had inherited Mavis, unfortunately, from his father, who thought the sun shone out of her, and she was therefore unsackable. 'Anything else? No other problems?'

'Not really, Mr Morrell . . .'

He eyed her closely. She had worked with his father for over twenty years and he knew she wished she still did. She knew more about the hotel trade than he did, was efficiency gone mad and, worse, privy to a lot of confidential information about Toby himself. There was a difficulty in retaining respect when the woman knew all there was to know about his teenage acne and his helter-skelter run through university. She certainly knew all about his relationships and had even had the nerve to offer her commiserations when the last one faltered. He was under strict instructions from his father not to forget the woman's birthday. . . .

'Let's have it,' he said, seeing she was bursting to say something.

'I know it's none of my business, but I'd rather you heard it from me, Mr Morrell, than anyone else.' Her smile, burdened with overlarge teeth, was malicious.

'Yes?'

'There's bound to be a complaint coming up about Fiona Jennings on reception. She's the dark-haired young woman. Rather flashy, I feel.'

'Yes, yes.' Impatiently, he glanced once more at his watch. She would win a prize for class sneak, Mavis.

'Surely people other than me have noticed that she's in grave danger of becoming over-familiar with guests? You know our rules about staff involvement with guests?'

'Of course. I invented them. Is she causing trouble?'

'She's just naturally flirtatious, I suppose. I've seen her hanging about the pool on her days off. And you know that is strictly banned.' Mavis smiled. 'Silly girl. A reprimand, I think, is called for. Possibly a word from you. Nothing more at this stage.'

'I'll decide what's to be done,' Toby said sharply.

'Of course, sir. Goodness, I never meant to imply otherwise.'

'I'll probably have a word,' he went on, although strictly

speaking it was a trivial matter and ought to be left to her supervisor.

He spent the time between nine and ten hovering between the breakfast terrace and the foyer, having a word here and there, smiling his smile, cracking the odd joke or two, dispensing a feeling of bonhomie. At ten precisely, he strode into the duty manager's office to see Alice.

'Before we start, Mr Morrell, a quick word on the celebrity front.'

'Have you got somebody?'

Her sigh was slight. 'I'm in touch with several, or rather their agents, checking availability. The rock star's come back with a no.'

'Has he?' Toby, who had classical tastes, was inclined to say thank God for that, but he saw he would have been better than nothing.

'Will you settle for a sports personality?'

'Anybody, Alice,' he said wearily. 'So long as it's a face. Somebody we know. We don't want any of those obscure sports. I don't suppose we could interest a minor royal? A very minor one would do.'

'I'm afraid not. They're booked up months ahead, sir.' She gave him a pained look. 'There's a ballet on in Plymouth. We could perhaps get one of the dancers. . . ?'

'Nobody recognizes ballerinas in plain clothes,' he said. 'Last resort that. What else was it? You have fifteen minutes to fill me in.'

'Fifteen minutes is all I shall require,' she said. 'The thing is, Mr Morrell . . .' She rose suddenly and walked across to her door which he had left slightly ajar. Closing it, she returned to her desk.

'I think we have a spy on board,' she said.

It was peculiar talking to a back-seat passenger. It made James feel like a chauffeur and it was disconcerting that he could not snatch glimpses of her but had to content himself with just listening. Sophie had a nice voice, calm and unhurried, and when she spoke to the baby, it charmingly changed tone, raised a pitch yet at the same time softened. It made him smile.

She could have sat beside him but Lily's seat had to be placed in the back and she insisted on sitting beside the baby.

'You've had your hair cut,' James remarked, flinging the comment over his shoulder, once they were on their way.

'Yes,' she said, and there was a note of caution. 'A bit drastic. I'm not sure now but it's too late.'

'It suits you,' he said firmly, well aware that women liked to be told that. It didn't matter an iota whether or not it was true.

'Thank you.' There was a smile in her voice. 'A little bird tells me that Ms Bell was a little the worse for wear last night.'

'Just a little,' James said. 'Quite an old girl, isn't she?'

'She had an army of servants waiting on her in Virginia,' Sophie said. 'Can you imagine that? She paints such a lovely picture of him, doesn't she? Oscar Lee Bell. The love of her life she tells me.'

'She has guts,' James said. 'Uprooting herself like that. That takes courage.'

Lily interrupted, letting out a single cry and there was some fussing and cooing to be done before they reached Totnes. The search for a parking space proved a headache, but at last they bagged one in a car-park in the lower part of town. Their subsequent disembarkation was, in logistical terms, equivalent to an army setting up camp. Sophie coped admirably with everything whilst he stood by, feeling useless, offering to hold Lily and relieved when it was turned down. Sophie could do the lot, single-handed, Lily perched on her hip.

They exited into the peaceful setting of The Plains, grateful for the leafy shade before they headed up the busy little street where most of the shops were. Full sun here and very warm. Sophie was wearing a long, loosely cut dress with a big-brimmed white hat and Lily was in striped lilac, her little bonnet with a frilly edge.

As they progressed, slowly because of the crowds on the narrow pavement, there was that happy, dated New Age atmosphere he remembered from his last visit and he commented on it as a group of out of time hippies passed. As they almost danced round each other, James exchanged a smile with them.

Beyond the East Gate in Fore Street, a busker had set up camp and was fiddling in a frantic fashion. Digging into his pocket, James tossed some coins in the cap in passing.

Casting a glance Sophie's way however, he saw to his surprise that she was not amused.

'Tuneless,' she said. 'You're wasting your money on him.'

'I don't know,' he said mildly. 'I didn't think he was too bad. Good luck to him.' He glanced back. 'Dog on a string, too. Did you see?'

'I did. And I'm surprised it's allowed. Down and outs, that's all they are.'

'Oh come on,' he said, showing his surprise now. 'What harm are they doing? I sometimes wish I had the guts to do it. Opt out like that.'

'It hardly takes guts: it's what they've chosen to do,' she said, her voice sharp. 'More fool them. It's all very well, James, but they can't have it both ways, people like that. They can't live like they do and then expect us to prop them up when they need it. Can they seriously expect us to pay for the tat they sell? And, as for begging, that is beyond the pale.'

'I haven't noticed any begging,' he said, his voice tight, too. 'The busker was trying to be entertaining.'

'One step away from begging, in my opinion. Anyway, begging's usually part of the package. I have no patience. They should get a job like everyone else.'

'Aren't you being a bit harsh?' he asked, smiling a little, not wanting to make too much of it, for they were in danger here of having an argument.

Thankfully, they were interrupted, having to separate to allow other people access to a shop and by the time they joined up again, she was talking about something else.

He chose not to pursue it. Why argue on such a sunny day?

Fourteen years ago, Victoria had, on the contrary, been quite enchanted with the free-and-easy lifestyle of travellers like these. She even bought one or two things from their stalls in the market, hand-made jewellery mainly. It was a good day all round. She had coaxed him into having some sort of discussion about the future over a marvellous lunch in a sea-food restaurant in Devisham and, to his relief, she had come round to his way of thinking. She agreed it was madness yet to think of a child. Although, and she smiled as she said it, he was not going to be too upset if the planning went haywire?

'No,' he said, managing a smile, although she sometimes overdid the little-girl image and over-estimated the effect. It did make him wonder though, that little planted warning, as to which of them was fooling the other. He could personally settle for two uninterrupted years before their planned family began, but could she?

'Are all women devious?' he asked Sophie now. 'I ask because my wife was. Is it inbuilt into the female constitution?'

'Absolutely not,' she said, smiling at him. 'What a thing to suggest.'

'Funny, that's what I thought you would say.'

Good-humouredly, he concentrated on steering the pram through the pedestrian traffic. Once you got the hang of it, it wasn't so bad and the baby had gone to sleep. James found himself glancing in shop windows, catching sight of himself in this new fatherly role and rather liking it. Once they'd exhausted the shops, they trekked down the street again towards the bridge over the River Dart and found somewhere to sit.

'Something wrong?' he asked, looking at her and recalling Victoria's faraway looks of old. They generally spelled trouble.

'No . . . well, yes, I suppose.'

He prompted her as the silence continued.

'The thing is . . .' She hesitated, pushing at her newly styled hair. 'It occurred to me that you might think I angled for this invitation to join you and I don't want you to get the wrong impression. I'm just after a bit of company, that's all, James. Nothing else.'

'It's OK,' he said gently. 'Perish the thought.'

'God knows I'm no teenager, and a holiday romance is the last thing on my mind.'

'Mine too,' he said, smiling through the lie. 'We both seemed at a loose end and that's all there is to it. It was a toss-up between you and Bea Bell and I can't stand the hats.'

'Can't you? I think they're lovely.' She reached over, lightly

91

touched his hand. 'Just as long as we're quite clear where we stand.'

It hung there for the rest of the day and they spent a considerable part of the journey home in silence.

'It's been lovely, James,' she said as the hotel came into view. 'If you don't mind, I think Lily and I will go straight upstairs for a rest. And I shall have room service tonight so I won't see you in the dining-room.'

Well, that was clear as crystal!

As they walked past the lounge, he happened to glance in and did an immediate double take. Who should be sitting in the lounge but Amanda Lester, taking tea it would appear with Bea. They were engrossed in deep conversation and absurdly not wanting to speak to Amanda at this moment, James hurried by and up to his room. He hated himself for wishing she had not come. Why had she come? True, he had urged her to take a few days away for she certainly needed a break, but he had not expected her to take him up on it.

The truth was and he acknowledged it reluctantly, the truth was that with Amanda on the scene, his style, if it existed at all, would be seriously cramped.

On the way down, Amanda pulled off the M5 south of Bristol for a break. A restaurant at a motorway service area was hardly the place for a bit of quiet contemplation, she reflected ruefully, fighting her way to a table.

She did not feel at all cheerful. On the contrary, she was torn once more by self doubt. Looking back, she saw that she had always reached decisions without much heartrending – which university, which course, which career and so on – and then simply gone with the flow. But with James . . . she had needed to be so strong this past year, for the events had well and truly knocked him into touch. Some of his friends, so called, had deserted him, embarrassed and not able to cope with it, but she loved him so much that she had no alternative but to stay and support him through it. She had seen the way Victoria's mother had looked at him at the funeral and seen he would get no help from that quarter.

Thoughtfully, she sipped her coffee.

By mistake, she seemed to have found a table in the smoking area but she could cope with that now. She thought about the past year, trying to put her thoughts into perspective.

The last time she saw Victoria, that most important last time, was a casual meeting in town. She had locked in the memory, gone over it since over and over again.

Amanda was buying a birthday present for her niece and having accomplished that, she was allowing herself a little browsing before returning to the car.

Stopping to adjust the parcel, a particularly awkward shape, she happened to glance in the window of a baby boutique and saw Victoria just on her way out. Having made eye contact, a meeting was inevitable.

'Hi.' They greeted each other with a kiss, with actressy enthusiasm, considering neither of them cared for the other.

'I was just looking round,' Victoria spluttered, peculiarly anxious as if she'd been caught coming out of a sex shop. 'A christening gift.'

'Did you find anything?'

'For what?'

'The christening,' Amanda said patiently.

'Oh no, I'll have to look somewhere else,' Victoria said. She was wearing a gorgeous dark-blue suit, a bit posh for shopping. 'How about lunch? I know this great Italian restaurant just round the corner.'

Amanda agreed, against her better judgement, deciding she would risk the possibility of a parking fine rather than snub her, for Victoria would take it as a personal insult and she would never hear the last of it. So they set off, Amanda feeling distinctly underdressed in jeans and top.

'You're looking well, Amanda,' Victoria said, as they waited for their meal.

'Thanks. So are you,' she said, politeness winning although it was not true. Victoria, always pale, looked paler than usual and the fidgety movements seemed worse, too. Her relatively cheery mood had evaporated on the way to the restaurant and, not for the first time, Amanda thought that poor James had his work cut out living with this woman.

'I'm a touch under the weather,' Victoria said. 'Exhausted. Working too hard, of course.'

'Me too. This is a real treat...' Amanda gazed around, soaking in the atmosphere. 'I must remember this place.'

'We've been here a few times. James wanted to take me to Italy last year but it's such a hassle by coach or train.'

'You should try flying. I don't like it much either, Victoria, but it's quick.'

Victoria gave her a look. 'Don't you start. I have enough from James. He doesn't understand at all but then men don't, do they? They don't understand what makes us tick.'

'I suppose not,' Amanda said awkwardly, not wanting to be seen to criticize James.

'I work like a navvy,' Victoria went on. 'All hours. I have to, in my position. My staff have no idea. I know I get paid for it, but the responsibility is awesome, Amanda.'

'I sympathize. I work all hours, too. Still, I love it and the challenge and there's a lot of satisfaction in it.'

Victoria eyed her closely. 'Oh yes, there is that.'

They smiled. Very brightly.

Amanda caved in first.

'Do you know, I sometimes wish I was like Ellie . . . free as air.'

'Henry's Ellie? Oh yes, she has it all, doesn't she?' Victoria said, the bitterness coming through. 'Career. Family.'

Amanda decided there was no point clarifying matters. Ellie's career was half-baked and she would be the first to admit it. Freelancing – period wallpapers – on a very relaxed basis.

'I want a family.'

'Do you?' Amanda fiddled with her glass, wishing she had never agreed to come to lunch.

'It was always in my scheme of things,' Victoria said wistfully. 'Don't you think I would have made a wonderful mother?'

'Well, yes.'

'James says it doesn't matter, that we're all right as we are, just the two of us. But it's not enough. Not for me anyway.'

They messed around a moment with rolls and butter, the importance of the conversation hanging in the air, the domestic movements automatic, giving them time to think.

'You have a lot going for you,' Amanda said, deciding on the jollying technique. 'You have a lovely home. You're very successful. And James loves you.'

'Does he?' Carefully plucked eyebrows were raised. 'Or does he wish he'd married somebody else? Some woman who could provide him with babies?'

'No he does not,' Amanda said, indignant on his behalf. 'What a daft idea!'

'It's so unfair,' Victoria said, picking at the pasta and seeming determined to make this a totally miserable lunch. 'Why me? My mother says she simply can't understand it. Infertility is not something we have in our family. And I'm not trying IVF for anybody. I'm not going through that.'

'Now look.' Amanda had had enough. 'There's no point moping. Think of all the things you can do without kids. They take your life over, Ellie says. It needs thinking about seriously. Frankly, I don't see that I'm going to bother myself. I aim to be a partner some day and it's going to be very difficult to combine that with a family. Maternity leave. Nannies. Horrendous.'

Victoria looked straight at her. Saw straight through her.

'And there speaks a woman who is probably as fertile as an oasis. Really, Amanda, if you can't say anything sensible, don't say anything at all.'

Restlessly, in the restaurant of the motorway services, Amanda breathed in the cigarette smoke and found she was ridiculously upset by the memory.

Poor Victoria.

That lunch that day had been a cry for help and she had not listened.

Two days later, Victoria had driven to Beachy Head and had jumped to her death.

Chapter Eleven

AMANDA checked in at The New Grand.

A porter whipped her bags away and she followed him to the lift, which deposited her, swishily silent, on the second floor. She left her unpacking for later and descended to the reception floor, finding her way to the lounge. The day looked tempting, still had a lot left in it, but she was very tired after the journey.

'May I join you?'

The old lady who posed the question was in a cream lacy dress with an orange and cream silk turban round her head. Very fetching! She sat down gracefully opposite Amanda and within minutes, she had ordered them a big pot of tea and some scones. Taken by surprise by the onslaught, Amanda, too tired to do otherwise, let it all drift by, answering the occasional question. She wished she could slip her shoes off and curl up more comfortably but The New Grand was just too grand for that.

Bea chatted to the young woman with the beautiful brown eyes and mop of dark-brown curly hair. A friend of Mr Kendall's, she quickly ascertained.

Expertly, she gave her potted version of life in Virginia with dearest Oscar but, when she sensed the girl was becoming bored, she swiftly changed the subject.

'Enough about me. What do you do, my dear?'

'I work in a law firm up in Leeds.'

'A lawyer like my Oscar?' She clapped her hands in delight. 'Wonderful. I must say, you do not look like a lawyer.'

'I'm not sure what a lawyer looks like.'

Bea regarded her calmly. 'The male of the species is attractively aggressive. Sure-footed and utterly confident. The female is exactly the same and that, I do believe, is a grave mistake. You are not quite built in that mould.'

'I'm not?'Amanda smiled, amused by the old lady's earnestness.

'You are not.' Bea smiled too. 'Let me assure you, my observation was meant to be a compliment. I very much dislike aggression in a female, other than to defend her young of course, when it is an admirable trait. I mistook your friend James for a lawyer but he tells me he is in graphic design. He will be so pleased to see you, won't he? Such a lovely surprise.'

Amanda agreed with that, but Bea watched her face as she talked of James Kendall, caught the underlying concern, and was quick to grasp the essentials of it.

A love triangle!

How absolutely wonderful.

Bea, unusually for her, in a navy dress and feathered hat, was extra watchful at dinner. There was sadly no sign of Mrs Willis. James, looking relaxed and tanning nicely, was accompanied instead by Amanda.

Amanda was clearly head over heels in love with him, written as it was in mile-high letters in her eyes. And he did not know. Men were capable of being such fools, unable to interpret the clearest signals. The woman literally glowed when she was with him.

She had taken particular trouble to look attractive this evening in a green, softly draped trouser suit that flattered her but, for all the notice he was taking, she need not have bothered.

He was being politely attentive of course, but he was preoccupied. Thinking no doubt of his little trip out with Mrs Willis and the baby. There had been a cosy look about them when they returned and Bea recalled how he had leaned over the pushchair and gently touched the baby's cheek before he left them. A tender gesture that had entranced the mother.

Bea, talking to Amanda at the time in the lounge, had spotted the arrival out of the corner of her eye but Amanda had not noticed. Bea was not entirely surprised. Her own powers of observation were rarely surpassed.

English ladies of a certain class were particularly good at that.

*

Room service was not a success that evening. The food was delicious but Sophie could only peck at it, leaving most of it and covering up the wasted food with a napkin, feeling guilty. Her mother's 'there are people out there, starving' came thudding back. Her mother was always right. She had warned her about Roger. You'll never keep *him* on a leash, she had said.

Sophie took stock of the day in Totnes. She knew she had taken fright at one point, been attacked by a sudden bout of impatience and extreme annoyance and it had puzzled James. She regretted, too, going on about holiday romances, making a complete idiot of herself. It was so embarrassing and she was not quite sure how to face him tomorrow, for the fact was, she knew, he knew, that they were close to embarking on the very thing she had so heartily disowned. She had made much too much of it and planted the thought in his head.

Giving Lily her feed, the baby snuggled to her body as she drank from the bottle, Sophie breathed easily and gently. She had never thought about Roger in the way she was thinking about James. She had been thrilled that Roger should look at her the way he did and she had wanted to show him off to her girlfriends, wanted to be the first in their group to get married.

What a daft reason!

Lily had stopped sucking, sated, eyes tightly closed, lashes long against the baby skin.

'I think you've had enough, young lady,' Sophie whispered, slipping the teat out of her mouth. It was enough to cause her to open her eyes a moment and fix Sophie with an aggrieved look, before sleepiness took over once more. Gently, Sophie laid her in the cot, looked at her for a while as she always did, taking in every tiny portion of her face.

Just then, without warning, that funny feeling came over her, that faintness, the onset of panic and she had to double up a moment, breathe deeply until it passed. She knew there was some sort of problem but she couldn't think what it was. Was she going mad?

'What shall we do about James?' she muttered, shaking off the

98

feeling and returning to normal, breathing more easily. 'Do you think we ought to cool things before it's too late?'

It needn't be such a big thing, she decided, as she undressed. They were grown-ups. They could have a fling without it being serious. She had Lily and she knew he was wary of that, and he had the memory of his wife and she was wary of that.

All these doubts.

Why was her life so complicated?

It had been a long time though since a man had held her in his arms and told her he loved her and she longed for that.

'You look very nice,' James said, over coffee.

At last! At long last.

Amanda smiled her appreciation. She had read somewhere not to underestimate the feminine approach. Apparently, according to an upbeat article in this glossy monthly, men still – yes, even in this new century – men could still be taken in by a bit of feminine fluttering. The article concluded by saying that, without exception, men melted if this approach was used to its full advantage. Women, it said, some women had forgotten how to flirt and they needed to wise up on it fast. There followed one of those ridiculous questionnaires on how you rated in the flirtation stakes and Amanda, feeling foolish, found a pen and dutifully answered, ticking the boxes that applied to her. She scored a miserable seven points, which meant she needed serious help.

Some women were born to do it and she was not one of them. She regarded this tarting-up business as a real pain but, if a thing was worth doing and all that. . . .

'You look nice.'

Better than nothing.

She had noticed him looking round though, maybe hoping that Mrs Willis would change her mind and come down to dinner. Frankly, it was insulting. She wondered briefly if he had kissed Mrs Willis for, damn him, he had never kissed her, not properly. He had held her close on a couple of occasions, but from disbelief and grief and she just happened to be there.

'Shall we have a breath of fresh air?' she suggested, picking up the silky fringed wrap, a floaty, far too glamorous affair. Even before it cleared her credit card, she knew it was a mistake, not her kind of thing at all. It would end up stuffed forlornly in a drawer and, next year, she would pass it on to a charity shop.

James eyed the wrap in neutral fashion, not seeming to appreciate that, Italian silk in autumnal shades, it had cost a fortune.

'Will you be warm enough?' he enquired.

'Of course.' She attempted to sweep the wrap over her shoulders in one deft movement, without knocking over the entire contents of the table. A bold but ultimately disastrous effort, as the wrap landed vaguely round her shoulders, hopelessly awry and she had to fiddle around making adjustments.

'You might have telephoned to say you were coming,' James said, as soon as they were outside. It was still warm, the pleasant heat of the day lingering and the sea beyond the harbour walls a calm silver. 'How did you get time off? I thought you said you were snowed under?'

'I decided you were right after all,' she said defensively. 'I needed a break. And Ellie kept on at me and she can be very persuasive.'

'Well, whatever the reason, you're here now . . .' he said, and she could have killed him for the offhand manner.

'How you do feel, James? Has it been as much of a shock coming here as you thought it might be? I suppose it's too soon to tell if this is going to work. This silly idea of Jennifer's,' she added crossly.

'Maybe it is. I'm still thinking about Victoria a lot. Memories are everywhere.'

'Of course they are. I was stupid when I said forget her. You never will.'

'You were only trying to help,' he said, with a reluctant smile. 'Even if you were a bit blunt.'

'That's me.' she sighed, glancing his way. 'I'm sorry if you didn't want me to come down. It wasn't one of my wisest moves, was it? I shall only get in the way.'

He did not deny it and she felt a chill in her heart and it was nothing to do with the night breeze blowing across from the open sea, feeling chillier now they were on a level with it.

'You've been just great,' he said. 'God alone knows how I'd have coped without you and you mustn't think I'm ungrateful but—'

'It's OK. Don't go on,' she said briskly. She knew a brush-off when she heard it and it was long expected – stupid fool that she was – and she had no option but to take it gracefully, even if she felt like crying and pummelling him with her hands. 'Why don't we walk up through town?' she said, anxious to be on the move.

'Just as you like.'

The view now was a complete waste of time, so far as she was concerned. The evening was finished, the whole holiday was finished for that matter, but somehow she had to struggle through because she had paid a sizeable deposit and there was no way she was going to lose that.

'You needn't hang around with me these next few days,' Amanda said. 'I didn't come down for you to hold my hand. I came for a short break and I have lots planned.'

'Are you quite sure?' he asked, the relief in his voice such that the chill in her completely iced over.

'Absolutely. I want to visit Plymouth and there are a couple of things I want to take a peep at over in Cornwall. I've never ever been to Cornwall.'

'Neither have I. I might come with you,' he said, spoiling things, not seeming to realize how she was trying to make this easier for herself.

'You're welcome,' she said, after a moment's hesitation. 'I could do with a navigator if nothing else.'

'I thought you were brilliant at directions. Henry says you read road maps for pleasure.'

She sniffed. 'He would say that. He's just peeved because he gets lost all the time. Men do,' she added, casting him a sly glance, 'but hate to admit it, and would never in a million years ask for directions.'

'Victoria was hopeless.'

Amanda sighed. She had hoped they might get through the remainder of the evening without a further mention.

'Or maybe she pretended to be hopeless?'

'What do you mean by that?'

'Nothing. It's just that some women are like that. Like to be fluffy.'

He laughed shortly. 'It's not like you to be bitchy.'

'Am I? I thought I was making an observation.'

'You didn't know her very well. You only knew her in a social sense.'

'I knew her well enough,' she said, feeling the need to apologize anyway. 'Sorry, I'm tired. Put it down to car lag.'

They were passing a smart bar and he suggested a drink. Amanda accepted and they drifted in, but somehow she felt he had done it out of duty, a peace offering for jumping down her throat, and she was miffed.

'What'll you have?' James asked, as they fought their way through a packed house.

'Gin and tonic, please,' she said, adjusting the slippery wrap. 'I'll find us some seats.'

Which was no easy task.

'This place is popular,' James said, returning with their drinks. 'We should have gone back to the hotel.'

'I like it here,' she said firmly. As he settled opposite her, for old time's sake and remembering Ellie's advice, she tried her version of a seductive smile and a look from lowered lashes, one she had practised hilariously but it predictably failed to get a whiff of interest. Well, to hell with him then.

'I'll get you back to the hotel as soon as we've finished this,' he said, looking at her with some concern. 'God, you look terrible. Absolutely shattered.'

She yawned. Gave up the ghost.

The fresh air outside woke her up a little and kicked off her fighting spirit once more. She liked a bit of competition, she decided, and she knew she had stiff competition from Mrs Willis. She had only seen her fleetingly but she had a bit of an anxious look, reminding her worryingly of Victoria.

She was not going to give James up so easily. Not without a fight. The fact that she had never had James in the first place was an irrelevance.

'Thanks for a lovely evening,' she told him, as they parted in the foyer.

'Thanks too. We should do it more often,' James said with a quick smile. 'Get yourself off to bed. You'll feel better in the morning.' He gave her a kiss on the cheek and propelled her to the lift, waiting with her until it emerged, murmuring a good-night as she stepped into it.

Only when she reached her room and was fumbling with the key, did it dawn that, somewhere, the wrap had made its silken escape.

And she would lose no sleep over that.

Toby had a harbour-view apartment, one of a rather functional if very expensive block built in the early nineties but it had spacious rooms, a security set-up second only to Fort Knox and it suited his purposes fine. It was furnished as he liked it – masculine but not aggressively so – and to hell with what that sniffy Louis would say. It was just a bachelor pad, although sadly it saw little action.

He rarely used the kitchen although he had been in the hotel kitchens often enough observing and had picked up a few tips in the process. It was the very in-thing, particularly with this practically insane new chef, always to be on the edge of panic, and stepping from the high temperatures and hot tempers into the calm air-conditioned elegance of the dining-foom was a shock to the system.

Toby chose to eat out most of the time and he also used the hotel to look after his personal items so he had a regular supply of clean pressed shirts and laundered sheets. He employed a woman to clean twice a week but it must be a doddle of a job because he was naturally tidy.

Since when was being tidy seen as a criticism? His last relationship of any significance with a slightly older but very attractive divorcee had ended in the usual blood-stirring row. Come to think of it, his relationships never just fizzled out, they exploded.

'Toby – for Christ's sake, get lost,' she had yelled. 'You're so bloody tidy.'

She claimed it was insulting to her that he could spare the time, before making love, to fold and hang up his clothes. Where was the passion? As a result of that, he made a valiant effort to pounce on her next time, surprise her with his impulsiveness and to hell with the state of their clothes, but he was past having sex on a polished floor and she made an unholy fuss about a splinter and the whole thing was a disaster.

She left him shortly after that.

What did women want?

At work or play, they were a terrible trial.

He thought about what Alice had told him. She had heard on the hotel grapevine that the *Harlequin Guide* had taken to an underhand method of inspecting their listed hotels. Yes, they continued to do the annual up-front one, but sneakily they also did a spot check using a – Alice's word – spy, a spy who stayed for a few days to get a wider picture. The other hotels could not offer much information and why should they, but he and Alice had put two and two together. Each time, during or shortly after a visit of a lone woman guest, their current inclusion in the 2001 guide was either confirmed or deleted.

It would be a disaster if they lost their spot. His father, who was scornful about all the expense of the refurbishment and mortified at the name change, would play merry hell. The *Harlequin Recommended Hotel Guide* lurked conspicuously in each of the hotels featured, home and abroad, a wonderful link-up and Toby knew that a lot of their bookings came from that source.

Alice was busy checking the current guest-list, looking to see if there were any likely 'spy' candidates. A woman alone, making a last-minute reservation seemed the best bet. If they could isolate her, then it would be all systems go to ensure that she had a very good visit. It was on-their-toes time for the whole staff.

Coping as he was with an Alice in panic mode, and the continuing lack of a celebrity, meant he still had not had a word with Fiona Jennings in reception, Mavis having laid that young lady's file on his desk.

Time enough for that.

He gazed out from the balcony across the darkening harbour with its calm sea and twinkling lights. Come Saturday midnight, the sparks of the fireworks display would join with the billions of stars in what had to be a clear bright sky. The fireworks alone were costing a bomb – literally money up in smoke – but that was that and another drop in the ocean.

Born as he was, with a hotel spoon in his mouth, Toby knew he ought to be able to ride out this storm of anxiety. He was letting it get to him. Good God, he had even found a grey hair this morning. It was still there because he couldn't remember whether or not you were supposed to pull them out.

If anything went wrong on Saturday, word would get round and it would set them back for years. If they lost their place in the *Harlequin Guide*, they would be sunk nationally and internationally. If they couldn't get hold of a celebrity, he, Toby, would be a laughing stock.

And to top it all, his stomach was playing up.

Jesus! Five days to go and counting. . . .

Chapter Twelve

JAMES awoke to a grey drizzly day but, optimistic soul, he thought he detected a smidgen of blue sky in the far distance; the forecast was vaguely promising so all was not lost.

He had quite enjoyed his little stroll last night with Amanda. She was, as so many people are, different out of context. He was used to her as a city girl and she seemed out of place here, paler and a little awkward. It made him realize how little he knew about her and perhaps over the next few days he might find out more. Victoria had always suspected there was more to Amanda than meets the eye.

He wondered about skipping breakfast but the temptation was too great and the sky was still heavy so he ambled into the dining-room, the terrace closed off because of the drizzle.

'Hello,' he said, bumping into Amanda at the buffet. 'Up early, I see.'

'I often wake early,' she told him cheerfully.

'Ah! You must be one of those irritating wide-awake-at-dawners,' he said with a smile. 'So am I. That makes us compatible.'

'We can't help what we are. It's something to do with the time of day you were born I think,' she said, escaping the table. 'Come and join me.'

She was looking more herself this morning, not so much make-up, wearing black trousers and an oversized white top. 'I thought I might drive over to Cornwall,' she said. Her look from those big dark eyes was pure innocence. 'You did offer to navi-

106

gate I seem to remember. Have you any plans?'

'Well . . .' He hesitated, wondering what Sophie would be doing with her day.

'Don't worry,' she said quickly. 'I'm sorry to be nosy. Of course, you probably have plans already.'

'No, nothing special,' he said, ashamed of his reluctance and hastily covering up. 'A trip to Cornwall will be great.'

Somewhere, here, away from the cosy familiarity of home, Amanda seemed a trifle dangerous. He could have sworn last night there had been a prowling look in her eyes. Victoria told him years ago that Amanda fancied him, but he had laughed it off. Now he was not so sure. And last night, in a painfully clumsy fashion, he had tried his best to pave the way for an eventual rejection.

He spotted Sophie and Lily heading for the lounge as he was waiting for Amanda who was set on ordering one the hotel's supposedly renowned picnic lunches. If it remained wet all day, she said, they would eat the picnic in the car.

'You two off somewhere?' Sophie asked, apparently unconcerned. 'We're huddling indoors until the rain stops then we might take a walk into town.'

'Amanda's insisting on driving me over to Cornwall,' he said, feeling the urge to explain. 'We have no idea where because neither of us have been before.'

'Should be interesting,' she said, holding Lily a little forward so that he could direct a smile at her. 'She slept through until six,' she said. 'Isn't she a darling?'

'She is. Hello, sweetheart,' he said, stroking the little hand but finding himself looking instead at Sophie, at the warm glow in her face, at the way she looked at her baby, and the way she looked at him, too.

He did not feel he was imagining it. They had gelled almost immediately as only potential lovers can, but the stumbling block was Lily. She was a lovely baby but she was such an important part of Sophie's life, not his, and that threw up a little barrier that had somehow to be resolved.

Why was life never straightforward?

He suddenly and totally unexpectedly wanted to say to hell with Lily and take Sophie in his arms, there and then. She looked lovely in blue, a long crinkly sort of skirt and a top tucked into a big broad leather belt.

'There's Amanda,' Sophie said, spoiling everything at a stroke. 'Have a nice time.'

'You've hit it off there, James,' Amanda said, driving confidently once they were sure of their direction. 'Ms Bell ... you know her?'

'Everybody knows her. Bea to her friends which seems to be everybody. A very sociable lady.'

'She thinks you two are made for each other. You and Sophie.'

'She should mind her own damned business.'

Amanda laughed. 'Come on then, any truth in it?'

'Not at all,' he said, not the least offended by the intimate tone of the question. 'You know I'm not ready yet.'

'You are when the right woman comes along.' she said. 'Victoria would not want you to mope indefinitely.'

He ignored that, snatching a glance at the road sign, which they had just whipped past. 'What did that say?'

'Missed it,' she said, quite unconcerned. 'We'll just drive generally west. And look, the sky's clearing. Didn't I tell you? We might be able to have an outdoor picnic. We can find a dryish spot and spread a rug and waterproof ...'

'How very British!' he said drily. 'I'd rather find a nice café.'

'Where's your sense of adventure?' she laughed, zooming past another sign that might have been useful. 'I'm not exactly an outdoor fan either, but I shall risk being bitten to death by insects just for the sake of a picnic.'

Silent for a while, he tried to enjoy the drive, although he would have preferred to be at the wheel himself.

'Sophie's separated from her husband,' he said at last, feeling the question hanging unspoken in the air. 'She was married at eighteen and he left her last year.'

'How awful. With the baby too. Men can be such bastards, James, with the solitary exception of you. You are such an angel.'

They laughed. Back to the easygoing toing and froing sort of conversation they were used to with no strings attached.

She headed for the coast, going left or right as the fancy took her, choosing places she liked the sound of and, ditching the map, he let her get on with it.

Sophie watched James leaving with Amanda. She could not make out that relationship one little bit. Long time friends and she fancied that, from his point of view anyway, they were just that. Amanda had a more proprietorial air and obviously thought a lot about him.

Those eyes shone for him just as she supposed once upon a long time ago, her eyes had shone for Roger.

After their whirlwind romance, they had got married and she became pregnant almost at once, a disaster of such magnitude that neither of them could believe it.

'For God's sake, Sophie, how the fuck did that happen?' was what her husband charmingly said on hearing the news. 'I thought you were sorted out.'

'I thought I was, too,' she said, close to tears. 'I don't know how but it's happened.'

Almost frantic with fear at the very idea of having a baby – physically having it – she suggested an abortion but, to her surprise, that shook him rigid.

He patted the sofa beside her, made her sit down.

'Steady . . .' he said quietly. 'It's not the end of the world.'

'It is,' she said, the tears welling. 'I don't want it.'

Suddenly he smiled the Roger smile that used to melt her to bits. 'Let's start again,' he said. 'Let's pretend you've just told me you're going to have a baby.'

'I just have,' she said irritably.

'And I reacted badly. It's the shock I expect. But, now that I've had time to digest it – a couple of minutes anyway – perhaps it won't be too bad. It's better in my circles to be seen to be settled with a family. Makes you seem a safer bet.'

Belatedly, he drew her towards him, held her close, told her she was a clever girl and that he loved her, although his initial reaction was a stab in the back and she was inclined to believe that's what he really thought.

During the pregnancy that followed, hot and sticky as September dawned, she faced the fact that she no longer loved

109

Roger, was not even sure she liked him. She could tell nobody, especially not her mother, who was sure to come up with the phrase 'you've made your bed etc'.

She continued with the secretarial course she was halfway through, finishing it just weeks before Mark Adam Willis was born. She had a job lined up and she desperately wanted to take it, get somebody in to look after the baby, but Roger dug his heels in. He would not hear of it.

'You are the right person to look after him,' he said. 'You are his mother.'

'And, if I go back to work, it won't change that,' she said. 'Lots of people go back to work and Mark won't be harmed in the least. It's better socially for babies to know lots of people.'

'That is utter crap.'

'I don't want to stay at home,' she said miserably. 'It's boring just looking after him. Can't we afford a nanny?'

'No, we can't. Not yet.' Roger was careful with money. He did spend it but on the things that mattered, things that could be seen. The right house. The right clothes. The exterior – the surface – mattered dreadfully. They could be down to their last tin of beans but nobody would see that.

Roger might be shallow but he was also stubborn.

'Well, if you insist, but I hope you realize I'm no good at keeping house,' she said, knowing she was on to a loser. The arrogance she had once found attractive was no longer so.

'I do realize. You're very sluttish, my sweet.'

'That's not my fault. It's him. His nappies. His things.' She sighed as Mark started up again. He had a voice like a little foghorn.

'See to him,' Roger said. 'Bloody hell, can't you shut him up? Feed him or something.'

'I'll make a bottle.' Wearily, she went into the kitchen. Bottles were a nuisance, but breast-feeding was something else, something she could not face. She was not maternal and that was all there was to it.

As she poured the mixture into the bottle, switched off from Mark's increasingly frantic cries, Roger came through and gave her a quick kiss.

'Got to go,' he said. 'Big meeting. And . . .' – a hesitation that she had come to know over the last few months – 'I might kip over at Ed's. Do you mind?'

She eyed him flatly. She knew full well where he would be tonight and it was not at Ed's. She didn't much care.

Mark continued to be a wretched baby. He suffered from childhood eczema, not life threatening but uncomfortable. He was red-faced, snotty-nosed and spent much of his time howling. In fact, nobody ever said what a lovely baby because it was patently an untruth.

As mother and son, sadly they just did not hit it off. She blamed it partly on his difficult delivery and her being immediately whisked away for urgent surgery. Roger, predictably, was away on business and had missed everything.

She had wanted a baby girl and, even though she put on a brave face, her disappointment did not ease as the weeks passed.

And then it happened.

She was weepy after a bad night and Mark had been a little monster all morning. Three lots of babyclothes soiled and a nappy so disgusting it made her retch as she dealt with it. And then, just as she was reaching for a clean one, what did he do but pee – a wonderfully directed stream – all over her and the new little babygro and vest she had laid out.

She threw him with some force, nappyless, on to the bed. He landed on the soft cover but within a scary inch of the very solid bedhead. For a moment, he lay puzzled before letting out an enormous yell of outrage.

Immediately, she picked him up and cuddled him. Seeing how his little head had flopped, she watched him minute by minute the rest of the day for any dangerous signs. By bedtime, she knew she had got away with it, but she told nobody, especially not Roger, who, despite his indifference, was never ever violent.

The guilt began.

And still remained.

'Oh dear, I can't make up my mind so I'll take both,' Sophie said to the assistant in the baby boutique off Harbour Walk.

111

'Thank you, madam.' The girl took some tissue paper from a drawer, began to fold the little garments, sparing a smiling glance at Lily. 'What a good baby!'

'Isn't she?' Sophie said, jiggling the pushchair and they both took a moment to look and smile at her. Sound asleep. Fat little cheeks bursting out of the frilly bonnet. A tiny wisp of hair escaping its rim.

'These are Italian designs,' the girl said. 'Gorgeous, aren't they? Worth every penny ...'

'I don't care what I pay for quality,' Sophie told her. 'And I don't care that they'll only last a few months. She's worth it.'

'I should say so. Mind you ...' – the girl took on a reflective pose – 'some little tots have it rough, don't they? Not loved. And when they ill treat them, I'm just lost for words. Such little innocents. And what do you think of that baby that's gone missing? Imagine doing that? Taking a baby that's not yours, putting the parents through all that. I know she's to be pitied, the woman who did it, and the mother was a bit daft leaving the baby outside the shop in the pram.'

'I never do,' Sophie said firmly. 'It's just asking for trouble, isn't it?'

'Absolutely. Still, she'll have learnt her lesson, poor thing. She'll never do that again. Assuming she gets her baby back that is. Let's hope it's not come to any harm.'

'I'm sure things will turn out all right. Thank you.' Sophie smiled a goodbye.

The girl's words had chilled her a little.

She glanced down at Lily.

If anyone took Lily from her, she would kill them.

'Oh, look, would you believe it, the sun's out,' Amanda said.

She risked a glance his way. He was a little withdrawn today but then she had seen the wistful look he gave Sophie. Oh yes, he wished he was spending the day with her instead and he was only doing this, humouring her, because he felt guilty. It really irked. She was doing her best to cope with it but she knew she ought not to have come down. Ellie did not get it right every single time.

James was supposed to be navigating but, distracted as he was, he was proving to be a bit hit and miss, even for her cavalier approach.

'It's true, I don't know what makes you and Henry tick,' he said, picking up on a previous point in their conversation. 'He keeps pretty buttoned up.'

'He told you about our parents though. Consider yourself honoured because he doesn't usually tell people.'

'Did it have an effect on you?' he mused. 'It must have.'

'Tell you later. We're here,' she said, turning down a very sharp bend to a car park of sorts beside the church. 'Ssh, this place is a secret. In an off-the-beaten-track leaflet.'

He laughed. 'That's a good way of keeping it like that.'

'We can take a solitary walk along the beach at low tide apparently.' She halted the car, flexed her fingers. 'Of course, I haven't a clue whether it's low tide or not. But we'll find out, won't we?'

They thought it a good idea to suss things out first before they humped the picnic hamper, very stylish, very New Grand, so they set off unhindered.

'James, this is heaven,' Amanda exclaimed, taking in the little whitewashed or pinkwashed cob-walled and thatched cottages. 'Chocolate boxy. Such a change from Leeds.'

'Yes, but that's where the money is,' he said thoughtfully. 'And our business contacts.'

'Does it have to be? You could set up down here, you and Henry. Ellie would love it and just think how nice it would be for the children.'

'You're suffering from holidayitis,' he told her. 'I think I'll stick with Leeds. I know where I am there.'

'Stick in the mud,' she said with a laugh. 'Just a thought. I knew you wouldn't buy it.'

The inlet, when they reached it, was wonderful, the sea in tempestuous mood, the white froth frothing against rocks with just a small patch of dark sand visible.

'High tide,' Amanda said needlessly. She lifted her face to the wind and the sun, taking off her floppy straw, as the wind threatened to do it for her.

'Close your eyes and listen,' James said. 'Hear it. . . ?'

'The sea?'

'Yes.'

They stood a moment, close together, eyes closed, listening and then Amanda felt his hand in hers. Warm. Strong. She opened her eyes, smiled.

'Thanks,' he said. 'Thanks for this last year. I meant it, what I said last night, I don't think I'd have got through it without you.'

'Don't . . . please.' She slipped free, spray tingling on her face, setting off across the rocks towards the bit of beach.

'You never answered my question just now, and you've made me very curious,' he said, catching her up. 'Did it have a profound effect losing your parents like you did?'

'I was too young,' she said. 'I've forgotten what she was like. My real mother. Somebody suggested regression therapy once and I was tempted, but it was dangerous. I was scared of dragging up something I might regret. Poor Aunt Enid. Mother. She's very good at bearing grudges.'

'She doesn't speak to Henry? Is it because he and Ellie are not married?'

'Got it. I hate it that she doesn't speak, doesn't see her grandchildren, but it's up to Henry to sort it out. I'd better get married or else. And have children, of course.'

'Is that what you want?'

'Maybe. Time enough.' Feeling this was becoming too cosy, she was glad to point out a likely-looking place up ahead for the picnic, a dry and sheltered piece of ground under the cover of a rock face. 'We'll set up camp here,' she said cheerfully. 'Can you go and get the picnic stuff?'

She watched him leave, striding easily across the rocks towards the village. The sun momentarily disappeared but it was a wisp of a cloud and it would be sunny again by the time he came back. She settled herself on a smooth rock and awaited the picnic lunch. The woman at the hotel who had taken the order had made a great deal of fuss, practically curtsying as she eventually handed it over.

'All part of the service, madam,' she said. 'Anything further you require, just ask. Oh, and the chef's put in a little surprise for you.'

They were extraordinarily nice.

Anyone would think she was someone special.

Bea Bell was at a loss as to why James had gone off with Amanda, leaving poor Sophie all alone.

Not that she seemed to mind much. She had spent the hour since breakfast, Bea observed, in the lounge thumbing through a selection of magazines, Lily playing for a time on a little colourful mat, shaking rattles for all she was worth.

Bea smiled a little. She could take or leave children, leave them more often these days when their crying and tantrums annoyed rather than amused, but Lily was such a pretty baby with those even features of promised beauty.

She felt her eyes closing, dozed off a while, woken suddenly by a voice.

'Oh, I'm sorry, did I disturb you?' It was Sophie, holding the baby in her arms.

'Not at all.' Bea roused herself, adjusting her hat, her bodice, her skirt. 'All alone today?'

'James has gone for a picnic,' she said, sitting opposite and bouncing the child on her knee. 'With his friend.'

'Amanda? She's a lawyer, you know. Odd job for a woman, don't you think?'

'Why? She looks like she might be a good one. She has a very capable air about her.'

'Yes,' Bea said drily. 'My Oscar would have had a blue fit. A male abode, Oscar's office. He did not like me to visit there. There was, you see, much tobacco smoke and some fearful spitting. He was afraid I might be offended.'

'How quaint!'

Bea considered. 'Yes, I suppose so. I approve of modern life very much, but some of the old-fashioned views cannot be faulted. In my opinion, what Amanda needs is a man.'

Sophie laughed. 'She might not agree with that. She's very successful.'

'Successful, but is she happy?'

Sophie lifted the baby around, on to her shoulder, started almost absentmindedly to pat her back. 'You think she would be happier giving up her career?'

'Possibly. My Oscar maintained that the world would be a better place if women knew their place.'

'Ms Bell – honestly, what a thing to say!' Sophie looked quickly around as if Bea had committed treason with the remark. 'Why shouldn't we have a role in life?'

'We surely do. Looking after our men and the babies when they come. I am proud to say I looked after Oscar. Not completely of course, for I delegated the household arrangements, but in essence . . .'

'But did he look after you?' Sophie asked, reminding herself that this old lady was of a different generation with ideas as firmly fixed as her own.

'He treated me like fine china,' Bea replied. 'And I was happy to play up to that.'

'It's brightening,' Sophie said, glancing out of the window. I think we'll get ready for our walk. Fresh air is so good for us.'

'She's a very lucky baby,' Bea said softly, eyes rather bright.

'Lucky?'

'She may not have a father, dear, but she has you. And you are quite the perfect mother.'

Bea watched Sophie as she crossed the room, still carrying the baby.

Watched and, for whatever reason, wondered.

Back in her sitting-room, checking through her jewellery, Bea noticed that a pair of ear-rings was missing this time. The double drop with the turquoise centres surrounded by a pearl and diamond cluster. Delightful pair and part of the considerable collection Oscar had inherited from his mother and grandmother.

Priceless.

Thoughtfully, Bea sat down in the armchair by the window, running a hand along the silky arm. The ear-rings were part of a set that included a necklace and were meant to be worn on grand occasions with a ballgown, preferably off the shoulder to show them off to their best advantage. Such a pity to lose the ear-rings.

Oscar, who had continued to add to the Bell jewellery collection throughout his life would be seething. When it came to gifts,

Oscar had little imagination, jewellery, jewellery, jewellery. Things specially commissioned for Bea, building up to the beautiful collection she now had.

On her way down the corridor, she met the little redhead coming her way, armed with the trolley that housed the assorted paraphernalia deemed necessary for cleaning. Spray polish Bea noticed with disdain. In Virginia, at the house, she – or rather the help – had used proper lavender wax polish that came in large round tins.

'Good morning, Mary.' she said with a smile. 'How are you?'

'A bit under the weather, Ms Bell,' Mary replied, and indeed she looked paler than usual.

'You should have stayed at home, rested . . .' Bea said, helpfully. 'Take a few days off.'

'Yes, but I have to be careful I don't get my pay docked,' Mary said, not quite knowing about such things but assuming the very worst. It was always best to assume the worst and then you might be pleasantly surprised.

'You mean to tell me that the rich bastard who owns this hotel would dock your wages when you are sick?' Bea asked, outraged.

Mary met her gaze. 'I suppose so,' she said doubtfully. 'I'm on a temporary contract,' she said, again not absolutely sure what that meant. 'And I can't afford to lose any money.'

'Disgraceful. I shall compose a stiff letter. I shall frighten that pompous arsehole out of his wits. He thinks I'm going to leave him all my money you know. And, as it stands at the moment, I am. I shall have to see my solicitor,' she added, almost to herself, aware she was being a little indiscreet. 'He's not getting a dime. Slimeball.'

'Can I do your rooms now, Ms Bell?' Mary asked, shocked at the language. Arsehole, had she said?

'By all means,' Bea said graciously. 'Oh by the way, I may have left my jewellery drawer ajar. Would you be so kind as to close it for me?'

Bea observed that the woman's face was a picture.

Chapter Thirteen

MARY kept remembering the dinner last night. It had left her with a bit of a tummy upset but never mind. He could really push the boat out, Dennis, when he had a mind.

He took her to a proper restaurant this time, in the very oldest part of town, a converted boathouse with a fancy name. French cuisine, apparently, and it was all a bit much for her, but she managed in a quiet way and Dennis, bless him, took it on himself to do the ordering, when he saw that the menu had completely flummoxed her.

It wasn't long before he got round to the ear-rings she had stolen from Ms Bell's drawer. It was a bit disappointing he should do that, for it left her with a nasty feeling that it was the only reason for inviting her to dinner.

'You've excelled yourself this time. They are valuable,' Dennis told her. 'The best thing yet. But my friend . . .' – he glanced round but there was nobody interested in their conversation – 'he thinks they're part of a set. Necklace and ear-rings he thinks. Did you happen to notice a matching necklace?'

'No, I did not,' she said quickly. 'I'm always in a rush, Dennis. I'm always scared to death she'll catch me at it.'

'The thing is, as a matching set it will treble the value,' he said. 'Even as it stands, we'll get a fair amount.'

'How much?'

'Mary, I can't say,' he said with a smile. 'Don't worry. I'll see you're all right. But, if you can bring me the necklace, it will be so much more. Pay for a lovely holiday.'

'Would it now?'

'Or whatever you want to do with it,' he said. 'Some redeco-

118

ration for your house.'

She glanced sharply at him. Her home didn't need it.

'I don't like digging about,' she muttered, getting down to the soup. It was a delicious green vegetable creamy soup, although they called it something else. 'It's dangerous. It's only a matter of time before somebody twigs. She's a wily old bird. Sometimes I could swear, Dennis, that she knows what's going on. She gives me funny looks.'

She looked directly at him. It was all right for him. He knew full well she wouldn't tell on him if it came to it.

'Fair enough.' He passed her the bread basket and she took another roll. 'Let's make this the last time if it worries you that much. Get the necklace for me and we'll call it quits. If you get too nervous, that's when you slip up.'

He had a nice smile, Dennis. He looked nice, too, in a dark suit and coloured shirt. Mary wondered when he would ask her back to his home. When he did, she thought it would be all right now to agree to it and, maybe, if he wanted, she might let him take her to bed.

Although, in the cold light of day, it was a different matter and she couldn't think what had brought that thought on.

Ms Bell saying *that* this morning – about leaving the jewellery drawer open – had given her a bit of a shock. It reinforced Mary's suspicion that she knew more than she was letting on. But if so, why didn't she say something?

Mary closed the drawer anyway, not daring to touch a thing, not today. Her nerves were shattered and Dennis would have to wait. In any case, it gave her a certain hold over him. After the dinner last night he had driven her home and leaned over to kiss her. Just a peck on the cheek but that was all right by her. His very gentleness was having a funny effect, making her want him.

Lily was being good, lying quietly in her pushchair, looking up at the sky.

Pushing the pram beside the harbour, Sophie chatted to her, showing her the big boats anchored there, pointing out seagulls, convinced that somewhere along the line the baby was taking it all in.

119

Sitting on a bench in the ornamental gardens, she enjoyed the comings and goings. She looked at Lily who was fighting sleep. She had lovely clear babyskin, was such a contented baby with a very happy nature.

So different from Mark.

If only Mark had been a girl. She had muddled through his babyhood somehow, with help at last when they could afford it. As he grew older, it was easier, for when he was eight, he went away to Roger's old school up in Durham and at last she was free to pick up the pieces of the life she might have had without him.

With Roger's business booming, they now lived in a large house in an avenue off The Stray. She could have settled for lunching and shopping which, in Harrogate, is a career in itself, but she wanted a job. Nervous and determined, deciding not to bother Roger with it in case it came to nothing, Sophie applied for her first job in years. Her subsequent interview was very odd and she got the job simply because the boss, very into star signs, was delighted that, of all the candidates, she was the most starrily compatible.

After that, working and enjoying it, she and Roger settled in some way to a moderately happy existence. Mark was doing well at school and relieved that, against all odds, he might turn out all right after all, Sophie was happy to leave him to it.

She might have known it was only a temporary lull.

A set-up too cosy to last.

The picnic was superb.

'They really push the boat out, don't they? I've never seen such a variety of little sandwiches,' Amanda said, crunching on an apple. 'The last picnic I had was a few soggy sandwiches, a Mars bar and a bag of crisps.'

'I can't even remember the last picnic I had,' James said, digging in the hamper and coming up with a tiny pastry delight. 'These are terrific. And look, a little box of handmade chocolates. . . .'

'Wow! I can't fault the hotel at all,' Amanda went on. 'You were right. It is pretty special.'

'I like the changes. Last time round, it was lovely too but, after fourteen years, it must have been getting a bit the worse for wear. Not any more.'

'Absolutely not.' Amanda fiddled with the hamper a minute, casting a glance at him. He looked so good, so relaxed and she knew that, if he by any chance thought about her as she did about him, then now would be the time to make a move.

And it was patently obvious he was not going to.

To him, this was just a pleasant interlude, nothing more. She had a legal mind and she ought to face facts. Love had to be balanced if it was to thrive, otherwise there was no option but to pass on it.

'Amanda . . .' The question was softly spoken, almost a caress.

'Yes . . .? What is it?'

'Why is it all so complicated?' He stretched out on the rock lazily looking up at the now clear sky. 'Here we are, you and me . . .'

'Here we are,' she repeated. 'Isn't it perfect? Normally we're squashed in a pizza bar grumbling about work. Isn't it nice to be here instead?'

He let out a sigh. 'We should do this more often. Forget about work. Chilling out, I think they call it.'

She laughed, liking the sound of it. Maybe all he needed was a bit of encouragement. Maybe she should stop the dithering. She moved closer to him, desperately wanting to wrap herself round him. Poor darling, he had suffered so much, far more than he deserved.

Suddenly, he sat bolt upright, making any plans of hers redundant.

'What do I know about Sophie?' he asked. 'Tell me that. I've only known her a few days. I know very little.'

Damn, damn, damn.

'Sometimes you don't need to know much,' she said, trying her best to be fair when she felt like killing him for how he felt. 'Go by instinct. Don't analyse things. Just give it a little more time.'

'You talk a lot of sense, Amanda,' he said, his admiration for this extremely irritating. Who wanted to be told she talked sense? 'Do you like Sophie?' he went on, earnest now. 'I value your opinion.'

She sniffed. Could not help it. 'What's it matter if I like her or not?'

'Then you don't?'

'I didn't say that. She's pretty and she loves the baby,' she said, hedging, and deciding she had had enough of this. 'Come on, we can't sit here all day. We have quite a drive back. Let's have a walk while we have time.'

He grumbled a bit and she nagged in a good-natured way, determined not to kill the day off yet. Where was her fighting spirit?

'When we get home, you and Henry should start going to the gym,' she told him, determinedly reverting to the Amanda he knew. 'Or you'll both degenerate into middle-aged has-beens.'

He dumped the hamper in the boot. Looked at her.

'And you, of course, are as fit as a fiddle?'

'No,' she wailed. 'It's my job. Deskbound. Courtbound. Whatever. I am seriously unfit.' She looked round the deserted car park, over to the quiet church. 'We'll take that path,' she said, pointing to a public footpath sign. 'Race you over.'

It was further than it looked, uphill at that, and they arrived there, laughing. Amanda, clutching her side, declared it to be a dead-heat because she said James had jumped the gun and she was at a disadvantage in her sandals.

It didn't occur until they were actually walking along the cliff top just what she had made him do. This wasn't Beachy Head, not exactly but . . .

Oh God!

She twittered on wildly, ranting on about all sorts of things, anything to get his mind away from the rough cliff path and, far below, the cliffs falling steeply and jaggedly towards the shore. Fall off here and your body would be smashed to smithereens. Just like Victoria.

'It's all right you know,' he said eventually, stopping her in her increasingly hysterical tracks. 'I know where we are and it's OK. I can't avoid cliff tops forever. This is what Jennifer wanted me to do. Confront things.'

'I'm sorry. I didn't know this path,' she said, taking a breath.

'Don't you start feeling guilty,' he said. 'If anyone's guilty, it's me. I can't have been much of a husband not to have noticed something was wrong. If she had told me, I would have said it honestly didn't matter. Sure, I would have liked children like Henry, but if we weren't meant to have any, then that was all right too.'

'James, stop it,' she told him briskly. 'We're not having all that again. She was ill. Remember, I saw her too and I didn't realize either. I just tried to jolly her along.'

'You're right,' he said with a weary smile. 'It doesn't take much to start me off, does it?'

'No. You're a real wet weekend sometimes. Cheer up, for goodness sake. Just look at that sea.'

'Fantastic. I've enjoyed today.'

'So have I, but I'm sorry for dragging you off if you really wanted to be with Sophie.'

For a moment, she thought he might deny it.

'I did hope to be with her,' he said. 'I quite like her.'

'What did I tell you? You can't plan these things. They just happen. And please don't worry about me, I have plans of my own for the next couple of days. As for tonight . . .'

'She usually has room service,' James said quickly. 'You and I can dine together.'

'I'd rather not,' she said, amazed sometimes that he could be so insensitive to her feelings. 'I need to be on my own for a while. I think I'll catch myself a meal out in one of those fish restaurants by the harbour.'

She drove back, James valiantly trying to keep the conversation going. It was a lost cause. She knew she would remember this day forever, a glimpse for her of what might have been. As for the future, she would brave this out a few more days and then she was going home.

Once there, she would get herself moved to a new place and decide what to do next. One thing was clear and she had better learn to live with it: James would not feature in her plans.

'Ah, Fiona – Miss Jennings – may I have a quick word?' Toby said, catching her as she came off duty.

'Certainly, Mr Morrell.'

He saw the anxious glance she gave her fellow receptionists and smiled what was meant to be a reassuring smile, as he led her through the foyer.

Stupidly, he had not even considered where to take her for the quick word. In fact, he had been on his way to see Alice and been reminded when he saw Fiona that he was due a word. His office, untouched by Louis, seemed too formal and dismal and it might make her nervous.

'Just a moment.' He picked up a staff phone, barked an order into it. 'Shall we go? They're bringing us coffee and cakes in the library. We'll find a quiet corner.'

'That's nice.'

She was looking good as usual, even after a shift, and he couldn't quite think what she did to the uniform, but it looked better on her than it did on anybody else.

The library was off an inner corridor, a little used room, that Louis had blessedly left well alone for libraries bored him. A restful scheme with the walls of books and the antique writing-desks. A cosy area with a low table was intended for perusal of books or the many upmarket magazines. No tat.

Fiona sat opposite, crossing her legs.

Toby averted his gaze, although in that fraction of a second, he had surely noticed stocking tops. That meant suspender belts! For a moment, it put him off his stride but only for the moment.

'How long have you worked here, Fiona?' he asked, although he knew exactly how long from having looked at the file.

'Three years in September,' she said at once. 'I started helping out in the general office and then I moved to reception. I like meeting people,' she added with a smile.

'And you are very good at it. I remember very well you starting out,' he said. 'In fact, I feel as if I know you personally. I like to think that we are one big happy family, a happy team with me at the helm.'

She nodded, but there was a doubt in her eyes and he knew he had to get to the point. He had the feeling she was not fooled by sentimental corporate claptrap anyway. Neither was he.

'It has been brought to my attention,' he began, more busi-nesslike, 'That you have been seen hanging about the hotel on your days off. Round the pool particularly.'

'Oh, Mr Morrell, I shouldn't have been there, should I?' she said at once, putting a hand up to her mouth in dismay. 'I'm so sorry. What must you think?'

'I think you must not do it again.' he said, rather enjoying this, pausing as the coffee arrived. She declined a cake and although they were his very favourite chocolate eclairs and they had an excellent pastry cook, he passed on one also. 'Between you and me, Fiona, the person who reported this incident is – well – considerably older than you and not nearly so pretty.'

She dimpled. Tugged ineffectually at her skirt, drawing attention to her slim, darkly stockinged legs.

'You're not sacking me then?'

'Heavens, no. It's hardly a sacking offence,' he said. 'Verbal warning. You are aware that the staff should not fraternize openly with guests and obviously if I have a further complaint . . .'

'You won't,' she said. 'I promise.'

'More coffee?' He struggled for ways to prolong the conversation. He needed an excuse to get her away from the hotel. He knew he was treading on dangerous ground and he was putting himself up to possible charges of sexual harassment but she excited him terribly, she had done so for months and he just knew from the way she looked at him that she found him powerfully attractive too. Toby believed strongly in making things happen and this just had to be. He reached for the coffee pot . . .

'No, thank you.' She stood up. 'If you'll excuse me, Mr Morrell, I'll have to go, or I'll miss my bus.'

'Bus?' Horrified at the very mention of public transport, a wonderful institution he thoroughly approved of in theory, he rose to his feet. His word with Alice could bloody well wait until tomorrow. She had isolated the inspector woman anyway and they were sweetening her up appropriately. 'I was just on my way home,' he said. 'I can give you a lift.'

'It's in the opposite direction,' she reminded him gently. 'Thank you so much, Mr Morrell, but I really don't want to put you out. You've been kind enough as it is, letting me off with a caution.'

'It's no trouble at all.' He steered her out of the library, finding to his consternation that, somehow or other, his hand had found its way to her waist. What with offering her a lift as well, he was operating in a world suddenly of very hot potatoes. As he saw it, he had already done enough to suffer horrendous consequences. 'In fact...' – he struggled with this, wondering how it would sound in an industrial tribunal – 'we're both off duty now. Fancy a spot to eat? Away from here of course.'

'I'd need to get changed,' she said doubtfully, giving him a shy smile.

He smiled too.

She had not said no.

The fish restaurant was in a small side street near the harbour. The whole area smelled or rather reeked of the sea and fish. God knows what Louis the decorator would have made of this interior – a fishy scheme of blue checked cloths and seashells but it did have a certain rakish charm.

Frankly, Toby disliked fish, especially shellfish, but there it was. You couldn't get away with not liking fish, not round here, and so it was something he kept very much secret from the local fish lobby.

He had driven Fiona to her home and been made to wait outside for close on half an hour while she got changed. Reflecting that she might have asked him in, he found curiously that he did not mind. This was a very awkward situation for the girl. She obviously found him sexually attractive – you could tell from the body language – but he was the boss and she was being careful.

They could deal with this and, if she did choose to blab to the staff, then what did it matter? Since when did it matter if a man showed himself to be a man, and a woman had never complained to him, unless you counted the last one and her obsession for doing it anywhere other than in bed.

Fiona was younger than he, but so what? Men of influence often had younger women around them. And Fiona was different.

If necessary, he would marry her and then none of this sexual harassment stuff would stick. It had to be treated seriously because it could mean thousands of pounds in bloody compensation. Hadn't he warned the male staff time and time again? Hands off. Don't call them darling and make sure there are no ambiguous remarks.

He failed dismally on all counts.

From the window of the house, ready for the last ten minutes, Fiona looked out at the gorgeous car.

She was very impulsive and she could not wait any longer. His asking for a private word had been the signal she needed. She had to get this fired up and running and, when she saw Mr Morrell looking at her stocking tops, she knew she had won. A glimpse of knicker and thigh had done the trick as she had known it would.

She could, she decided, get away with it. She could start off a relationship with Mr Morrell and still continue to see Tony for the time being. Tony was frantically energetic in bed but otherwise a bit slow and stupid. Tony had visions of them getting married and living happily ever after when they could afford a place, which was sometime never in her books. She was not going to end up married to a fisherman-cum-boatyard-repairman living in one of the cottages on Wharf End, making ends meet, having a couple of snotty-nosed kids and having to buy her stockings in a bargain pack from the supermarket.

She had watched Toby Morrell for years, from afar, and he was lonely. After his last relationship had ended, he was devastated. He was a man who needed a wife and she was more than happy to volunteer. He needed a bit of loving attention and some good old buttering up.

If she played this right, she could have it all: money, her own car, be able to stay in hotels like The New Grand as a guest rather than a crummy receptionist. She knew she was reaching for the stars hoping for marriage instead of just a quick fumble but, as she checked her appearance in the mirror, she knew he would give a lot to have her. She would play it very cool and act shy. Men adored that. Especially men like Toby.

Ready. She ran her tongue over her glossy lips.

Steady. She undid the very top button of her jacket.

Go.

Fiona tapped on the car window, waking him from his reverie, a vision in a white trouser suit, her hair glossily black in that neat style of hers.

'I'm sorry to make you wait so long outside,' she said breath-

127

lessly, 'but my flatmate is out and it . . . well, it didn't seem right.'

He noticed her lipstick was very shiny.

'No, of course not. Quite right, too.'

'This must be our little secret, Mr Morrell,' she said as she climbed back in, her delicious scent preceding her. 'I shan't breathe a word, of course. I can be very discreet. The other girls will be so jealous.'

'Toby – call me Toby,' he croaked, rocked by the heady perfume and her proximity. Hell, he actually felt like pouncing on her here and now in full view of the entire population of this hamlet. His car had attracted some attention, some villagey stares, but then that was the point of it.

'Toby,' she repeated softly. 'You've no idea, Toby, how long I've wanted to call you that.'

He engaged gear and shot off smoothly, showing her what the car could do.

Once at the restaurant, she made him wait again whilst she trickled off to the ladies, reappearing freshly lipsticked and making a few heads turn.

And now, at their table, she was attracting more glances. He had forgotten how nice it was to escort a really beautiful woman. Those last two had been definitely the worse for wear.

'What will you have, Fiona?' he asked, wondering if he should help explain the menu to her. 'Don't worry about what anything costs. Have what you want.'

'Are you sure?'

He smiled at the shy hesitation. 'Absolutely.'

She glanced at the menu and, after the briefest glance, proceeded to rattle off, with great authority, her choice.

Quite obviously, she had gone for the most expensive dishes willy nilly. Toby, not minding, consulted the wine list, instantly deciding that his own list was infinitely superior. This lot had a cheek to be charging what they were for inferior stuff. Catching himself weighing up the prices, he stopped himself hastily. He was not going to start acting like his father. His personal finances might be deeply up the Swanee just now but it was temporary, a cash-flow problem that would soon be resolved.

As they waited for their food to arrive, Fiona charmingly chatting on, he noticed that, at a solitary table by the window, that rather attractive, dark-haired inspector woman from *The Harlequin Guide* was lurking.

He swivelled round slightly, hoping she had not noticed him, although cutting a fine figure as he did, accompanying the most beautiful woman in the room, it had to be a forlorn hope.

It took the edge off his appetite.

Dropping James off after their trip, Amanda made her way upstairs. She felt hot and sticky and needed a shower. Unfortunately, she found herself in the lift with Sophie and the baby and the pushchair and assorted bags.

'We've been shopping,' Sophie explained, as Amanda held the door open and they started to walk down their corridor. 'Have you been in town yet? There are some lovely little shops.'

'Not yet. Not shopping as such,' Amanda said tightly. She hardly dared look at this woman, this woman who had grabbed James's attention in just a couple of days.

'Did you enjoy your day out?' Sophie asked, stopping at her door and fumbling with her handbag.

'Very nice, thanks. The weather was good and we had a picnic on the beach,' she said. 'And then a walk.'

'Lovely.'

Amanda hesitated, but her essential good nature, which could be such a pain, won and she smiled. 'I think James might be quite pleased if you dined with him tonight. He asked me but I fancied a meal out.'

'I prefer room service,' Sophie said, releasing the door at last and pushing the pram through. 'But, if I can arrange a baby-sitter, I might make an exception.'

Amanda nodded, smiled at Lily, left them to it.

As she walked to her own room, the feeling persisted that there was something of Sophie in her over-anxious manner that reminded her very much of Victoria.

Amanda was waiting for her main course, something interesting done with plaice, when she saw the hotel owner Mr Toby Morrell come in accompanied by one of the receptionists at the hotel.

She watched the little charade with amusement. Goodness,

the girl was making a lovely play for him and he was puffed up like a peacock with pride. She would have scored top marks in that ridiculous how-to-flirt quiz.

And didn't it just work every time.

Men!

She left them to it, thoughts drifting back to Sophie, wondering if she was dining now with James, wondering what James was telling her. The thought he might be telling her *anything* irritated like hell.

There was something wrong with Sophie but she couldn't put her finger on it. She felt it in her bones and she was sure it was not just a bad case of jealousy. If James did it again – got caught up with the wrong woman – then he was on his own. He couldn't expect her to be there a second time. She could not face another rescue package. There was a limit to how many times she could counsel and console for, when she did that, she wanted more than anything to hold him close, stroke his hair, feel his arms round her and tell him she loved him.

More than anything, she wanted that.

Chapter Fourteen

Wednesday

'SORRY I couldn't manage dinner last night,' Sophie said, meeting him just outside the foyer. 'Lily was a bit hot and bothered and I thought she might be catching a cold but she's fine today.'

'Good.' James dutifully admired a thoroughly happy-looking Lily before they set off. Looking through the tourist leaflets at the reception desk, he had come across some gardens nearby that sounded as if they might be worth a visit. He was not interested himself in gardens but Sophie had said she was, so there it was.

'Amanda said you had a lovely picnic yesterday.'

'We did. Lots of fresh air. It made me very sleepy. I was off before my head hit the pillow.'

'Me, too,' she said, hiding a yawn. 'Sorry. I kept waking to check on Lily. She was fine, of course, but . . .'

He laughed and, for a while, they concentrated on finding their way up a variety of frighteningly narrow banked-up lanes to the garden.

'Amanda thinks I'm mad to come back here,' he said. 'What do you think?'

'She knows you better than me,' she said. 'I know I wouldn't want to go back to where I spent my honeymoon.'

'Hmm. When things go wrong, wouldn't it be great if we could turn back the clock? Start again. Do things differently this time around. If I'm honest, all our troubles started on honeymoon.'

'Did they?' she said, deciding this time she ought to probe a little. She had guessed that Victoria was not as perfect as he made out. 'Tell me about her.'

'She was complex,' he said, after a pause so long that she thought he was not going to answer. 'And the longer I knew her, the more complex she became. And she brooded on things.'

'Don't we all?' Sophie commented with a little laugh. 'My husband is not complex at all. He is just a total swine. Very simple.'

'I don't want to give you the wrong impression about her,' James went on hastily. 'When I say complex, I mean just that. In many ways, we had a good marriage.'

Sophie glanced at him, smiling a little. The man protesteth too much maybe.

James turned into the gardens at last.

'I hope you're not going to be bored,' he said.

'No, I am looking for lots of ideas for my garden.' she said eagerly. 'I have a proper cottage garden at home.'

'And where is this cottage?'

'Near York.'

'My neck of the woods then.'

He spoke to the man on gate duty, was handed two tickets and told where to park. Sophie heard the man refer to her as 'your wife' but they made no mention of it as James parked the car.

Once Lily was in her pushchair, sunhat on, they set off.

'I had a lecture on gardens the other evening from Bea Bell,' he said, allowing her to pause and examine various plants. 'She described them very well. They sounded beautiful. She supervized things.'

'Her role in life,' Sophie said. 'Personally, I like to do things for myself. I like to know what's what.'

'You don't have anyone to help you with Lily then?' James asked. 'What are your plans when you go back to work?'

'Look, if you don't mind I'd really rather not talk about that,' she said. 'I'd rather talk about you. Please . . .'

'What do you want to know?' he asked, sitting on one of the stone benches that were placed at strategic viewing points. Formal beds here on level ground, before a steep woodland path leading down to a stream, which they could hear but not yet see.

'Where do I start?'

'Tell me to mind my own business,' – Sophie folded the rain-coat she was carrying and sat down on it – 'but it might help if you tell me what Victoria died of?'

'I thought you talked to Amanda,' he said. 'Didn't she tell you?'

She shook her head. 'Why should she? We just talked in passing. A few minutes. Nothing in particular.'

For a moment, he looked at her and she thought he was not going to answer. She minded that, even though she knew she was not being straight with him either. It was so confusing, but her mind was playing all sorts of tricks on her these days, hiding something from her.

'My wife committed suicide,' he said, voice low but calm. 'She drove to Beachy Head and jumped off the cliffs. Just one more statistic.'

'Oh my God!' Sophie gasped, felt his shock returning as he spoke, could not trust herself to speak. Instead, she reached for his hand which was cold.

'She left a note,' he said. 'For me. Disturbed mind, the coroner said, so a lot of it didn't make sense but the gist of it was that she never came to terms with our not having a baby. I thought she had. . . .' He gave her hand a squeeze to say thanks. 'I can't believe I didn't notice how she was. She had her job and was very successful. She seemed content. We were planning to move house. That's what's difficult: we were actually making plans for the future.'

'How terrible for you.'

'I told her it didn't matter. The baby thing,' he said. 'What more could I do? I told her she hadn't to feel she was letting me down.'

'That was probably a mistake, James. We women sometimes turn things round. She could have taken it to mean that it did matter.'

'Could she? Good God!'

'Sorry. I'm supposed to be making you feel better.' She smiled a little, thinking how unfair it was, how easy it was for some women, thinking of Roger's aghast 'How the fuck did that happen?'

'She was godmother to two babies. Acted very naturally with them.'

'We hide our feelings. Our true feelings.'

'Even from those we love?'

'Especially from them.'

He stood up, took the brake off the pram and moved on, past the water gardens, into the herb knot where a strong minty smell wafted up. Sophie walked beside him, thoughtful and very quiet.

'We had breakfast that morning,' he said, reluctant to let it go now that he had opened it up. 'She cooked it. She made a bit of an effort in fact. My favourite. Porridge followed by scrambled eggs. I remember saying . . .' – his voice faltered a little – 'what have I done to deserve this? And she said that I had made her as happy as anyone could have and that it wasn't my fault at all. Later, it did seem a bit profound for seven-thirty in the morning. And then, just before she went out, we had this stupid row. Nothing serious, just a tiff. About nothing, just something we'd read in the paper that we didn't see eye to eye on. Anyway, whatever it was, she huffed out and we never kissed goodbye. She even slammed the door.'

'Don't, James,' Sophie said, eyes misting over as she looked at the beauty and softness of the garden. Nature helped. Something stirred in her own mind, but again, it was as if a curtain was half pulled across and she could not remember why she experienced sadness.

'After all that, instead of driving to work, she drove all the way down to the south coast,' James went on, walking rapidly down the path. 'Imagine driving all that way with one thought in her head. I keep wondering how she found it. She was hopeless at finding her way to places.'

Sophie sighed. Let him go on.

'No danger of making a mess of it. Too bloody high. It was not a cry for help, Sophie, it was the end. Oh, and she took her teddy with her . . . she had this teddy, you see,' he said, embarrassed. 'Her mother's never forgiven me. She blames me for everything.'

'Oh James . . .' She gave up the pretence of being interested in the garden and took his arm. 'I'm glad you told me. You needed to get it off your chest.'

Lily chose that moment to wake up and let out an enormous yell and it was a necessary distraction and time to bail out for lunch.

On the way back, he was quite chatty, much cheered, but the revelation had sobered her. She had seen, and liked, his vulnerable side. She was warmed by his patience and knew this was a man who would treat her well. Look after her and Lily. She should have met him years ago. But just now, for some reason, it would be unwise to be involved. There was Lily to think about and she was more important than anybody else.

Lily was worth ten of her son Mark.

When Mark was fifteen, all was going swimmingly. He was still doing well at school and had become very like his father in looks.

They still lived in the house in Harrogate, which she loved although it was massively big. Roger liked to show it off, entertain his colleagues and people who mattered at lavish dinner parties, people who were always strangers to her.

She knew she made a satisfactory job of it, was a good corporate wife, and she had learned what to say and more importantly what not to say. They used to eat rather splendidly in the enormous high-ceilinged dining-room at the rear of the house that looked on to the lovely garden. Their house was one of the blessed few that possessed a rear garden and for more energetic walks, The Stray was nearby.

Her career was treated with disdain by Roger who never wanted to discuss it, but it gave her money of her own and that little nugget of independence.

And that niggled the hell out of her husband.

So, as soon as the trouble with Mark started, he blamed her.

'You're never at home,' he said. 'The boy doesn't know where he is.'

'He's at school most of the time,' she pointed out. 'And he is fifteen, Roger. He can cope on his own now.'

Sadly, that did not turn out to be true and drugs reared their head. Not the hard stuff, as Mark was quick to acknowledge – that was for losers – but hard or not, it meant the threat of expulsion and with it all chances of decent grades.

'You speak to him,' she urged Roger. 'He'll take notice of you.'

'Bloody hell, Sophie, he never listens to me,' Roger said, and for the first time she saw in his face a kind of desperation.

He was right of course. You couldn't just ignore somebody, more or less, for fifteen years and then take up the reins and expect them to do what you wanted. Mark, in the throes of a spectacular teenage rebellion, ultimately took no notice of either of them.

He missed out on college. He refused to retake. He messed about thereafter with a variety of jobs. He travelled. He hardly ever rang. Sophie called those years the wilderness ones for that's what they were. Never knowing where he was, she feared the worst. Once he rang from Bangkok and she had visions of drug smuggling, following by beheading or a lifetime in a filthy cell.

She kept all this from Roger, who was furious that his son had let him down, and their marriage teetered on the brink of divorce, but they drew back from it and decided to try again, Sophie arguing that, with Mark being as he was, he needed a stable background to come home to. She had to make amends for her neglect. A bit late in the day for maternal feelings to surface but there it was, although they were accompanied by despair.

And then, last year, things finally came to a bitter head.

Roger left home.

And Mark came back.

Getting ready for dinner, James felt a sort of relief at telling Sophie about Victoria. It was not something you could keep secret for ever and he had the feeling that he and Sophie might be heading for seeing quite a lot of each other when they got home.

Easy does it. He was not sure yet how she felt, very early days, and of course there was the baby. She had looked lovely today. He liked the new hairstyle, the way she kept pushing strands of it behind her ears. She wore little jewellery although her wedding ring was very firmly there.

He remembered the annoyance when Victoria had first taken to removing hers.

She was giving him a lift to the office and idly glancing at her hands on the wheel, he noticed the oddly blank look about her fingers.

'Where's your ring?' he asked. 'You haven't lost it?'

'No, I haven't lost it,' she said irritably. 'Credit me with some intelligence, James. Would I lose my wedding ring?'

'Why aren't you wearing it then?'

She sighed. 'I knew you'd be like this. The fact is I've noticed a lot of my contemporaries are not wearing rings either. As far as my professional career goes, it shouldn't matter either way. Totally irrelevant whether or not I am married.'

He was puzzled but hardly annoyed. If she felt the need to make some sort of statement . . .

'If we had children, it would be different,' she went on. 'I would always wear it, but then, if we had children, there would be a point to it, wouldn't there?'

Thank goodness, they arrived at work then so the odd conversation ceased. At MacMillans, he kept a low profile, avoiding her as much as possible, and, to her credit, she gave him a wide berth too. The difficulty was that, knowing who he was, his colleagues had to bite their tongues before they said anything about Victoria. In the end, it had prompted him to move on, take up Henry's offer, although Victoria had been annoyed at his removal to what she saw would be a rival set-up.

'We shall feel like industrial spies,' she said. 'I hope that anything I might say about work will be kept confidential.'

'Oh come on. Of course it will. And I don't want you making overtures to our clients either.'

'As if . . .' She tossed her hair, shorter now as were the skirts of her all-powerful suits.

Having said that, she then proceeded to poach his ideas with abandon and, like a fool, he allowed it. Incensed at losing a particularly valuable client to her, he confronted her with it and predictably got short shrift.

'For goodness sake,' she hissed. 'I'm your wife. You wouldn't stop me, would you, darling?'

She was removing her blouse at the time, holding on to eye contact, more at ease with her body now, using it in fact to get her way. He knew it and was powerless to do anything about it because she was Victoria and he loved her.

'People will put two and two together,' he said, knowing he had lost the argument before it had begun. 'Promise me you won't nick my ideas again?'

'I promise,' she said sweetly.

She was in a pyjamas phase, black or red silk, and the teddy – and he was becoming increasingly uncomfortable with it – was bizarrely sporting a matching black or red silk bow.

And, all the time, it had been an icy front.

All the time, she had been heartbroken.

'You don't often come down for dinner,' he said to Sophie, meeting her on the way to the dining-room. 'Care to join me tonight?'

'That would be nice, James, although please don't feel you have to,' she said with a smile.

She was wearing a red dress and a touch more make-up than usual. James knew with some amusement at the antics of females, that she had gone to some considerable trouble. The bright lipstick was a spot-on match for the dress and, looking at her, as she sat opposite, he suddenly wanted to kiss her.

'Good evening.' Bea Bell paused beside them, in a lace confection with another of those hats. She glanced at Sophie, smiled. 'My dear, I adore red. Not a popular colour in Virginia – too hot – and Oscar disliked it intensely so I never wore it. Such a pity I always thought.'

She clattered off and they exchanged a smile.

'Have you ever been to the States?' Sophie asked. 'I must say, Bea has quite whetted my appetite.'

'On my own. A couple of times. To Boston on business,' James replied. 'Victoria refused to come with me. Did I mention she was scared of flying? She liked to keep her feet on the ground.'

'I don't like heights either,' Sophie said, instantly colouring. 'Oh sorry, I didn't mean that to sound like—'

'My fault,' he said. 'She was frightened of heights so why do what she did?' He shrugged. 'No more talk of her tonight, please. Let's concentrate on us.'

Yet despite an enjoyable meal and a very good wine, he still felt cheated. As soon as any aspect of Sophie's life was touched on, she clammed up. For God's sake, he wasn't expecting a blow-by-blow account of her life, but he did think she might tell him *something*. By coffee, which they would take in the lounge, he was determined to make a breakthrough.

'Your husband's called Roger . . . is that right?'

She poured the coffee, gave him a look.

'He runs a recruitment agency,' she said, passing him a cup. 'It's very successful, although just now he seems to have taken leave of his senses. Mid-life crisis. Thoughtfully she stripped a mint of its wrapping as she spoke. 'He met this woman and he's gone to live with her. She's much younger, although that doesn't bother me. It all seems very settled.'

'Are you divorced?'

'No. We haven't got round to it. I don't suppose either of us will want to get married again.'

He sipped his coffee, wanted to ask about Lily but dared not.

'I suppose I should tell you that we have a son Mark,' she said after a long moment. 'I'm not trying to keep him a secret, but I just don't talk about him. He's grown-up.'

'Oh . . .' He realized that she was capable of having a grown-up son but it still took him by surprise. 'What does he do?'

'Nothing if he can help it,' she said with a sniff. 'Believe me, James, you count yourself lucky not to have kids.'

They finished their coffee in silence and then he suggested a walk.

'All right. But I'd like to check on Lily first. Come on up.'

The room, curtains partially drawn, was warm and quiet, Lily asleep.

Sophie smiled at the girl who was sitting.

'She's been fine,' the girl whispered. 'A little sweetheart. Good as gold.'

Sophie led James over to the cot where the baby lay. She was sprawled, flat out, arms stretched.

'She's got a funny bald patch on the back of her head,' Sophie said. 'But I think her hair's coming on quite well, don't you?'

'Yes. She's very pretty.'

'You do understand, James . . .' – she spoke very quietly, almost to herself – 'how much she means to me.'

139

She looked at him and, to his surprise, he saw tears in her eyes.

'What's wrong?' he asked. 'Do you want to tell me?'

'Not now. Please be patient a while longer.'

They left quietly, taking the blue-carpeted stairs down to reception, where Bea was just emerging from the dining-room.

'Off for a stroll?' she said. 'How lovely.'

They felt her eyes on them as they went by and, once outside, Sophie laughed.

'She gives me the creeps,' she said. 'I can't make her out at all.'

Nor I you, James might have said, felt like saying. She had asked for patience and he would try to give her that. They walked, not by the shore, but up into town, stopping off at a little wine bar for a drink, not the same one he had taken Amanda to although it would have scarcely mattered.

'I promised I wouldn't think about work whilst I was down here,' James said. 'In fact, I promised my partner I would forget it.'

'And. . . ?'she smiled. 'This sounds ominous. You haven't forgotten work, have you?'

'Not quite,' he admitted. 'I had to jot down a few ideas the other day. But the thing is . . .' He hesitated, for it seemed an imposition and possibly a mistake to ask her and Lily to accompany him. 'I phoned a friend of mine earlier. Dave Price. He lives out near Salcombe and I've had a standing invitation to visit for a while. He's asked me to lunch tomorrow and he's asked you and Lily along too.'

'Does his wife know?' she asked with a slight smile. 'She won't be too happy if we turn up out of the blue.'

'That's no problem. They have staff.'

She raised her eyebrows. 'That sounds very grand. Will you be talking shop?'

'A little. But I'm sure his wife will keep you entertained. She mentioned something about a swim. They have a pool.'

'Their own pool? My goodness. What does he do?'

'Dabbles in everything,' James said, pleased that she was warming to the idea. 'He's always on the look-out for something new. He's hoping to set up a mail-order business – yachting and leisure clothes – and that's where we come in. He needs help

140

with brochure design.'

'All right. I will come but on one condition.'

'What's that?'

'I hope your friend realizes you and I are not an item, James. I wouldn't like there to be any misunderstanding.'

It was beginning to irritate him, this constant reiteration that they were just friends. What did she expect him to do next? Because they lived not too far from each other, he did hope they might follow up things when they got home, so this was not just a holiday fling – it wasn't even that yet.

'What about Lily though? I hope they won't mind a baby. She's not too fussy who she's sick over.'

He grinned. He would surprise her. Dave and Elisabeth had a little boy, a toddler. It would be baby talk galore for the ladies and perhaps he and Dave might slip away to the snooker-room and have a couple of frames and a beer for old time's sake.

He and Sophie arranged to meet after breakfast next day. But, this time he escorted her back to her room and they parted at her door with a kiss.

'What do you mean? He's got somebody else?' Ellie's voice was close to frantic. 'I knew it. I should have come with you. I would have come with you if I didn't have to look after absolutely everybody and everything in this house. Henry, the children, the dog. Crumbs, Amanda, what have you been doing?'

'Nothing. I've done nothing.'

She was beginning to regret calling Ellie at all, but, after breakfast, she had returned to her room and didn't know quite what to do next. She contemplated visiting the gym and sweating out all her frustration but thought better of it.

She knew Ellie would be home, having delivered the children to school. Ellie's morning routine was sacrosanct. She would be having a few moments with the paper and the remains of breakfast and Amanda just needed to talk. Ellie was so sensible. Ellie knew all the answers.

'Who is this woman?' she demanded, indignation in every word.

'She's called Sophie Willis,' Amanda said with resignation. 'Late thirties, early forties I suppose. And she has a baby. A lovely little thing.'

'A baby? And James has fallen for her, you say?' Ellie gave a huge despairing sigh. 'I find that incredible. Is she a single parent?'

'How would I know? It's not something you ask straight off, is it? She calls herself Mrs.'

'That means nothing. I call myself Miss and I have two children. It infuriates Henry.'

'I thought you said he was slow on commitment. That is not true, Ellie; he'd marry you tomorrow if you'd let him. Why don't you?'

'And risk spoiling everything?' The voice was wistful. 'You're a divorce lawyer, Amanda. Are you so naïve? I like to keep him on his toes and this way I can. Anyway, stop changing the subject. We have a strategy to plan.'

Amanda, smarting from Ellie thinking her naive, gathered her thoughts together.

'I knew it was a mistake coming here,' she said. 'He'd just been out for the day with this Mrs Willis when I got here. He was not exactly thrilled to see me.'

'But you said you'd been out together since then?'

'For what it was worth. We had a day out in Cornwall, upmarket picnic, lovely spot, you know the sort of thing. And then, I spoilt it all. I suggested a walk and would you believe we ended up on a cliff path.'

'Cliff path? Oh, how could you. Not the best idea in the world, darling.'

'Exactly. He was all right about it, said he had to face up to it. Maybe that psychiatrist was right after all. And maybe Sophie is helping.'

'Bollocks! Where's your fighting spirit? We shall see her off. You don't just give up at the first hurdle.'

Amanda laughed. 'It's lucky nobody's listening to this, Ellie. And, anyway, it's hardly the first hurdle. After all, he was married when I first met him so it's never been plain sailing. If I'd had any sense, I would have given up on him and married somebody else.' She gave a huge sigh, wishing she was up in Leeds with Ellie, sitting at the kitchen table with a big mug of coffee. 'Why do we torment ourselves, Ellie?'

'Because, for better or worse, we damn well fall in love. I've given up trying to make any sense of it. That's how it is with Henry. I know he's hardly Pierce Brosnan, God knows, but I wouldn't want anybody else seeing me when I tumble out of bed in the morning, or anybody else holding my hand when I'm being sick down the loo, or peering up my nether regions in the delivery room.'

'Ellie, must you? You have a funny way of putting things.'

'Maybe, but if you can't see your man in that situation, then forget it.'

'Whatever happened to romance? Doesn't that feature?'

'Oh yes.' Her voice softened. 'Henry can be terribly romantic once he's been prodded and reminded and heavily hinted at.'

They laughed at that and then Amanda hesitated. 'Look, Ellie, I hope I'm not just saying this because I'm jealous as hell, but I can't help thinking there's something funny about Sophie.'

'Funny?' Ellie pounced on that. 'How funny?'

'That's just it. I don't know,' Amanda confessed, looking out of her window and seeing that James's car was gone. 'I'm sure she's being secretive. About what I have no idea.'

'Secretive?' Ellie perked up. 'This is interesting. Gives us something to play with. People are only secretive for one reason: she's obviously got something to hide.'

'What if she has?' Amanda flopped down on to the bed, phone clutched to her ear. 'I'm fed up with it all. I am playing gooseberry here, Ellie, and I've had enough. Just going down to dinner is assuming sinister proportions. Will James ask me to join him, or worse, ask me to join the pair of them? Should I do that? Could I cope with that? I'm a nervous wreck.'

'And while you're standing there agonizing, she's bulldozed her way forward without a single thought in her head other than she's out to get him.'

'They've gone out to visit a garden.'

'Really? How very middle class and National Trust of them. Serve him right! He hates gardening.'

'They've taken the baby with them, of course. He's starting to get very fatherly looking.'

'Where does she come from? This *woman*?' Ellie asked, very nearly spitting out the word.

'Somewhere near York. She was married to a guy called Roger who's in the recruitment business and I understand they separated last year. Before baby arrived anyway.'

'Good. You've done your homework.'

'I just found out in passing,' Amanda said, not wanting to sound as if she had gone to any great trouble. 'One of the other guests, an old lady, is a mine of information. She's got me filed away, I'm sure, as a lovesick fool. She sees right through people. A mind like a razor. She thinks there's something odd about Sophie, too.'

'Does she now? I shall find out what I can,' Ellie said confidently. 'Willis is not too common a name, so it shouldn't be difficult. I'll look her up in the phone book for starters. Near York, you say? I'll take a drive round, chat to the neighbours. It's amazing what you can find out from being friendly.'

'You'll do no such thing,' Amanda said, horrified at the prospect. 'No, I mean it, Ellie. Promise me you won't.'

'Spoilsport,' Ellie said. 'I love delving into things.'

'I know you do and I wish I hadn't said anything. You'll get yourself in trouble one of these days from nosing around. I have to accept it, don't I?'

'If he's fallen head over heels in love with her, then yes, but I don't believe he has. This is simply infatuation combined with the holiday thing. He loves you and I have a sixth sense about these things. The only thing that's holding him back is Victoria.' She paused for breath. 'I could always ring her ex. Recruitment business, you said? I can always say I'm starting up a business and would appreciate some help with recruitment. Or I could say . . .' – her voice rose with the thought – 'I could say I was a friend of Sophie's and I could say—'

'Stop it.' Amanda was beginning to feel desperate. Once Ellie got a hold of something, she was difficult to control.

'I don't like mysteries,' Ellie went on. 'I need to speak to the husband, and on the phone, he'll be off-guard. I'll get back to you.'

Suddenly, Amanda was furious. Fighting mad. 'If you dare mention my name—'

'I shall be discreet. You and I are James's guardian angels. She sounds like she could be another Victoria. Some men never

144

learn.'

Considering the matter when she'd hung up, Amanda wondered why she had set all this in motion, for that's what she had done, naïvely or not. Ellie had lost her vocation. Once she got a sniff of scandal, she was off. It had happened before and it would happen again. She was nosy gone mad.

Although, as she tried to justify things, Amanda felt a bit better. After all, she was doing all this for James. She just knew in her heart that Sophie Willis was not the right woman for him. If she had been, then she would indeed have given in gracefully and left well alone.

Wouldn't she?

Who was she kidding?

Bea Bell had had a most delicious day. The beauty salon on Front Street was a little haven and the girl who regularly attended her, her chambermaid's daughter Lucy, was most attentive with soothing hands and a good listening ear. Arriving in time for her appointment, she was whisked away by Lucy and prepared for her pampering.

She always had the complete works, a full day, and the salon provided an excellent light healthy lunch with a glass of white wine at the halfway point in the proceedings.

Bea allowed the lotions and the girl's soft hands to smooth her aged back. She must think her the oldest of old crones and perhaps she did not like to touch Bea's body but she gave no sign of it.

Today was a special day and she made a point of telling Lucy directly she was on the massage table.

'Your fifty-fourth wedding anniversary,' Lucy said. 'How wonderful! 'A little silence and then she added, 'Congratulations, Ms Bell.'

'Thank you. My husband is alas dead as you know, but I still regard it as a day to celebrate,' Bea told her, as Lucy kneaded her shoulders. 'There would have been jewellery today. He loved to buy me presents.'

'How sweet!' Lucy prodded a little. 'You have some tension here, Ms Bell. I'm not hurting, am I?'

'Not at all, my dear.'

Relaxing later, under hot scented towels as her feet were prepared for the pedicure, Bea listened to Lucy and the girl's rather elaborate plans for the future. Poor soul. Pie-in-the-sky dreams, but who was she to deflate them?

For her anniversary present to herself, she had bought a new dress for this evening. Shades of cream. Swirls of vanilla and chocolate. And with it, she would wear her cream and silver cloche.

Lucy fell silent as Bea did, allowing her to drift off.

Pleasant dreams . . .

Chapter Fifteen

'I'M told the *Harlequin* inspector looked pretty glum at breakfast,' Alice informed Toby in the privacy of his office. 'She's been hanging around the hotel ever since.'

'Hanging around?' Toby frowned. 'Any complaints from her?'

'Oh no. She hasn't complained about the food and the house-keeper is keeping a particular eye on her room making sure it is attended to rightaway. We're replacing towels and linen daily and we're leaving little packs of chocolate biscuits on her coffee tray.'

'Careful. She might smell a rat,' Toby said thoughtfully. 'Hanging around where exactly?'

'She's gone to the library. Reading,' Alice added, as if it were a strange thing to do. 'Looks official stuff. Scribbling in a pad, according to my source. I got one of the receptionists to have a quick peep, Mr Morrell.'

'Well done. I think I might have a word. Discreetly, of course. In fact, I'll do it later this morning.'

'Thank you, sir. I was hoping you'd say that,' Alice said. 'Incidentally, Chef's on top form now that he's ironed out a few things in the kitchen. We've had some glowing reports and honestly I think we might well swing it.'

'We'd better.' He wished he shared her optimism. 'Any news on the celebrity front?'

'All in hand, sir.'

As she was in her chillingly efficient mode, he let it by, although he glanced at her suspiciously. After his round of golf on Sunday, which he had for once comprehensively won, he had an emergency plan up his sleeve celebrity-wise: a woman who would be instantly recognizable, because she had achieved fame via one of those dubious docu-soaps, a woman who was known to Dave Price, but he hoped it would not come to that. He did not want to scrape a favour from that particular quarter. That man had too many fingers in too many pies and Toby's worry was that he would move into hotels, for lay people always thought it was a piece of cake.

He dismissed Alice, trying to concentrate on what he had to do next but thinking only of Fiona. She had held out her hand as a gesture of goodbye when he took her home after the meal at the restaurant but, when he made to draw her to him, she had very firmly moved away and closed the door in his face. Being frozen out and made to look like a spotty youth was a ridiculous situation to be in at his age and totally unacceptable.

It also excited him to hell. He was ashamed of the clumsy gesture anyway. What had he been thinking of going at it like that, trying to kiss her after one meal, but she had looked delicious, good enough to eat, and he had wanted to nibble her all over. And she had the most unusual greeny-brown eyes with long silken lashes, although she had a habit of not looking directly at him most of the time. Shyness, he suspected, shy because he was the big boss. He realized with a jolt that he'd been hankering after Fiona for the last three years. He had watched her grow in confidence on the work front, so that she was now one of the senior reception team and a force to be reckoned with. A local girl with more than enough minor qualifications to show she had an intelligent enough head on her shoulders for, after all, a relationship was not only about sex.

Now that the ball was rolling, he had to keep up the pressure or she might feel he had lost interest. He wondered if he should invite her to the apartment for dinner or would it seem a little premature for that? She was off duty for the next two days, but he had insisted she gave him a contact phone number and it suited him rather well that she wasn't in her usual place at reception this morning. She had promised discretion, but he knew what girls were like and surely she wouldn't be able to resist telling them that Mr Morrell had wined and dined her, given her a ride in his limousine, escorted her home and behaved like a perfect gentleman.

God! He was playing it close to the wind. Hadn't his father warned him about women? He thought gloomily of all the sexual harassment cases he had read about lately. They were never out of the papers – women being awarded thousands, hundreds of thousands – because the boss had put his arm round them, admired their frock or patted them on the behind. And if you touched their breasts, went anywhere within tit distance, the price of the compensation soared and the headlines made a meal of it.

He thought longingly of Fiona's breasts. She was softly rounded, a great shape, a womanly shape. He wanted her. Not on his polished floor but in his bed with freshly laundered, white linen sheets. He wanted her opposite him at the breakfast-table too, beside him in the car. He wanted to buy her things. Take her places she had never been. He wanted to see those lovely eyes light up in delight.

One thing was sure: he had to get her off the staff list quickly. Once she was no longer an employee, there was no problem, other than her being out of a job of course. He thought of her sharing that nondescript house in that village that had somehow escaped the idyllic tag of most Devonian villages. She needed taking out of all that.

She needed rescuing.

And he was the man to do it.

The phone call to Ellie had not helped at all. All it had succeeded in doing was getting Ellie into one of her well-known ferreting-about moods that might well end in tears.

Amanda tried to do some work in the library. Turning to work was a last resort to knock some sense into her and soothing at that, just a few files she had brought with her on the off-chance. Thinking about other people's problems and ways to resolve them was just the tonic she needed.

The library was very quiet and she had been largely undisturbed, although it looked very much now as if Mr Morrell was intent on doing just that, smiling his way across the room towards her.

Quickly, knowing the personal content of the files, she closed her work, looked up at him.

149

'Good morning, madam,' he gushed, in that way of his. An immaculate little man in expensive clothes, he swanned around nimble-footed in his shiny black shoes. 'And how may I enquire, Miss Lester, are you enjoying your stay at The New Grand?'

'Lovely, thank you,' she said.

'Good. And how are we treating you?'

'Fine,' she said, anxious to get back to her notes. 'I was just about to order another pot of coffee. . . .'

'Allow me.' He was instantly alert, catching the eye of a junior member of staff who at once bustled up and listened to a murmured command. After that, to her consternation, he sat down opposite.

She thanked him for ordering the coffee, and desperate for something to say, resorted to telling him in some detail about her visit to Cornwall.

'Delightful county,' he said. 'Pity about the people. . . .'

'I found them charming,' she said.

'Well yes, they are, of course,' he said hastily. 'Noble folk, the Cornish, salt of the earth and so on, and they make wonderful ice-cream and pasties. The building contracting firm who have done such a magnificent job here were from Cornwall.'

'Congratulations to them . . .' She looked around the library. 'It's a nice idea, Mr Morrell, to have a quiet room like this. Somewhere to slip away to.'

'We try to cater for all manner of guests,' he said, catching a glance at an expensive watch. 'And we have done our very best to ensure that the alterations were accomplished with the minimum disruption to our guests. May I say that we are very proud of our inclusion in *The Harlequin*—'

'What's that?'

He smiled. '*The Harlequin Recommended Hotel Guide*, Miss Lester. Wonderful publication. We treasure our position.'

She nodded. 'It's not a publication I'm familiar with.'

'Quite.'

'Although I think there's a copy in my room,' she said, as she remembered. 'Thick glossy book, isn't it?' Doubly anxious now to be rid of him, she glanced at her watch. 'Where has that coffee got to?'

'Where indeed?' He stood up, looked as if he was about to

rush out and make it himself but, fortunately, it appeared at that moment. Silver service, pretty cups and several tempting slices of cake.

'I didn't order cake,' she said to the girl.

'Compliments of the management,' Mr Morrell said, breezing the girl aside. 'Now, I trust all is in order, madam. If you need any help with your report . . .' He gave an odd looking glance towards her closed notepad.

She smiled, not quite understanding. 'I'm not working on a report,' she said. 'They are personal papers. I'm a solicitor and I'm just catching up on some paperwork.'

'Good. Good.'

He did that little swivelling action of his and disappeared. Strange man, likeable in a way, although his fussiness would drive her to distraction.

Knowing she ought not to, but beggaring caution today, she slid the pastry fork into the creamy sponge.

'Any joy?' Dennis asked Mary, coming into The Whistling Kettle, just as she was cleaning the tables, prior to going home.

He sat down and she got him a cup of tea and an ashtray, checked with the boss if she was OK to go, before sitting down with Dennis and breaking the news. No, there was no joy with the necklace. She hadn't had the chance yet, but she would see what she could do tomorrow.

'Geoff's sister rang up this morning,' she told him. 'Reckons she's seen him again on television. At a race meeting, somewhere or other. It's daft because he was never interested in horse racing. What would he be doing there?'

He sighed. 'You shouldn't take any notice of her. She's always seeing him somewhere, isn't she? Wishful thinking.'

'Yes, but just suppose. What if he is still alive?' She leaned forward intently. 'What is he up to, Dennis? Is it another woman? Is he one of those bigamists, do you think?'

He laughed. 'What! You mean, has he staged his disappearance? You are joking, aren't you? From what I know of Geoff, he couldn't work out something as complicated as that before the next Millennium.'

Mary felt a moment's indignation on her husband's behalf.

No, they would not have got on, either of these two men. Geoff would have thought him a bit soft maybe.

'But, if he was a bigamist, his other wife could have worked it out for him,' she said, 'There might be an insurance fiddle. I've read about such things. She might be a scheming sort.'

'Oh come on, you're grasping at straws,' Dennis said. 'It's dangerous talk. Face facts.'

She sniffed, unhappy with the way he just dismissed it. 'Lucy's always on at me to face facts. But there aren't any and that's what's wrong. It's not knowing, Dennis. It's eating me up, not knowing. If his body turned up, well, it would be a relief. If there was something concrete, I could get on.'

'Mary . . .' He reached for her hand and she wished he hadn't because it was sticky from disinfectant. 'Put him out of your mind. Promise?'

'Well . . .' She slipped her hand free, wiped it on her apron and wondered if this was him stepping up the pace as Lucy would say. Mary was in no rush but they had been at this stage for ages and ages and it was getting nowhere. He needed a bit of a push. Maybe she should make a move, egg him on a bit. After all, they'd known each other long enough now for a bit of a kiss and cuddle.

'Fancy the pictures tonight?' she asked. 'I believe there's a good film on down in Plymouth and I've not been to the pictures for ages. It would be nice.'

'You're right. It would be nice.' He grinned at her. 'Tell you what, I'll run you home now and be back later to pick you up. We could maybe have a quick bite afterwards, make a proper night of it.'

'Lucy will think I'm never in these days,' Mary said with a smile.

'And then, when you get the necklace, we could have a weekend somewhere,' he said, as they went out to his car. 'London perhaps.'

'One of those theatre weekends?' she said, belting herself in. 'We could see a musical. That would be lovely, Dennis.'

She worried about it though on the short drive home. And, as she got ready to go out, she worried more. A weekend away sounded a bit serious.

'Don't worry if you're late back,' Lucy said, supposed to be helping her get ready. 'I shall know where you are. And if you want to stay over, it's all right,' she added with not a trace of embarrassment.

Mary did not say anything to that.

How could she stay over anyway? She wouldn't have a nightie with her.

They were coming out of the cinema at the Barbican Leisure Park, exiting with the throng on their way to the car park when Mary spotted him. He was alone, wearing jeans and a brightly patterned sweater, his back to her. But she just knew it was Geoff. He walked like Geoff, loping along, hunched just a little forward.

He climbed into a maroon car a few rows away and drove off but not before she had urged Dennis into his and ordered a pursuit.

He did not fuss, merely grinned, reversing swiftly out of their slot, sneaking in front of several other cars with a prior claim to a forward place in the queue, catching up fast at the exit road. Dennis drove a nice car, not brand new but solid. The sort of car she felt safe in and Dennis was a good driver.

'I never thought I'd hear those words, "follow that car",' he said, having an instinctive knack for following, dropping back so that they were not immediately behind. 'I can't believe I'm doing this. I'm getting to be as daft as you are. Your husband's dead. How can he be at the pictures?'

'I know. But it *was* him, Dennis. Don't you think I don't know the back of my own husband's head?'

'Yes, but what would he be doing here? It's too near home.'

'Who knows?' she said anxiously, her eyes trained on the maroon car that was now three or four ahead, noticing with alarm that they were approaching a junction. 'Watch the lights. He might get through.'

'He has got through,' Dennis said, having to stop as they changed to red. 'Sorry, Mary, I can't jump a red light, but don't worry, we'll pick him up. I know this road and it's dual carriageway ahead and there aren't any turn offs for a while.'

'I hope you're right.'

153

She said nothing more, just drumming fingers on her handbag in her agitation, willing the lights to change, letting him concentrate on positioning himself in the right lane for overtaking. He was a confident driver, swinging the car smoothly and, sure enough, before long, they could see it ahead of them again, the maroon estate car, a bit posh for Geoff to be driving. They'd only ever had second-hand vehicles because he fancied himself as a mechanic and didn't mind having a tinker with them.

'Write the number down,' Dennis said. 'You'll find a scrap of paper in the glovebox. Got a pen?'

She fussed with her bag, dumping everything in her lap in the search for a pen. And then carefully, she jotted the number down as Dennis called it out. This would be dead exciting if it wasn't so awful.

It made an odd end to the evening. The film had been good, a romantic comedy set in San Francisco, which was a really good place to have a car chase with all those frightening hills. There had been just the one bed scene when they'd been half under the covers at that, although there had been no mistaking what they were doing. A lovely actress with a big smile and nice eyes and the man – well, no wonder she'd fallen for him.

She and Dennis had not held hands – they weren't teenagers – but they had dispensed with the seat arm and sat close together and she thought she detected a bit of interest. When she was a teenager, she had been with Geoff and they had held hands and he had put his arm round her and kissed her too, fumbling with her top if they were in the back row. Daft beggar that he was.

That little love scene in the film with the two of them being so tender, never mind that they were just acting, had put her in the mood to be honest and she hoped that he might ask her back to his place tonight, nightie or not.

So much for all that. All gone out of the window as soon as she saw Geoff and now here they were on a wild goose chase through Plymouth, heading out of town northbound and goodness knows where after that.

'People who go to the cinema don't go far to get home,' she said, wondering where Geoff lived and why he had done this to her. If it was him, if they confronted him when he got out of the

154

car, she wouldn't half give him hell for putting her through all this, imagining him at the bottom of the sea and so on. It wasn't as if they'd been able to have a funeral with a body in a coffin when they could have said a proper goodbye. Sometimes, she did go to the end of the harbour, by the wall there, where the water was dark and deep and wonder.

'He's turning,' Dennis said, slowing and changing gear. 'Private housing estate by the look of it.'

They were right on his tail now, both cars in the central section of the road waiting for a safe moment to turn. He turned first and then, after a few seconds, it was safe to follow. The maroon car was at the bottom of the private road, indicating left and Mary's heart hammered as Dennis did the same, the indicator clicking as if in rhythm with her heart.

'He'll see us,' she said, panicking. 'He can see us in his mirror, can't he?'

'Yes, but how often do you notice who's behind you?' Dennis said, sensibly enough. 'As car chases go, Mary darling, this is all very sedate.'

He had called her his darling. Biting her lip, she glanced his way. She knew he was trying to make her lighten up but it was very hard. Suddenly, she thought of this from his point of view. Here they were on their way to a relationship and here she was going on and on the whole damned time about her husband. Dennis was some man to put up with it. Most would have walked out by now. Of course, she knew she was useful to him, with the jewellery, but she knew that was separate.

'He's stopped,' Dennis announced, drawing into the kerb and pulling them to a halt too. 'Outside the house with the blue door.'

The door of the maroon car opened and the man stepped out, reaching over the seat for a bag and hoisting it up and out. He was very like Geoff, same height, same colouring, but this time she could see his profile clearly and she knew it was not him.

She felt very foolish.

'Well?' Dennis said. 'Do you want me to instigate a punch-up? I don't know that I'll be much good at that. He looks bigger than me.'

His smile made her smile.

He knew.

She realized she was relieved.

It could not be Geoff because Geoff was dead.

And she was glad. At last, she could grieve for him.

'Let's go and find something to eat,' she said.

Earlier in the day at The New Grand, Toby had enjoyed his usual Wednesday ploughman's lunch in the simplicity of the coffee shop. Afterwards, he did a little walkabout. The new chef was settling in, still shouting but in a more restrained fashion. He was a cook of distinction and Toby had sampled a selection of menus recently which were all superb.

Still, it was unwise to let the man grow too big for his apron strings. In the heat and confusion of the kitchen, Toby carefully positioned himself out of harm's way.

'Everything all right for the party, Chef?' he enquired.

Chef, a man of few words, shrugged and dipped a spoon in some sauce.

'Wonderful!' he breathed the word, blowing a kiss to some white-overalled soul. 'The party . . .' He returned his attention to Toby. 'Of course. Everything edible will be out of this world. They will still be talking about it in the year 3000. You may leave that to me. Now, if you please, sir, you are bare-headed in my kitchen and a threat to hygiene.'

Faced with the choice of leaving or donning the white cap someone was bearing his way, Toby smiled and left.

Who did that man think he was?

A genius, of course, and, judging by the comments they were receiving, he wasn't far wrong.

After leaving the kitchen, Toby enjoyed the calm of the principal reception rooms before finding himself in the foyer itself, checking the display of summery flowers in the vast silver goblet in passing. The goblet, atop a massive glass-topped circular table, took pride of place in the foyer. According to Louis, the decorator, it led the eye forward and beyond to the classic sweep of the stairs.

Toby felt reasonably pleased with life today. He had received a letter from the building contractors, to his surprise not demanding payment within fourteen days but offering to reduce the amount owed because of the unfortunate cinnamon-effect cream on the exterior walls. Wrong tins of paint were blamed, a direct result of yet another Millennium mix-up with labels at the paint factory. Actually, the slight difference had been much admired, but Toby was not about to tell the contractors that. He would pay them a proportion of their bill in good faith.

He had telephoned Fiona, sweating a bit as he dialled, inviting her to his apartment tomorrow for lunch. He thought it had gone well, the invitation, hitting the right casual note. Of course when she arrived, the friends would be mysteriously delayed and she would probably guess his intentions at that point, but, by then, she would be most impressed and would surely stay.

Their secret.

Toby frowned, wondering about that. How soon would it leak out? How soon before she turned nasty and took him for what she could get? She could claim he had seduced her and, if things went according to plan, she would be quite right.

He called in on Alice to bring her up to date.

'You need not concern yourself any more about the inspector,' he told her, sitting down and accepting a cup of black coffee. 'It's all sorted.'

'Ah. You had a word then?'

'I did. Delightful lady. Her cover story is that she is a solicitor.' He laughed. 'You can't believe these people, can you? They must think we were born yesterday. She even had the nerve to pretend she didn't know *The Harlequin Guide*. Kept her report under lock and key too. I couldn't get a glimpse of it.'

Alice smiled. 'You've got to hand it to her. She is very cool. Did she seem reasonably happy?'

'I wouldn't say that. Not exactly.' He frowned, trying to recall her words. 'I found her pleasant but melancholy. Let us hope it is purely a private matter.' He suspected it was PMT but he was not going to say that to Alice and risk her feminine wrath. 'She was at some pains to say how pleased she was with the hotel. She cannot fault us on service.'

'When is she due to leave?'

'Sunday, I believe,' he said, dismissing any negative thoughts. Nice woman. She would be fair to them and although she had

157

had a teeny bit more attention than normal, he had no qualms about that. It was a ruthless business and he would lose no sleep over other hotels who lost their slot. Just tough.

'So we'd better invite her to the party? VIP reception, do you think?'

Toby considered. 'Why not? I've invited the guests who are occupying the promenade suites and one or two others. Organize an invitation for her and a guest. She ought to see us in full swing.' He watched as Alice made a jotting in her pad. 'Any other problems?'

'Nothing major, sir.' Alice flicked through papers, as she remembered something. 'Although, the resident pianist has resigned, Mr Morrell. Blames lack of interest. Says it's like playing in a morgue.'

Toby clicked his tongue. Damned artistes! They were all alike.

'See to it promptly,' he said. 'Call the agencies. Do the interviews.'

She looked blank. 'I have no musical qualifications, sir.'

'You have ears, don't you?' he said, not in the mood with this Fiona thing hanging over him for complications. 'Get the applicant to play a few tunes. Listen. If it sounds OK, hire him.'

'Or her?'

'Whatever. We must have a live pianist and it's up to them to get people to listen. Jazz it up a bit. Although, damn it, they're supposed to be playing background music. Don't hire anybody with a personality, for God's sake. Now, is that everything, Alice? I'm knocking off early. Oh, and let me know as soon as we get confirmation of our place in the new guide. It might be on its way now. We'll make an announcement on the board, open a bottle of champagne to celebrate. Get a mention in the local Press.'

'Leave it with me, sir.'

He left it to her.

She had better not make a cock-up.

Thursday tomorrow and Fiona was coming to lunch and, just now, he could think no further than that. He was a fool to have asked her this week when he had so much on his mind.

He nipped into his office, simply to cross another day off.

Looking out of the window, he saw it was glorious. Would

you believe that fool of a weather forecaster promising severe storms for Saturday? The woman was clearly unhinged and unprofessional to boot. She had got her isobars mixed up for it had never looked so settled.

With a sigh, he hung the calendar back on the wall.

Three days to go and counting. . . .

Chapter Sixteen

Thursday

AMANDA felt guilty as she joined James for breakfast. The telephone conversation with Ellie and Ellie possibly shooting off to dig the dirt on Sophie was very guilt-inducing.

'You do love breakfast, don't you?' she remarked, as the waiter arrived with what looked like grilled everything. 'I can't face much usually. On Sundays, I have a glass of water.'

'Not good for you,' he said, tucking in unapologetically. 'And don't tell me you're on a diet. No need.'

She sipped her grapefruit juice and smiled. She supposed she could count that as a compliment if she had been fishing for one and she had not. She wondered what his plans were for today, but she was resigned to them including Sophie and the baby and not her. Today, in rebellion after the peculiarly inactive day of yesterday, she was going to drive to Torquay, shopping, spending, lunching. She would cheer herself up and buy some new clothes, a couple of suits for the office and something sexy for lounging around. And when she got home, she would start going out more, do things, meet people and you never know – eventually she would forget James or, at the least, learn to live without him.

'Sophie's coming to Salcombe with me to Dave Price's today,' James said, looking just faintly uncomfortable. 'You remember me mentioning him? He could be putting some business our way. And that's just between the two of us. I don't want Henry knowing yet.'

'I'm hardly likely to tell him,' she said, peeved that he should think she would. 'I don't envy Sophie. You two will be talking shop the whole time.'

'Part of the time. His wife will keep Sophie entertained. They live in a mansion from all accounts. A pool and everything.'

'I see.'

He put down his knife. Looked at her.

'What's the matter?' he said. 'I know you, Amanda, and I know that look. You don't like Sophie, do you?'

She hesitated, ran a finger round the rim of her glass. 'Since you ask . . . no.'

'I might have known I could rely on a straight answer.'

'You did ask.'

'And you might be a tad diplomatic,' he said, his expression tight. 'I don't understand you. You never liked Victoria either and you made no secret of that.'

'She didn't like me,' Amanda said, looking round helplessly as it dawned they were on the brink of a row. 'I tried with her, James, I really tried. But she was very odd with me. With everybody in fact.'

'I don't want you saying things about my wife,' he said, plate pushed to one side.

'Oh don't you?' she said, feeling herself hot with indignation. 'Well, that's just too bad, James. It's time you faced the truth.'

'You finished? Then let's go outside to continue this.'

She followed him, slowing her pace deliberately as he fairly tore out. Bea Bell was watching them and suddenly her presence and the knowing look infuriated Amanda. Unable to stop herself, she paused in passing, and leaned low over the table.

'Yes, we are having a row,' she hissed. 'Satisfied?'

'I'm sorry, my dear. Were you addressing me?' Bea enquired, drawing haughtiness around her like a cloud.

Mortified to have upset the old lady and wanting to apologize, to explain, Amanda had no choice but to rush after James who was disappearing at full pelt, catching him up just outside.

161

'How dare you make me run after you like that?' she stormed. 'You're making an unholy fuss about nothing.'

'Am I?' His eyes were steely, shot through with ice. 'I thought you were my friend, Amanda.'

'Oh, for heavens sake,' she said. 'What is this? You asked me a question, I answered it honestly and now this. Would you prefer if I lied? Did you want me to say I think Sophie is the most wonderful woman in the world? The prettiest? The best dressed? The most honest?'

'What do you mean?' He picked up on that as she had known he would, for it had been a mischievous, throwaway line. 'Are you saying she's not honest?'

Amanda took a breath, setting off towards the swimming-pool and the sun-chairs that surrounded it. Wearing a long cotton skirt for her shopping trip and a white top, she plumped herself down and he followed suit. The pool was very blue, the tiled floor shimmering and moving slightly as the water caressed it, sunlight shining on and through.

'You want me to be happy, don't you?' he asked at last.

'Of course I do. You know that,' she said, feeling tears prick at her eyelids and fighting to control them. 'You've been through hell, James, you deserve some happiness now.'

'Well then?' He managed a smile. 'What's the problem?'

If he needed to ask, then there really was no chance. He did not know how she felt. He had not guessed. He genuinely, crazily, believed all that baloney about being just good friends. So, who was the fool then?

'It's early days,' he went on. 'Me and Sophie. And there's Lily, of course. But there should be no problem with that. She's very sweet.'

'Be careful,' she said. 'Sorry. But you know what they say about holiday romances. As I said to Ellie. . .'

'You've been discussing this with Ellie?' he asked, eyes dangerous. 'Have you?'

'I might have mentioned it,' she said defensively. 'We are both worried about you.'

'Look, Amanda, can we get something straight?' he said. 'Stop interfering. You may not have liked Victoria and I admit she was difficult but you have no business at all discussing this with

Ellie, or saying things about Sophie when you know nothing about her.'

'Do you? What do you know? What can you know about someone in a few days?'

'Perhaps that's all it takes. A few days.'

'For what? *Love*? You're talking about love,' she said, feeling a whole flurry of mixed emotions rising within her. 'Oh James, I sometimes wonder if you've ever been in love.'

'Leave it,' he said. 'I'm not expecting too much yet, but I am hopeful that, when we get home, Sophie and I will get together again and take it from there. Anyway, she's still married to Roger.'

'OK, I'll leave it,' she said. 'But don't say I didn't warn you. And I'll have you know' – she hated this but she was too far gone to stop – 'Bea thinks there's something odd about her too.'

'I'm off.' He stood up abruptly. 'We must get off to Salcombe. Perhaps we'll catch up before you go home.'

'I'm not supposed to be going home before Sunday,' she said miserably. 'But I'll probably go before then.'

She wanted to ask if they could still be friends but that was pathetic.

They would never be lovers.

And their friendship, even if they did manage to resurrect it, would never be quite the same again for she had bared her soul too much.

She slipped back into the hotel, avoiding Bea Bell to whom she really would have to apologize, and picked up what she needed for her shopping trip.

Her credit cards and a steady nerve.

Sophie made up her mind that, before the day was out, she would tell him. She was aware he might react badly and she was resigned to it. She enjoyed his company, but if it came to a choice between him and Lily, there was no choice.

'Are you all right?' she asked, directly she saw him. He looked jumpy and she had spotted Amanda in the foyer, jingling car keys, very conspicuously avoiding looking at them. She contemplated asking what the problem was but decided against it. Why start the day in a bad mood when it might very well end in one?

'Are you booked in until Saturday or longer?' he asked.

'I'm booked in provisionally for another week,' she said quietly, sitting in the back of the car with Lily, 'But it's flexible. I can stay longer or go before then.'

'I have to go back. I have to work for my living.'

'It's been lovely meeting you, James,' she found herself saying, ridiculously, as if they were about to go their separate ways this minute. 'And perhaps we might meet up again sometime when we get back home.'

He laughed shortly. 'Oh! I see.'

'No, you don't,' she said. 'You don't see at all. I am a very complicated woman and I think you've had your share of them. We have to be careful we don't rush into something that might not work.'

He cursed softly at a traffic incident ahead, slowed and then stopped, snatching on the handbrake. He risked turning to look over his shoulder at her.

'It's time we talked. Would you believe me if I told you there hasn't been another woman since Victoria?'

'What about Amanda?' She smiled slightly. 'Bea thinks she's in love with you.'

'That woman. Does she interfere in everybody's life?'

'I think so. It's the only thing left for her. Think about it, James: sooner or later, most of us are left alone.'

'I like Amanda,' he said. 'Although she can be very annoying and she gets these stupid bees in her bonnet about things that don't concern her.'

'Has she been saying something about me?' Sophie asked, as a little warning sounded.

'No, of course not,' he said. 'Now, before we go any further, I'd better give you the run-down on Dave.'

A smart change of subject.

'He's been very successful as I said.'

'So have you. Don't let it get to you.'

'Is it so obvious? I am jealous, Sophie. I know we're doing quite well, Henry and I, but we're not in his class. He ended up on some list – top earners of the South-west, something like that. Funny character. He dropped out after school. Really dropped out. In fact, I suppose at that point he could have gone either way.'

'Like my son,' Sophie said. 'He dropped out, too, but in his case went down not up. Ended up busking, begging, you name it.'

'Is that why. . . ?' he hesitated. 'Is that why you minded so much? In Totnes?'

'Yes.' She watched the back of James's head. 'Mark's never had a proper job yet and he's twenty-one. Can you believe that?'

'He's got time,' James said.

'What? To pull his socks up? I don't think so. Anyway, I don't want to talk about him; it depresses me.'

They were silent as James struggled with the directions before they at last pulled up in front of the house amongst the gentle slopes that they had spotted from some distance away. The views from up here of the pretty little harbour town itself were outstanding and the house was white, all a dazzle in the sun.

'Well?' James looked at her. 'What do you think?'

'I think it must be worth a million,' she said. 'Don't you?'

'At least. Elisabeth will give you a guided tour whilst we talk business. Oh by the way, they have a little boy. Freddie I think.'

'How old is he?' Sophie peered out as they neared the house. It was spectacular and she found herself curious to see inside, to see what this Elisabeth had done with it. She glimpsed an outdoor pool, oval, with seats and sun umbrellas, as James drove round the back to park the car.

'Don't look so nervous,' he told her, as she lifted the baby out. 'Enjoy the day.'

'No, I'll carry her,' she said, as James started to undo the pushchair.

Lily's little face was hot and she had two bright red spots on her cheeks. Teeth? She nuzzled her head a little grumblingly into Sophie's neck and Sophie smoothed her damp hair.

'We'll get you something to drink in a minute, darling,' she said, as they walked towards a rose arch where Elisabeth Price was waiting for them, leaning on a stick, foot in plaster.

*

165

Sophie took an instant dislike, not to Elisabeth, but to Dave. He was short and slight with longish, rather lank, fair hair and a very feeble beard. He had cool, oddly colourless eyes and she hated the up-and-down look he gave her when they were introduced and the way he kissed her immediately, as if they were old friends.

Elisabeth, as well as having a badly twisted ankle, was tiny and oriental, almond-eyed, and the little plump boy holding on to her good leg was Freddie. Lily and Freddie were placed close together a moment by way of introduction, but ignored each other and everyone laughed, the ice broken.

'I was playing golf on Sunday with Toby Morrell,' Dave told them. 'How's he treating you? Hotel up to scratch these days?'

'It's very good,' James said, looking at her for confirmation.

'Yes it is,' she said. 'There's a big party on Saturday to celebrate its refurbishment. Fireworks, I believe, and a mystery celebrity.'

'A *very* mystery celebrity. He's been let down badly,' Dave said with a grin. 'We were invited but, thank God, we have another engagement. I can only tolerate Toby Morrell on the golf course. The bloody fuss he makes about that hotel . . .' He shook his head in amazement. 'Anybody would think it was the Ritz and Raffles combined.'

'He runs it very well,' Sophie said stiffly, feeling absurdly loyal to the little man. 'I shouldn't think it's that easy.'

Dave gave her a look then turned and winked at James, a gesture that did not pass unnoticed.

'Ready?' he enquired of James. 'Spot of business, ladies. I'm sure you can amuse yourselves for a while.'

Sophie felt like slinging him a sharp left hook for that remark, but his wife seemed unperturbed, giving her a smile and limping towards the pool where iced drinks were waiting. Lily's bottle was produced and Sophie gave her the drink she so wanted.

'This is such a nuisance,' Elisabeth said, indicating her foot. 'You'll never believe it but I really did slip on a banana skin out on the road. Dave says he's going to sue the council for letting things spill out of the rubbish bins. He'll kick up an awful stink.

But . . .' – she smiled brightly – 'I say, forget it. Life's too short for squabbling. There's no harm done although I can't swim for a while and I love to do that. Don't let it stop you, Sophie. You're welcome to have a dip. I can lend you a bikini.'

'No, thanks.' Sophie was relieved in fact. 'It's not easy with baby.'

'Doesn't she like water?'

'We haven't been swimming,' Sophie said. 'But I think she will. She loves her bath anyway.'

'Freddie's been coming in the pool with me since he was a few weeks old, and at first he could swim, but then for some reason we missed our sessions for a few weeks and when we got back in, he had lost it. Isn't that maddening? I have to watch him like a hawk now because he's still keen to get in and has no fear and might go in the deep end.' She glanced across to where her son was playing. 'I do worry. I think we may get it covered over until he's older, but Dave is reluctant. He's very proud of it.'

Despite the oriental appearance, her English was faultless and, as they talked, she told Sophie that she was half English, half Japanese as her father, a senior civil servant, had met her mother when on business in Japan. She was brought up in England however and felt very English.

And then, that topic exhausted, they were soon on to the very subject that mothers get on to.

'Did you have a horrible time with Lily?'

'Did you with Freddie?' Sophie volleyed the question back with a smile, recognizing that Elisabeth was desperate to tell all.

'Horrific,' she said. 'Twenty-three hours of hell. Never again. I told Dave straight, no more. Luckily he's not bothered. He's got what he wanted now, a boy, after two grown-up daughters from his previous marriage. He dotes on Freddie.' She fumbled in her bag and withdrew a packet of cigarettes. 'I know I shouldn't but would you mind?'

'No.' Sophie tried to take in all this luxury, the house and the extensive, beautifully cared for grounds. She closed her eyes a moment, enjoying the gentle warmth of the sun on her face, not too powerful but infinitely soothing. Dave must be earning a fortune to have all this.

'It started with computer software,' Elisabeth said, reading her mind. 'Then it expanded and he shot off in various directions. Don't ask. It's all a bit technical for me. He's always away. He flies to the States regularly, like hopping on a bus now. And he has his helicopter for shorter trips.'

'Helicopter? You mean his own? Goodness, I am impressed.'

Elisabeth smiled. 'Boys' toys,' she said. 'He's just got his pilot's licence. Would you like a trip later? Show you this house from the air?'

Sophie did not answer, busy disentangling Lily from her arms where she had fallen heavily asleep. She gently placed her back in the pram, covering her with a lightweight cover and adjusting the canopy to shade her from the sun.

She caught Elisabeth looking at her quizzically.

'My husband and I are separated,' she said, feeling she must explain in part. 'I'm here on my own. We needed a break.'

'I'm sorry. He must miss the baby.'

She could not face a further explanation, left it at that, uncomfortable though as Elisabeth continued her appraisal with her beautiful Eastern eyes.

'I didn't quite catch how James introduced you. Are you and he together?'

Sophie sat up, startled. 'No, we are not. We only met this week.'

Elisabeth raised amused eyebrows. 'So? It only takes a few minutes to know, doesn't it? I knew straightaway with Dave. He's such a livewire and I love that and I love his energy. He also . . .' She hesitated a moment. 'He has this vulnerable side that he likes to hide. What's James like?'

'Nice.'

'Yes, isn't he? I understand he's doing very well. Dave wants him to do some work for him, something I'm not allowed to discuss.' She looked at Sophie thoughtfully. 'He seems to like you a lot.'

'Maybe he does, but we're neither of us completely free,' Sophie said, pushing her glass over as Elisabeth refilled it from a jug.

'James is. He's a widower.'

'He still thinks about his wife.'

'I can't imagine why. I never met her but Dave says she was a bit odd. Dave wasn't the least surprised when we heard that she

168

had killed herself.' She pulled herself up short, grimaced. 'He has told you, I hope?'

'Yes, he has.'

'Between you and me, Dave says she was hard-faced,' Elisabeth went on, refusing help and leaning over at a very awkward angle to lift a suddenly disgruntled little boy out of his playpen. 'All designer suits and briefcases. Business was all she thought about.'

'What do you do?' Sophie asked, tired of all these bitchy references to Victoria. It was well established by now that Victoria had been very difficult and it was time people forgot about it.

'I help Dave with his business interests. This and that,' she said vaguely, casting a shrewd glance Sophie's way. 'I don't want to intrude, but is there no hope of you getting back with your husband?'

'None at all. It's over with me and Roger.'

'Then you should forget him,' Elisabeth said firmly. 'Forgive me, but it doesn't look like that to me. Are you still a little in love with him?'

'No,' Sophie said, totally surprised if that was the impression she was giving. 'I wouldn't go back to him if he got down on bended knees.'

'Wouldn't you? If you say so . . .'

'I do say so,' Sophie said tightly. 'Let's change the subject please.'

'Sorry. I read signs the wrong way sometimes. So, if you and James—'

'He's an attractive man,' Sophie interrupted. 'But so far, that is all. Would you mind if we didn't talk about him any more?'

'Sorry again.' Elisabeth glanced at her watch. 'My turn to prepare lunch today. I've given the help the day off.'

'Let me help.'

But it seemed Elisabeth would not let it drop, the subject of her and James, even as they prepared a simple buffet lunch.

'Isn't it nice that you live near each other up there. You'll be able to meet up when you get home,' she went on. 'I imagine he'll be the persistent kind.'

'We might,' Sophie said carefully. 'It depends on James.'

'From the way he looks at you, I would think it depends on

you.'

Sophie glanced at her sharply but she was preoccupied with slicing cucumber and made no further comment. Just as well, for the men returned at this point.

'Sorry I kept him,' Dave said, cornering Sophie as she carried a plate to the table. 'My fault. I wanted to show him the new car and we had to have a quick drive.'

'Quick being the word,' James said. 'I think Dave's a failed Formula One driver.'

'I'm a failed nothing,' Dave said, his laugh short.

James collared her too for a private moment.

'I hope you weren't too bored,' he said.

'No.' She smiled, thinking that, if Roger had done something like this, left her high and dry to spend time with a woman she had little in common with, she might have been annoyed. Somehow, she seemed more able to forgive this man.

'I thought you might enjoy a bit of girl talk,' he said, his smile mischievous.

'I could kill you for that remark,' she said lightly. 'But you're forgiven instead.'

'I am?'

On impulse, because he was such a nice man and had had such a rough ride lately, she reached up, kissed him.

'How about a ride in the helicopter after lunch?' Dave asked. 'Just you and Sophie, James. Elisabeth will look after the children.'

'Great.'

Sophie managed a smile. There was no way she was going up in a helicopter piloted by this man. How could she, a lone mother, risk it?

She knew it was bound to put a damper on proceedings, as Dave went on and on about it throughout lunch and she tried unsuccessfully to drop hints about her reluctance. It passed him by and she knew she would have to be firm and say thank you but no.

When she did, James stood by her, declined too, but Dave took it like a personal insult, a slur on his capability to pilot the blessed thing, and the lunch ended on a sour note.

Elisabeth tried to retrieve the situation, suggesting they retreat to the sunny conservatory for after-lunch drinks. James excused himself a moment, heading for one of the many bathrooms and the three adults settled themselves on chairs, Lily playing quietly on the rug in front of them with some soft bricks, and Freddie . . .

Where was Freddie?

It was just then that all hell broke loose.

Chapter Seventeen

TOBY checked the food and then his appearance. He was in casual gear for lunch, light-blue cashmere sweater and dark, slimline trousers, standing sideways to the mirror to check his stomach. God, he was very nearly slim these days compared with his podgy youth and at this rate, his face would soon be looking fashionably haggard. Bit to go though ... he put the weight loss down to his panicky lifestyle. There was nothing like a spot of frantic pandemonium with no time to eat to shed the pounds.

He was bloody nervous. He had never felt like this before. She loomed in his thoughts. All he could think about was Fiona. She was years younger and beautiful and he wondered what she really saw in him. He hoped, above all else, she liked him. He hoped the attraction was not just because of the power he exuded, his position at the head of the pyramid, his decisiveness, all the things that were supposed to be a real turn on for the ladies.

He really hoped she liked him.

One thing was sure: there would be no pouncing and having it off on the floor with Fiona. For all that sexy exterior, she was surprisingly innocent but then he suspected most girls didn't know half as much as they pretended. They talked about sex a lot, all the time if you believed those titillating magazines they read, those soul-searching TV programmes, but did they honestly do it all at the drop of a hat, like they did on plays on television? An introduction, a quick coffee, a bite to eat and they were back at a flat, naked and at it.

A TV producer's fantasy to boost ratings, he felt sure, and he was not going to make that mistake with Fiona and scare her off. They were not exactly strangers, for he had known her for three years, but this was a crucial step up.

Anticipation flurried within, as he drove out to collect her and bring her back. She seemed not the least surprised that they were alone, giving him a bemused smile, and he made only the barest attempt at excuses, telling her rather that she was looking very lovely and that he considered himself honoured that she was here as his guest today.

She admired his apartment, his taste with genuine pleasure, and he poured her a drink, making sure she was quite comfortable before disappearing into the kitchen, where he just had to make a few finishing touches to the meal.

Fiona, listening to agitated kitchen sounds, took her time examining the room. She really did like this apartment although there would be one or two changes she would make given the choice and chance. At work, she had decided to keep quiet about Toby. To her own surprise, she was developing a strange bout of discretion. And, surprising herself, she had found it necessary to put an end to the thing with Tony. She had ended up having to spell it out, when he seemed not to understand what she was saying. She had not, of course, thought it wise to mention Toby. Tony, Toby, the names might be similar but they were poles apart.

Toby was different from her usual men. Older. A little world-weary. But classy for all that. She had lain awake last night, worrying about it, asking herself if she could really go through with it. If it came to it, could she marry purely for money?

Coldly, she calculated the pros and cons. For instance, if you caught him at the right angle, Toby was not so bad-looking and he did have quite a nice smile, the private one that is, not the one he used on the guests and staff alike at the hotel. His beautifully cut clothes made the best of his shape. He was courteous which she did like and, if she was his wife, the door was open to so many new experiences. Those boutiques, whose windows she could only afford to gaze in just now, would be available for Mrs Toby Morrell.

On balance, she could live with the cons. She would insist on making love with the lights out, so that she could let her imagi-

173

nation run riot. She would plead shyness. He would love that.

She wanted a proposal of marriage, quickly, before the momentum dried up.

Nothing less.

Mary Parker felt as if it was a load lifted from her mind.

Acceptance.

After all this time, she had finally accepted that Geoff was not going to come back and now it was time to plan what was to happen in the future.

'You were late last night,' Lucy said, not exactly accusingly at breakfast. 'Are you working today?'

'Yes. I've swapped a shift.'

Lucy sniffed. 'They have you down for a mug at that hotel,' she said. 'You should get extra when you do that. For your inconvenience.'

'I'm only going in at ten and I'll be finished by one. And anyway, I don't know why you're so bothered: it's me who's doing it.'

'I don't like to see you exploited,' Lucy said. 'One day, when I get my own salon, you'll see how I treat my staff.'

Mary raised her eyebrows, decided not to dash young hopes. How would she ever afford her own salon? She sat down and wondered how to tell Lucy about what had happened last night.

'Did you enjoy the film?'

'It was very good. Lovely couple they made.'

Who?' Lucy laughed. 'The film stars you mean?'

'Well, yes.' She realized it was a daft thing to say. Film acting was not real. Just make-believe, like she had been indulging in make-believe of her own these past months. 'I thought I saw your dad when we were leaving the cinema,' she went on, deciding to come straight out with it. It was enough to make Lucy look up from her glossy fashion magazine. 'I made Dennis give chase in his car.'

'You didn't?' Lucy's eyes widened. 'What? A car chase through Plymouth?'

Mary nodded, shamefaced. 'Daft, wasn't it? We followed him home to this housing estate. Nice house. Blue door with a cherry tree in the garden.'

174

'And?'

'It wasn't him, was it? It had a look of him from the back, but it wasn't him. Anyway, it made me feel a bit silly if you must know. Dennis was very good about it. He laughed but in a nice way. Took me for a meal afterwards and then we went back to his house for a cocoa and then he brought me home.'

'A cocoa?' Lucy laughed. 'After all this time? I bet you gave him no encouragement.'

'I did not,' Mary said hotly. 'And you shouldn't be saying things like that, Lucy. It's none of your business what I do.'

'You've got such an old-fashioned attitude. Anybody would think you were sixty not forty. You are a fool, Mum,' Lucy said, but kindly.

'Maybe I am. Do you know, Lucy, the honest truth is I was ever so glad when it wasn't your dad. If it had been him, you see, it would have meant he'd been double-crossing us and I didn't want that. I'd rather he was dead than that. Now . . .' She sighed deeply. 'Well, now I can get on with other things. Start again.'

'With Dennis?' Lucy asked gently.

'We'll have to see.'

Lucy smiled, a bit flushed suddenly. 'I'm glad you've seen it like this. He seems all right, Dennis. What's his house like?'

'Untidy,' Mary said. 'Needs a good clean. And cluttered. Half his stock is in there, I expect. It's all higgledy-piggledy. Big old-fashioned stuff. Antiques.'

Lucy looked round their very tidy room. 'He has a shock coming then,' she said. 'Once you get your hands on it.'

This morning, she would see if she could get hold of the necklace for Dennis. She was glad it would be the last thing because, excitement or not, it was getting dangerous and she was bound to be found out and have her name in the local paper.

As she went into the hotel staff entrance, she saw Ms Bell taking the sun on the veranda, morning coffee and toast by the look of it and she also looked as if she was settled there for some time.

Good.

Pushing the cleaning trolley along the corridor outside Bea's room a little while later, she flicked a duster over picture frames

175

and across skirtings in the corridor a minute, just letting her nerves settle. Then she went into Bea's private rooms.

The bedroom reeked of scent as did the bathroom. Ms Bell left the rooms tidy but very dusty, what with her talc and her loose face powder. Mary fussed around for a while, changing the bed and towels, flashing round the bathroom. She could not bear a messy bathroom and Dennis's last night was a shocker. Not dirty, not quite, but not up to her standards. He needed somebody to tidy up a bit. Not that he wasn't neat and tidy in his own appearance, so the state of the house had been a surprise.

She checked the corridor again, listened for the lift, but everything was quiet, that lull in the day when the guests are all dispersed.

All clear. Ms Bell was well settled downstairs and, if she did need to freshen up during the day, she tended to use one of the powder rooms on the reception floor.

Heart thumping nonetheless, for she would never get used to this, she tiptoed across to the dressing-table and opened the drawer where the jewellery was kept. There it was in its glittering heap, half of it tangled up, the rest in little bags and boxes.

Mary saw what she was looking for at once. Dennis had asked if she wanted one ear-ring to make sure of the match but she had said no. Gently, she picked it up and could not resist holding it against her neck, although it needed a fancy ballgown and looked daft against her house uniform. She put it in the pocket of her cleaning overall and gently closed the drawer.

She didn't know later why she did it but she did. She went over to the wardrobe, picking out the lovely cream dress that hung there protected by a see-through cover.

It was a wedding dress surely, lacy and very soft, yet surprisingly heavy like all good materials. She unzipped the cover to get a closer look and carefully lifted it out. Taking complete leave of her senses, she quickly slipped off her overall and slipped into the dress, taking great care not to tread on the hem, as she adjusted it.

It fitted her very well, a bit slack round the waist but all right. Lifting up the skirt, she rustled across the room and tried the necklace on once more. Oh yes, this was more like it, this time it was perfect, shining against her skin, even making her eyes shine too with its sparkles. This was the real thing and it felt wonderful. The only real diamond she had ever owned was the tiny one in her engagement ring. It had never really mattered that it was so little for it was all Geoff could afford.

If only Dennis could see her in this . . .

She never heard the lift rising or the door opening.

Chapter Eighteen

AMANDA hit town for a spot of retail therapy. A new business suit, neat but that important bit different, a beautiful ivory jacket plus some new evening wide-legged pants, and some disgracefully useless shoes and matching handbag in Italian leather. She only drew breath when she was practically at the limit, carrying her purchases into a department store to ease her aching feet.

Ellie caught her on her mobile.

'Just to tell you that I rang the ex.'

'Ellie, you didn't?'

'No harm done,' Ellie said indignantly. 'I didn't leave a name. I just said I was an old friend of Sophie's.'

Amanda drew a sharp breath. 'And. . . ?'

'And I'd met her down in Devon, her and the baby, and that she'd happened to mention the recruitment agency and, as I live near Leeds, I thought I'd check them out. Put some business his way.'

'You have a nerve. What on earth did you hope to achieve?' Amanda asked, feeling some small admiration for her sheer gall. 'Go on then, what did he have to say?'

'Nothing,' Ellie said, clearly unhappy. 'As soon as I mentioned I'd seen Sophie and the baby, he became very abrupt. Snapped at me. Wanted to know whereabouts in Devon and which hotel. So I told him.'

'Oh. Maybe you shouldn't have?'

'He took me by surprise. And then he hung up. What a way to run a business! He might have passed me on to a colleague.'

Amanda did not bother to remind her that she had not actually needed recruitment advice anyway, but she did wonder

178

what Ellie had said to upset him so much.

She spent the rest of her coffee break wondering just what it might be, the scenarios becoming more and more bizarre.

'You are losing it, Amanda,' she said aloud to herself, as she drove back to the hotel. One or two things about the future were shaping up in her mind and a move down here was uppermost. Why ever not? It was lovely, warmer and prettier, and she could buy herself a small cottage – she had peeped in a few estate agents' windows – for a more modest sum than she would have imagined. She certainly could not contemplate living within dinner-party distance of James and Sophie, if they ever got together, wondering if Ellie would cut him dead, too. Good heavens, there was a limit to civilized behaviour.

A complete new start.

It sounded good and, just thinking it, made her feel a little better. All this stuff about broken hearts was pure bunkum. Hearts could be bruised maybe and hers had been, but it was time for her to snap out of it and to get on with things. She had to stop acting like such a wimp.

Carrying her packages through the foyer, she was accosted by the duty manager – Alice – according to the name tag.

'Goodness, you're heavily laden.' she said, clicking fingers and having a young man in uniform instantly appear. 'Take these parcels up to Number 27,' she said briskly. 'Would you like coffee and a selection of cream cakes in the lounge, madam?'

Bereft of her parcels, feeling a little bullied too, Amanda consented.

'You wouldn't have any curd tart rather than cream cakes, would you?' she asked, feeling a sudden urge for the fabulous concoction that Ellie rustled up with such ease. 'Or something like it?'

A look of panic crossed the woman's face.

'Absolutely,' she said. 'Nothing is too much trouble. It will be with you directly, madam.'

Idly, she picked up a magazine in the lounge and waited for her coffee to appear. She would cut back on the caffeine when she got home, restrict herself to no more than four cups a day. She found she was wondering about some of the cases she had left high and dry, hoping her assistant was coping. It was, for a

179

moment, tempting to ring him to check, but she decided that nothing was vital and, if he was really desperate, he could ring her. He could deal easily with a decree nisi that was expected. Another case she was involved in was one of those about-turn ones where the wife was the high earner and the husband the stay-at-home. She was acting just as high-handedly as the husband might do in a similar case, spitting outraged feathers about money and the allocation of accumulated funds, splitting hairs about possessions. Amanda did not like the woman, for whom she was acting, and a long and bitter wrangle was promised.

Oh, the joys that awaited her!

She glanced at her watch, realizing her coffee was taking an age. She did not mind being relieved of her packages but she did mind being almost frog-marched in here and then kept waiting.

And then, just as she was about to give up on it, it arrived brought in by Alice herself, all smiles.

'Is this all right?' she asked, indicating the pastry case with a soft meringue-like filling. 'Sorry, we couldn't come up with exactly what you wanted but I do hope it's an acceptable approximation.'

'It looks lovely. It's not the same, but I realize this is Devon not Yorkshire. Thank you for trying.'

'Not at all. We are here to help.'

Amanda smiled. She couldn't for the life of her understand why but, everytime she came within speaking distance of this woman, she seemed to initiate a panic.

She thought back to the words she had had with James first thing. She ought to have known better than criticize Sophie. Red rag to a bull. If she had been trying to think of a way to drive him into Sophie's arms, then she could not have done better.

'There he is!' Elisabeth Price pointed into the distance. 'Can you see? Over by the hedge. How did he get there? Was anybody watching him?' She took a breath and yelled his name.

Freddie was toddling along across the lawns plumb in the direction of the pool. Toddling, yes, but in that funny rapid-legs-all-over-the-place way that meant he was covering a fair old distance, going even faster it appeared when he heard his mother call his name.

'Oh my God! He thinks we're playing a game. Run and catch. Dave, go and get him. He's getting too near the pool.'

Sophie heard Elisabeth's agonized cry but did not stop to hear anything else. Freddie was a long way off already and she had to get to him before he got to the pool and fell in. She kicked off her shoes as she ran and, in an instant, she was back to her youth, that same pounding in her ears, that same hell-bent concentration, everything else shut out so that she was in her own little world. Her goal the finishing line or, in this case, the edge of the pool.

She covered the distance, the old techniques pulled out of nowhere, shamefully out of condition, handicapped by the skirt that flopped round her ankles but yes – she could still do it. She could still give practically anyone else a good run for their money. Wherever Dave was, behind presumably, he was nowhere near. And she was gaining on the little one fast.

She managed to call out his name, trying to tell him to stop, but she was aware that effort of speaking was losing her precious seconds. He did stop as he heard her, for a fraction, looked round and waved his little hand before, all of a giggle, he carried on, legs working overtime so close to the pool now that she knew she was not going to make it and she couldn't swim either.

A final heart-bursting sprint.

And then, together, they both fell in.

Shallow water, shallow for her, and with her feet on the bottom, she scooped Freddie up in her arms and lifted him high out of the water.

For a moment, they both spluttered and coughed.

'Again,' he laughed, his chubby hands tugging on her wet hair. 'Run fast, lady.'

It didn't dawn until later that Dave was still back at the house, rooted to the spot, with Elisabeth collapsed in a heap beside him, beside herself. It was James who was now running towards her, his face tired with relief by the time he reached them.

'Sophie, darling . . .'

'Wet in the water,' Freddie was saying. 'Wet socks. Wet hair.

181

Wet lady.'

They looked at each other, virtually ignoring the chattering little boy as James helped her up the steps and wrapped his arms round her shivering body.

'You were right not to say anything,' James told her on the way back to the hotel. Sophie was wearing a change of clothing, courtesy of Elisabeth, but they had refused the offer to stay over. They felt intrusive because of the chill atmosphere between husband and wife. Dave had thanked Sophie, of course, for saving his little boy's life but not as profusely as might be expected.

'He froze,' Sophie said with the smallest of smiles. 'It's not unheard of, especially if it's your own child. Shock, I suppose. And I certainly didn't want a big thing made of it. I only did what anyone else would have done. If you hadn't been in the bathroom, you would have done it too.'

'Elisabeth said she's never seen anybody move so fast before,' he said. 'They'll cover up the pool now, of course. Or teach him to swim.'

'If he'd gone in the deep end . . .'Sophie shuddered. 'I would have gone in too and I can't swim and Lily . . .'

'But he didn't go in the deep end so don't dwell on it,' James said, pulling off the road into a lay-by, killing the engine, taking in the summery scents of the field through the open window. Lily was asleep and, for once, Sophie was sitting beside him. She opened her door and let her legs dangle out.

'Quite a day,' James said. 'Are you sure you're all right? You've had a shock.'

'We all had a shock. I'm fine, James. Don't fuss.' She spun round, looked at him. 'But you've lost the contract, haven't you?'

He shrugged. 'I'm not sure we wanted it. Henry would not have liked his ideas at all. There are some clients you can work with and some it's better not to. It's no big deal to have lost it.'

'Dave couldn't stand the humiliation of you knowing about that little episode today,' she said. 'That's all it is. And now he has to face Elisabeth and what she feels. He'll feel guilty and he'll keep wondering if his little boy would have drowned if I hadn't been there. Freezing like that can happen to anyone but

182

the trouble is Dave thinks he's too confident for it to happen to him. Confident people like him have a very long way to fall.'

'You're very good at this, aren't you?'

'Oh yes. I'm good with other people's problems, but not so good with my own.'

'Do you want to talk about it?'

'If I do tell you, you might not feel the same about me,' she warned, knowing she had no choice. 'Just when things might have . . .' She glanced his way, smiling. 'I do find you attractive, James.'

He took her in his arms then. Warm and comforting and, for a moment, she hid there but then, as he touched her chin and raised her face to look at him, a kissing look in his eye, she knew it was more than time.

'There's something I have to tell you. It's about the baby.'

'What about her? She's not ill?'

'Oh no, she's all right. It's just – I may have given the impression that she's mine. My baby.' She tried to smile as she heard his gasp of disbelief.

'What do you mean? She is yours.'

She moved out of his arms and he let her.

'James, you've got to help me,' she said, trying to stay calm, even though his face, not surprisingly, was registering complete shock. 'They must not get her. They can't have her. I'll kill myself first.'

He turned away from her, started up the engine, clipped his seatbelt on.

'I'm taking you back to the hotel,' he said abruptly. 'You can tell me the whole story on the way and then we'll do what has to be done.'

Chapter Nineteen

'WHAT do you think you are doing?'

Bea Bell stood in the doorway, quite astonished at what she saw. For a moment, coming in from the shadow of the corridor, she thought she was seeing a vision – a ghost. A ghost in a wedding gown.

'Oh, Ms Bell . . .' Mary stood there, still as anything, not making any attempt to take the dress off, looking rather beautiful in her fragile way.

'It suits you,' Bea said drily. 'You look like a bride, my dear. It was my bridal gown, you know. It's very aged, like me, and you must be very careful as you take it off. Would you do that now, please?'

Mary, pink-faced, was already unfastening the very many fabric-covered buttons with fingers that seemed clumsy and, with a click of her tongue, Bea went forward to help.

'So many buttons,' she murmured. 'A work of art. Hand made by my aunt. ' She noticed the necklace, noticed too that Mary had clasped it to her chest as if afraid that Bea might see it. 'Shall I unfasten that?' she asked. 'And then you can get changed back into your housedress and we can have a talk.'

'I can't stay. I'm still on duty, Ms Bell,' Mary muttered, standing in a pool of creamy material, which she very carefully stepped out of. Bea, although she had quickly averted her gaze, noticed she was wearing a white brassiere and pink knickers and Bea, who had worn matching lingerie all her life found herself oddly sorry for the woman, whose habitual flusteredness had taken on a whole new meaning just now. 'I'm really sorry. I shouldn't have done it. You won't report me, will you?'

'No, I will not. As for you being on duty, you may leave that with me. I shall inform your housekeeper that I requested additional work from you today and that will be that. They will do nothing to offend me, Mary, for fear that I will leave. I pay an exorbitant amount of money and they can ill afford to lose it. Now . . .' She crossed to her comfortable armchair and sat down, waiting for Mary to dress hurriedly and hang up the bridal gown.

'Were you going to steal the necklace?' she asked, when Mary was at last settled or as settled as her anxiety would allow.

'Oh no, never . . .'

Bea shook her head. 'Don't lie. I have a record of the things you have stolen from me and I very much suspect that you need the necklace because it belongs to the ear-rings. Am I right?'

There was a brief unhappy silence.

'Yes, Ms Bell.'

'Good. At least we have established something. What did you do with them? The stolen goods? Did you sell them through a fence? Isn't that the word?'

'Dennis . . .' She stopped, coloured. 'I shouldn't incriminate him, should I?'

'Why ever not? You poor girl, led astray like this. Your own dearest husband was lost at sea . . .'

She waited for Mary's nod, gave her an encouraging smile.

They waited for the kettle to boil and Mary, glad of a chance to hide her face and have a bit of a think, fussed with the tea things. She might end up in prison and then what? What would happen to Lucy? Oh she thought she could manage, but could she?

'Tell me about this man. This Dennis,' Bea said when they were drinking their tea as calmly as you like.

'He's very nice.' Mary told her about the way it was, and then about Geoff, about the car chase through Plymouth the other night.

Bea clapped her hands. 'How exciting! And now that you have accepted that your Geoffrey is dead, what will happen with Dennis?'

'I don't really know. I'm still married until they find a body,' Mary explained. 'But I dare say we can wait.'

Bea smiled, finding she was liking this woman more and more. A fool, of course, for doing what she had done but just that. There was nothing malicious about the act. She just wasn't very bright but she had produced a nice, very pretty daughter.

She could make a huge fuss. Mr Morrell would have kittens if this news broke just before his grand reopening. One of his trusted staff stealing from a poor old lady.

She looked at Mary, at the frightened eyes. Once more, she exercised the power she had been using all her life.

'I'm going to let you off,' she said, lifting the necklace from her lap and passing it over. 'Take it. Give it to your man and let that be an end to it. There will be no more. Say nothing, of course. This is our secret, Mary.'

'Oh, I couldn't.' Mary fingered the necklace, saw the dazzle of it. When she looked up, there were tears in her eyes and a silent sorry barely escaped her mouth.

'Do it for me. If it makes your Dennis see you in a new light, so much the better. I love a happy ending, my dear.' She looked out of the window on to the bright day. 'It worries me, Mary. I was still relatively young when Oscar departed. And look at me now? What will he think when we meet again? I had such beautiful hair and he used to adore it.'

Mary searched eagerly for words of comfort for the old lady with no hair. 'He'll think you're very grand, madam,' she said shyly. 'He'll think you're a real lady.'

Bea nodded, getting up slowly and a little painfully and going across to where the dress was hanging up once more, reaching for it and holding it against her body. Hearing the unmistakable sound of gentle ladylike weeping, Mary chose the moment to depart.

Sobered by events, very sobered by events, James could hardly take it all in as he drove Sophie back to the hotel.

'Lily's not my daughter: she's my granddaughter,' Sophie finally told him. 'And that's the truth.'

He tried to take it in. 'That's all right.' he said. 'I could be a grandfather too, at my advanced age. Just about.'

'It's nothing to do with my age,' she snapped. 'I've never pretended to be younger than I am. I'm nearly forty, James.'

186

'I don't understand,' he said. 'Why not tell people? After all,' he smiled encouragingly, 'you look pretty good for a grand-mother.'

'I'll tell you.' She was briefly interrupted by the baby, waking and crying in a grumbly sort of way, sleepy though and with the motion of the car soon settling off again. 'I'd like you to listen and not pre-judge.'

James, though infinitely weary, listened. Was he fated to go through life with women like this? Why couldn't he have a woman with simple tastes, easygoing and just happy?

He listened anyway.

He owed her that.

'After failing at school, Mark disappeared on us for a time. Roger said not to worry. After all, he wasn't a child any more. We didn't hear for a long time and I tried not to worry for he'd never been one for telephoning home every night. But then, it was coming up to Christmas, and a friend of mine went to visit relatives in Bristol and who should she see wrapped in a blanket on the pavement with a begging bowl—'

'Mark?'

'Reduced to that and there was no reason for it,' Sophie went on briskly. 'I took the first train down and found him straight-away on the same bit of pavement. Scruffy and cold. I begged him to come home and stop this nonsense.'

'My God! That must have been tough.'

'Tough? It would have been heartbreaking if I'd had any feel-ings left for him by then,' she said. 'But I was past all that.'

'What happened? Did he go home with you?'

'No. He did not. He just told me to go away and I did.' She hesitated, wondering if she should mention the fifty pounds she had pressed into his hand. Conscience money, of course. 'Roger said we should forget him. We'd done our best and we couldn't do any more. We couldn't hold his hand forever. Something like that . . .' She paused as that awful panic came over her again, listening to her own breathing until it calmed.

'Go on,' James urged, as the silence lengthened.

'And then, another Christmastime, just as Roger and I were in the process of splitting up finally and I was in the middle of moving house, there he was again. It was like a scene from the nativity. This couple turning up on the doorstep, unannounced. A girl, very pregnant, with scruffy hair and a butterfly tattoo on her arm. Oh, and the most beautiful eyes. She looked so surprised as if she had no idea why she was here at my house with Mark.'

'I see,' James said, picturing the scene. 'It's her baby. And Mark's. And you've been looking after Lily for them?'

'You could say that. Looking after her indeed. They abandoned her. The girl hadn't even seen a doctor throughout the pregnancy so it was a miracle that everything went so well. She was completely clueless and I had to organize everything, the hospital admission and so on. I was there at the birth because Mark would have none of it. Just like his father,' she added with a sniff. 'It was another miracle that the girl was not on drugs so at least she did have some sense. She was surprisingly healthy in fact.'

'So, she had the baby,' he prompted, determined to get the whole of the story.

'I took them back to my cottage. She wasn't a natural mother at all, scarcely looked at the baby. Then, days later, she packed her bag and went away, don't ask where because she didn't say, and then Mark went after her, saying he'd be back and could I hold the fort. Hold Lily he meant.'

'I'm beginning to see. And now they want her back. Is that it? You've looked after her and now they want her back?'

'The girl's gone. They don't know where. Mark knows but he won't say. In any case, he's with someone else now, a girl he calls Sage Willow and they want the baby.' She reached over and touched the pastel-coloured blanket that covered Lily's feet. 'They want to take her with them to live in this . . . this *commune*,' she could hardly bring herself to say it.

To her dismay, James laughed.

'What's so funny? It's tragic,' she said. 'It's in this big house in Wales, a run-down country house that they've taken over. One of the group has got some money and he's donated it to the cause and bought the place. All these weird people live there, James. Mark says some of them are teachers and they will educate the children. They pool their income. They have books but no television; they grow their own vegetables, sell the surplus to local markets; make craft items, for goodness sake. That sort of thing.'

'Maybe it won't be so bad,' James said. 'It's just an alternative lifestyle, Sophie.'

'I might have known you'd say that,' she said. 'But I don't agree. I cannot allow Lily to go. At home, at my cottage, she has her own little room decorated in lemon with stencilling on the furniture. A little chest, the cot, the wardrobe. All her soft toys. She has everything she needs. I shall put her name down for the local primary school because it has such a good reputation, but then I thought private education after that. She's going to make me so proud of her.'

'To make up for her father?'

'How dare you say that?'

'How else can I put it? Aren't you listening to yourself?'

'I knew it. You don't understand. You don't understand about babies. I'm the one who's looked after her, right from the start. I can afford to give her the better life. And I'm not giving her up without a fight. Especially not to my own son.'

'We're here.' James drove round into the car park. 'I'm coming up with you, Sophie. I want you to ring your husband now and tell him where you are. And your son. Don't you realize they'll be worried sick? And Mark has a right to know where Lily is.'

She agreed, but said she preferred to make the call in private.

For a moment, he caught what could only be described as a wild and sly look in her eye which greatly disturbed him.

He was not sure he trusted her.

Amanda caught him as he was escaping the lift.

'You look as if you've seen a ghost,' she said.

'If you knew the day I've had . . .' he began.

'What on earth's the matter?'

'I'm not sure I can tell you, but I fancy some fresh air,' he said. 'It seems very stale in here.'

She followed him out. 'Then you didn't enjoy your day?'

'Disaster from start to finish,' he said. 'Well, not quite. Sophie saved a child's life in fact.'

'You're joking? What happened?'

189

'It was Dave Price's little boy Freddie. He nearly drowned in their pool. Sophie went running after him and they both fell in. She can't swim either she told me later. Luckily, it was the shallow end.'

'But how extraordinary. That was a fantastic thing to do,' Amanda said, taking it in in a daze. 'Is Freddie all right? Is she all right? Shall I go up to her?'

'No,' he said sharply. 'You stay out of it. I know Ellie's been snooping – don't bother to deny it. I want to know what she's found out about Sophie. Has she been in touch with Roger?'

'Well, yes,' Amanda said, seeing no point in hiding it. 'She just rang his agency, told him she'd seen Sophie and the baby here in Devon and he more or less hung up on her.'

'So he knows she's here?'

She nodded. 'Is it a problem?'

He ran a hand through his hair in a tired gesture. 'I can't believe it. She's in a helluva state. I'm frightened for her, Amanda. After what happened to Victoria . . .'

'Why is she in such a state?'

'Because of the baby.'

'Lily? What are you talking about?'

'Bloody hell, Amanda, it's private. She made me promise—'
That did it.

'Right,' she said, furious. 'So, you won't let me help?'

'It's not that. I'm not sure anybody can help.'

'But you don't trust me, do you? Well, that's it I'm afraid. I have had it up to here with you, James. Yes, I was sorry, of course I was sorry when Victoria died, especially like that. Who wouldn't be? But I'm sick of it now. Sick of you not trusting me. And sick of you getting it wrong with your women every time. I should have said it before: I loved you for what you were, James, and it's hard to cope with what you've become. What's the matter with you? Why these women? Why can't you be normal, find yourself an ordinary woman who'd be happy with you and even have your kids?' She laughed. 'To think that I once thought it might be me, but then, I'm much too ordinary for you, aren't I? I'm even happy most of the time. I could have made you happy too, James, but I've had enough of playing second fiddle.'

'Now wait—'

'To hell with you. I'm off home. And you might as well know, that as soon as I can, I'm getting a job down here and settling here. On my own. I don't need you.'

She had silenced him as if she had shot and wounded him. Hurt and bewildered him. He looked – and this satisfied her immensely – he looked shattered.

She got her breath back. Smiled.

'You loved me?' he asked, his amazement truly amazing.

'Yes, you fool,' she said, delivering the *coup de grâce* as she turned. 'And you might notice the past tense, James.'

Chapter Twenty

Friday

'MR Morrell.' Alice fairly shot into Toby's office. 'You're never going to believe it.'

'What?' He felt a moment's apprehension, which evaporated as he caught the excitement of what could only be good news.

'You know "Holidays Inn, Holidays Out" that new programme on television?' He nodded. He tried to keep abreast of the holiday shows and this was one of the few that concentrated on all kinds of UK holidays.

'Well, you know Sasha Rogers-Reed, the presenter?'

'Not alas personally,' he said with a smile. The woman was a publicist's dream. A former model, she was in the news just now because she had signed a book deal – enormous sum – for a steamy novel she had yet to write. As well as literary aspirations, she had a penchant for off-the-shoulder gowns and the Crown Jewels came a poor second to her collection of outrageous sparklies. She had long flowing blonde locks, a dazzling smile and a fashionable accent. She wrote a column, or somebody did, in some downmarket rag and was forever on panel games and suchlike, acting the part of the dumb blonde with some panache. The very mention of Sasha Rogers-Reed would have the local Press drooling. Seeing Alice's expression, Toby dared for the first time to hope against hope.

'Don't tell me, Alice, that they want to feature us?'

'Yes.' Alice's smile broke out, dazzling enough but nowhere

near Sasha's standards. 'They'll be filming next week for showing later in the year. It's the usual format. Devon on the cheap, moderate and four-star. Her researcher rang up, very apologetic about such short notice but I took it upon myself to assure them it was no problem for us.'

'Absolutely not. Well done,' Toby said, his admiration for too-tall Alice growing by the minute.

'Anyway, sir, Sasha will be here tomorrow and so I asked the researcher if Miss Rogers-Reed would be available tomorrow evening to perform our reopening ceremony and the answer is she will be thrilled to do so. She has promised us a dress to remember and will be notifying the Press accordingly.'

Toby just managed to restrain himself from a very unexecutive desire to punch the air and yell 'Yes!'

'Well done again, Alice,' he said. 'Things are looking up. We now have a celebrity and the weather forecast is improving. We only have a slim chance now of catching the storm.' He glanced out at a calm unhurried sky which tomorrow night would be shot through with sparkles of exploding and falling lights. The French windows that made up the entire side of the Clovelly Room would be open so that guests could wander on to the terrace to view the fireworks display.

Champagne and fireworks at midnight.

When Alice, in a tizzy of excitement, had gone, Toby took the still unopened letter from his desk drawer, the private and personal letter that had arrived in the morning post. It was a heavyweight cream envelope with the Harlequin crest on the back. Inside, the fate of The New Grand.

He held it up to the light, trying to see inside, searching for a good sign, a congratulations, but the envelope was too thick and nothing showed through. If it was good news, if the inspector – who seemed in no great rush to leave – had given them the thumbs up then they would milk it for what it was worth tomorrow. However, if it was the boot, the raspberry, then they would be well advised to bury all mention, now and forever.

Toby sighed.

This was worse than examination results. In examinations, he always managed to scrape through.

He flicked the switch on his phone.

'No calls please,' he told Mavis. 'And don't disturb me for the next quarter of an hour.'

He reached for his paper knife and slit the letter open.

Fiona slipped her letter into its envelope, sealed it. It was her letter of resignation and a calculated risk. Toby needed a kick up the backside and if he thought he might be losing her, it might do the trick.

Toby wanted her, she knew that, but whether he had marriage on his mind or a bit of fun was entirely another matter. The only way, therefore, to play it was to keep her legs firmly together. After all, it was supposed to have worked for Anne Boleyn with King Henry, although that lady blew it afterwards by not producing a son.

Oh yes, a smitten man was a vulnerable man.

Toby had invited her to the VIP reception tomorrow evening and she had purchased a new ankle-length dress from Next, black, simple, which fitted like a second skin. Flat shoes, so that she could just about gaze *up* at him.

She fingered the envelope thoughtfully.

Already, she had decided on a single whopper of a diamond for her engagement ring.

Amanda decided to spend the day looking round the area at a few cottages. The idea of moving here, pie in the sky at the start, was taking shape. Why not? Why ever not?

She could get a job here, for she had already done a provisional check with a few agencies. The thought of remaining in the Leeds area, albeit in a new house, with James within spitting distance was not a happy prospect. He was heading for living the rest of his life in an endless, hopeless search for the right woman and she was no longer prepared to pick up the pieces.

She concentrated on the job in hand, which was a preliminary look at several likely sounding cottages. She was a bit too cynical to believe completely in the idyllic village and the cottage with roses round the door concept, although it was hard not to be swept away by some of the romantic descriptions and pretty-pretty photographs.

Reality was a little different and the practical difficulties soon emerged, her critical eye unmoved by the agent's enthusiasm of what a little hard work and a modest few thousand pounds would achieve. She found it difficult to see beyond what was actually there, preferring to leave creative thinking to James.

By lunchtime, she was somewhat dispirited.

She arranged a further couple of viewings in the afternoon and found a coffee shop in Dartmouth, in which to sit and mope, ringing Ellie from the car, letting it slip what she was up to.

'Moving down there permanently? Are you completely mad?' Ellie shrieked, as she had known she would. 'What about James?'

'What about him? He's history. I told him more or less to take a running jump.'

'What? You hang on in there, do you hear? What's the latest with Sophie?'

'Dying a death I think, but that's really not the point any more, Ellie. He just thinks of me as a friend and that's not going to change.'

'Dying a death, you say?' Ellie perked up. 'Something's happened to put him off then?'

'It's no business of mine. Of ours,' Amanda pointed out. 'And it never was. This holiday has been brilliant when I think about it. It might have taken me years to come to the same conclusion back home.'

'Promise me you won't do anything hasty. Don't buy a house without giving it serious thought.'

Amanda laughed. 'I'm not buying one today. These things take time, you know that. I'm just looking. No harm in that.'

'You are running away, Amanda, that's what you are doing. When are you coming back?'

'I was coming back tomorrow, but I've got this invitation to a party at the hotel, the VIP reception, and I've decided I might as well go along. You never know who'll be there. It's a good excuse to wear my Harvey Nicks.'

'That sounds great,' Ellie said, although her lack of enthusiasm was very evident.

The afternoon brought bright sunshine and a cottage in a breathlessly silent dip of countryside, that lived up to its lovely name, Lilac Cottage. On paper and in truth, it was fairly near perfection, give or take a shambolic garden, but Amanda had watched more than enough gardening programmes to think she could cope with that. She could already see a pretty little lawn surrounded by masses of softly pastel flowers and scented roses and she could see herself wandering round snipping gorgeous blooms for indoor display. Maybe a water feature too. . . .

With the softly romantic vision spiralling out of control, Amanda was unable to hide her delight from the keen-eyed agent's representative. She would get back to them, she said.

'It will go fast,' the woman said, grasping the details to her bosom and giving a warning sniff. 'I wouldn't hang around too long if I were you, Miss Lester.'

Back at the hotel, she avoided everyone, catching a glimpse of Sophie and the baby and a shimmering Bea Bell, but not seeing James at all.

Up in her room, she watched a hopelessly romantic period film, a superbly directed costume drama. At least, you knew what was what and where you were in those days with roles so clearly defined. Wiping away the give-away tears, she concluded that no woman in her right mind in the twenty-first century would stand for such treatment from such arrogant, pig-headed men. Although – she smiled a little – being courted like that, in such a carefully controlled way was somehow so much sexier than the often unspoken assumption these days that you would be more than willing to go to bed in exchange for a glass of wine and a cheap meal.

Still romantically anaesthetized, she ordered room service and ate a solitary meal.

James spent some time in his room after Amanda had left him that morning, hunched over his desk, thinking about her.

He had put Sophie and her problems aside. Talk about pouring cold water over his feelings! He hardly knew her and it was just as well this had pulled him up sharply. She had said Roger was on his way tomorrow to pick them up and he had to believe her.

Sophie was another man's problem and he had to step aside and let Roger deal with it. If that made him feel guilty, too bloody bad. He was fed up to the teeth with guilt.

Amanda ... he thought of her this morning giving him a much needed what for. He thought of her bright annoyed eyes, of the shocking words that had escaped her lips. She had loved him once, she said, and he wondered if she could love him again. Did he live on another planet where women and their emotions were concerned? Being without Amanda, living life without her being there, was suddenly unthinkable. She was always there, someone to ring up, to grumble at, to listen to. Looking back, he saw she had been there too when he was married, someone to chat to, friendly and easy, but in those days, silkily tied as he was to Victoria, he had not allowed it to happen, put thoughts like that firmly to the back of his mind. He remembered their first meeting so very clearly, Henry's office, dancing at the door, being introduced, holding her hand and then, looking after her as she skittled out, momentarily knocked off his stride.

She had looked fantastic this morning as she shouted at him and told him to pull himself together. First time she had actually said as much. That little remembered hankering for her started up, spluttering and igniting, firing up now, and this time he did not allow the memory of Victoria to interfere. After a year, at last her image and influence were fading. Sometimes, without looking at photographs, details were blurring. . . .

He had taken poor Amanda for granted for so long and he now knew that he had let her down very badly. He now knew, slow-witted fool that he was, that he loved her. He loved her but she was a stubborn soul and the way she was feeling now, it would take a lot to persuade her that he had had a change of heart.

Quickly, he downed his coffee and picked up his room keys.

A grand gesture.

That just might swing it and he had nothing to lose by trying.

'My dear, all alone?' Bea Bell enquired of Sophie, who was sitting with Lily on the veranda.

Sophie nodded. She was pale and quite interesting today and the baby was a delight as usual in a pink smocked dress.

'I'm going home tomorrow,' she told Bea. 'Back to reality.'

'Ah well, it comes to all of us or almost all,' Bea said, dangling a hand over the baby's pram and allowing the baby to grasp her finger. She tried, unsuccessfully, to pick up a resemblance between mother and baby but then she had never been very good at it. To her babies were just babies. 'And what of James?' she went on, retrieving her finger before it was sucked into the baby's ever ready mouth. 'Is he returning home also?'

'I have no idea. My husband is coming to collect me.'

At a loss, puzzled by the practicalities, not least because Sophie had transport of her own, Bea fell silent. The secret this woman held within her was overwhelming her.

Pity about the little romance she had played out in her mind. James and Sophie. Such a lovely ring to it. A handsome couple too. Of course, she must not forget the other woman who featured in his life, Amanda, so she did not altogether dismiss a happy ending. Although, Amanda, legal mind and all, would be like her Oscar who had been incredibly stubborn on occasions so, in her mind, the odds of a happy outcome lengthened.

'Why?' Toby asked, holding the resignation letter in his hand. Fiona, looking upset, was opposite him in his office, having requested an urgent meeting. She was wearing a dark suit, its severity redeemed by a short skirt, over a crisp blouse and she looked utterly delectable. Off duty, so it was a surprise to see her. 'Why are you resigning?'

'Because . . .' She raised tearful eyes. 'Don't you see, Mr Morrell. . . ?'

'Toby, please, ' he said quietly.

'I can't go on,' she said. 'Not working here. Not when you and I are so close. It doesn't seem right somehow.'

He nodded. 'I agree. It does have its difficulties, particularly if our relationship is to continue. . . .' He smiled, searching desperately for reassurance.

'I know. And I would so like it to carry on,' she said, blushing and lowering her gaze.

'What will you do if you leave?' he asked. 'This is so sudden after all these years. I will, of course, give you an excellent reference.'

'Thank you. Would you mind very much if I did not work my notice?'

'That's fine. Leave it with me. I'll speak to your senior,' he told her, wondering if it was too soon to step up the pressure. It suited him fine that she should resign, for that would solve all the potential problems about workplace harassment, but he wanted to make sure he saw her again.

'I might try my luck in London,' she said, fiddling worriedly with her hair. 'I should have no trouble finding a job, not with your reference, Toby.'

No. God, no. He hadn't meant that. He'd meant her to look for another job here.

'Don't be hasty,' he said. 'Have a break for a few weeks before you do anything.'

'I have to eat,' she told him with a smile. 'I'm afraid I can't afford to be without a job for long.'

'You are still coming to the party tomorrow?' he asked, for it was important she do that. He needed someone to share the joy, or possibly the despair, with him and, come midnight, he did not want that someone disappearing like Cinderella on him. He had after-plans.

'Of course,' she said. 'I wouldn't miss it for the world. I'm as proud of this hotel as you are, Toby.' The 'Toby' he noticed was now slipping very naturally off her tongue. 'It's going to be a terrible wrench for me to leave.'

'We are all very proud,' he murmured, remembering the wonderful news from *The Harlequin Guide*. Not only were they still included, they had won the annual golden star award for best improved, which would be presented here at Christmas. Another big event to organize and a headache and a half promised, but well worth it. 'And it will be a wrench to lose you, Fiona.'

'Thank you.' She bit her lip, looking so sweet that he wanted to take her in his arms there and then. He would have risked it were it not for Mavis, hovering nosily in the outer office, fully capable of bursting in with any old excuse at any minute. For a mad moment, Toby wondered what the hell she would do if she burst in and found him and Fiona engaged in a passionate encounter on the desk top.

He coughed, adjusted the cuffs of his shirt to cool that particular image.

'Have you something to wear for tomorrow?' he asked,

embarrassed to be asking such a question of a woman, but knowing that they worried about things like that.

She hesitated.

'Come on,' he said, fishing in his wallet. 'You and I are friends, good friends I hope, and you will be there as my guest. Do you need to buy a new dress?'

'Yes. I want to look my best.'

He had no idea what decent frocks cost. A hundred? Luckily, he had just drawn a substantial amount of cash, useful stuff to have on occasions. Three hundred pounds in all.

'Fiona, I do hope you won't be offended but I feel responsible for your present situation,' he told her clumsily, finding difficulty in expressing himself. 'Would fifty pounds be enough?'

'Yes. I ought to be able to get something for that if I look carefully,' she said, her voice hesitant.

Damn it. Not enough.

'How much then?' he smiled. 'Don't be shy. I want you to be my special guest, Fiona, and you will have to look special, too.'

'Two hundred,' she said instantly. 'That should cover it.'

For a second, the slightest second, he wondered. He was singularly clueless with women and the workings of their minds. But hadn't his mother told him that they liked to be pampered, never mind how much they might deny it? And hadn't his father told him that they liked to be treated like princesses?

Courtesy, his father told him, costs nothing.

But dresses do.

Without a quibble, he handed over the money, adding another fifty for luck, recklessly telling her to keep the change.

He left soon after, determined to bloody relax tonight if it killed him. Not a bad day although he was nearly £300 down. Still, she was worth it. Fiona would not disgrace him and he needed a beautiful woman hanging on to his arm. Successful men everywhere had beautiful women on their arms and in their beds. Look at Dave Price. He was nothing to write home about and yet he had that lovely Elisabeth.

He tried on the new cream jacket he was to wear tomorrow evening, together with the new shirt, tie and black trousers. The jacket fitted perfectly and he had been assured by his tailor that, with nearly all the other gentlemen in black, he would stand out, as he needed to stand out.

He would buy Fiona a spray of orchids.

He was scared stiff of asking her to marry him.

She would laugh at him for, although he had known her in theory for three years, he had only asked her out a few days ago. Much too soon. And a rejection was just not on.

Always, in the past, he had agonized about the right moment to spring the question. And each time, there had been a silence, shock probably and then a rapid recovery.

'Toby, it's terribly sweet of you and I'm very flattered but . . .'

And so on.

But the same old story.

They never told him the truth, of course: that he was too short, too fat, too ugly and now, getting to be too old.

He needed a financial shot in the arm after all this. He wondered what the chances were of Bea Bell popping off and leaving him her loot within the next few months. She had, so his father said, hinted hugely that it was what she intended to do. The trouble was she was looking very perky these days so that seemed a forlorn hope and there was always the terrible possibility that she could take sudden umbrage and go somewhere else.

Everything was under control in full frantic last-minute swing. The Clovelly Room looked a picture in pink and gold elegance. Chef was in one of his perpetual rages again, hell let loose in the kitchen, a creative rage that signified masterpieces were promised.

Tomorrow was it.

The final countdown had begun.

201

Chapter Twenty-One

Saturday

TOBY was at the window directly he awoke. Clear skies.

'Thank you, God,' he breathed.

Sasha Rogers-Reed was due sometime this afternoon and she had alerted the Press as promised. Alice had received details of the dress by fax. A shocking pink clinger apparently, with a transparent side panel, a little adventurous for Devisham but Toby did not care. The mayoress's well-known sensibilities were no concern of his.

The hotel was glowing anew in the morning sun and the cinnamon flush was growing on Toby. The lawns were manicured to within half an inch of their life and the beds were weed-free, the gravel freshly raked. Inside, the housekeeping staff had been on overtime, polishing and dusting to fever pitch. All the reception girls were sporting cream carnations and Toby was wearing a cream rose in his lapel today and the Millennium inscribed gold cuff-links bought by the most recent ex-girlfriend.

'All ready?' he enquired of the porter, and then of reception. 'Miss Rogers-Reed is to be dealt with directly she arrives and give me a shout at once,' he instructed. 'On no account is she to be left dangling.'

Alice was blessedly in efficient mode this morning, carrying a clipboard, asserting herself charmingly.

'No hitches,' she assured Toby.

Confidence booming, he strode across the shiny foyer, where

the housekeeper herself was putting finishing touches to the flowers. Later, he was to reflect how unwise it was to count chickens for, within the hour, the perfection of the scene was to be dimmed by the unwanted addition of a body.

Mary had the day off and was glad to be out of it, for they were running round like scalded hens at the hotel preparing for the fancy party tonight.

The horror of being found out by Ms Bell was still with her. She would never do it again, steal anything, that was for sure. If Ms Bell had not been so understanding, she might have been in a police cell by now, awaiting trial, reputation in ruins.

The thing was she was not at all sure that Dennis would have lifted a finger to help. And that niggled. She had to find out what his feelings were for sure and so, when she next saw him, before she admitted to him that she had the necklace, she was going to ask him where they stood.

She wasn't asking much. She just wanted to know if he was interested in her as a person, a woman, and not just a supplier of stolen goods. If Lucy knew what had been going on, she didn't know what she would say, but she wasn't about to tell Lucy. She was ninety-nine per cent sure of Dennis but even the most honest men could go peculiar at times and she didn't know much about Dennis, for he kept pretty much to himself. As far as she knew, he had never been married, but she liked to think that he had perhaps been jilted at the altar at the last – something unbearably romantic like that – something that was too painful for him to talk about. Something he would tell her about one day.

She had promised to pop into The Whistling Kettle this morning for a couple of hours, but she would have the afternoon free and she might call in at the antique shop and see if she could catch Dennis in.

They were just tailing off the breakfasts when she got to the café, the other girl working flat out, and Mary helped with the clearing away and cleaning the table tops. As cheap cafés go, she reckoned it was not at all bad, cleaner than most anyway, and the food was all right too, or at least they knew what the customers wanted and provided it with no fancy extras. It might well be chips with everything as Lucy said, but they were the best chips in town. Mind you, she'd never dined up at the hotel but they wouldn't be called chips there, not even if they were chips.

After an hour it slackened off a bit, and she took the opportunity to have a break taking a cup of tea over to a table and sitting down, noticing a friend of hers just coming in. She waved Jenny across and then she fussed a bit, getting her a cuppa and ordering some rounds of toast.

Jenny, as usual, enquired after Geoff and it was the usual story. Nothing to tell, but Mary made it clear this time that she was getting over it, getting used to it, and told her that she was thinking maybe of trying to organize a little memorial service for him, if the vicar would let her.

'That would be nice,' Jenny said, patting her hand. 'We could all come along and think about the good times. We wouldn't be wearing black, would we?'

'Oh no, as bright as you like.' Then, flustered, she found herself telling Jenny about Dennis. 'Of course, we can't do anything until Geoff's been declared dead,' she said, making it clear there would be no funny business. 'But it's just nice to have somebody.'

There was a little silence and, opposite her, Jenny flushed, put an extra sugar in her tea and stirred it furiously.

'Oh, Mary, you're not getting serious about him, are you?'

'Not serious,' she said quickly. 'But it's been a year, Jenny, and Lucy keeps saying—'

'You don't know, do you? Has nobody said?'

'What?' Her heart thumped.

'I don't know how to say this but there's no future to be had with Dennis. Not for a woman anyway. . . .'

It took a moment to dawn.

'He can't be,' she said indignantly. 'How could he be? We've been going out together. He's taken me to restaurants and the pictures. How can he be . . .' – she lowered her voice, mouthed the word – 'gay.'

'I don't know him that well,' Jenny went on. 'But I heard from somebody who does. He goes to this club in Plymouth where they hang out. This nightclub. I'd leave well alone if I were you, Mary. It'll just end in grief for you and you've had enough of that.'

Of course. He had been just using her, as she had half suspected, which seemed just now to be a particularly despicable thing to do. She would have it out with him, tell him what she thought of him and there was no way now he was having the necklace. She would give it back to Ms Bell before she would let him have it.

She did not cry until she had finished work and was walking past the harbour to the beach. The salty air was warm and moist on her cheeks, mingling a bit with the tears that just about spilled over. She had always controlled her crying.

She must have been stupid. As if a man like Dennis – if he'd been a proper sort of man that is – would have been interested in her, a worn-out woman with a past and no future. And what really got to her was that he'd had the nerve to criticize her place, turn his nose up a bit, when his place was nothing to write home about either and, on top of that, needed a good clean.

Geoff had never complained about the state of their little house, had loved it like she did, always told her she knew how to treat a house, was happy to go along with whatever she did to it.

She walked right across the shingle to the hard ridged sand at the water's edge, not caring that her shoes were getting damp.

Looking out to sea, to the distant waves and the silvery horizon, Mary closed her eyes so that she could feel the gentle warmth on her face and smell the wet sand. They had come here, years ago, when they were first married, walking here – great long walks – and then Lucy came and then the dog.

And now, there was just her and Lucy.

'Geoff Parker,' she whispered, looking at but not really seeing the sea, wondering whereabouts he was, 'I could kill you, you big daft beggar.'

After breakfast, James went back upstairs to call on Sophie. He couldn't let her disappear without saying goodbye, without wishing her luck, without a last little look at the baby. And he had no wish to interfere with the reunion that she would soon have with Roger.

She opened the door, fully dressed, suitcases sitting on the floor, Lily slumbering in her pram.

'Oh, it's you,' she said, her tone dead. 'I suppose you'd better come in. Do you want a coffee or something?'

'No, I've just had breakfast.' He smiled, awkward because she was. 'I just came to say goodbye. You'll be getting off quickly I expect when Roger gets here.'

She nodded. 'I haven't slept a wink, worrying.'

'You're bound to,' he said, trying to be sympathetic but feeling a bit irritated still.

'They are not having her back,' she said. 'Mark and this woman of his. Roger will have to tell them as much.'

He nodded. Poor old Roger. He could see no solution to this, no way out. The baby needed to be with her father and, as he saw it, if it meant going to the commune, then that was that. Somehow, Roger was going to have to persuade Sophie.

'I'm sure you'll sort things out amicably,' he said, regretting the stiff words as soon as they were said.

'Are you?' she laughed. 'What do you know about it? You have more confidence than me, and you don't even know my husband. He will take Mark's side, I just know it.'

'Well, perhaps . . .' James hesitated. 'Perhaps it's the right thing to do. Think about it, Sophie. They'll only be in Wales. It's not exactly the other side of the world, is it? You can visit. And Lily belongs to your son. You wouldn't stand much of a chance in a custody court. Amanda would know about that.'

She looked at him, studied him carefully as a child studies a grown-up, without embarrassment.

'Who said anything about custody?' she said at last.

'That's what it could come to,' he said softly, cursing himself for starting on this. He was supposed to be out of this one and here he was, still hanging in there, trying to come up with impossible solutions.

'You're right,' she said, face crumpling. 'Of course you are. We can visit. Every week. I'll still be able to see Lily often, won't I? She's not going to forget me.'

'That's right,' James said quickly. 'She'll look forward to seeing you, especially when she gets a bit older.'

'I'll still have some influence, won't I?'

'You will.'

'Thank you, James.' It was as if she was noticing him for the first time. 'Shame, isn't it? You and me? We weren't meant to be. Another time, we might have been. I know we only met a few days ago but it went well at first, didn't it? I did think . . .'

'Me, too,' he said. 'So much for holiday romances. Let's face it: we are both emotionally knackered, Sophie, and we wouldn't have stood much of a chance.'

'Like lost souls clinging together,' she said, reaching up to plant a kiss on his cheek. 'Thanks again. I hope you will be happy, James. Probably with Amanda.'

He wondered why she had said that, as he strode back down the corridor, feeling as if his duty was done.

Must be the female intuition thing, he decided.

After he was gone, Sophie woke the baby, picked her up and cuddled her. Lily was sleepy but very content, breathing softly and gently.

'My baby . . .' She held her close, brushing the bits of hair from Lily's forehead, smiling into her eyes. 'You're getting to be such a big girl. What am I going to do without you?'

She held the baby against her shoulder, holding and stroking the back of the little soft head and, without warning, that occasional stab of fear pierced her, causing her to flinch as if in physical pain.

What was it? What was wrong about this? A vague memory of being in church, of a little white coffin, of singing 'All things bright and beautiful' . . . and Mark crying . . . her son crying . . .

She would have to learn to deal with this. She would have to return the baby to Mark and that woman of his, Pussy Willow, or whatever her stupid name was, and hope that they would love her as much as she did.

Carrying the baby in her arms, she went over to the window, watching out for Roger. He had sounded quite frantic when he had phoned her last night.

'What the fuck are you playing at?' were his first words to her.

'I'm taking a break,' she told him sharply. 'What else?'

'Don't you know what's been going on?' he asked. 'Is that baby all right?'

'I thought you'd never ask,' she said. 'Of course she is. Lily is beautiful.'

'Oh Sophie, my darling . . .' He had sounded choked. 'What am I going to do with you?'

'I don't know why you're getting so het up,' she told him. 'I intended coming home in a few days. And since when have you cared a fig anyway?'

'I'm coming down to get you,' he said. 'Stay there. Don't bloody move, whatever you do.'

'I'll be here,' she said, puzzled by the anxiety in his voice. What was the matter with him? 'We'll have to use both cars to get to Wales,' she said. 'I've told James about it.'

'Who's he?'

'James Kendall. A nice man I met this week.'

'*What* did you tell him?'

'About Mark and Lily and you. About Lily having to go to the commune. I don't want to give her up, Roger, I don't think I can. You'll have to work things out with Mark. Talk to him for once. I can look after Lily and he and this Willow woman can come and see her whenever they like. Oh please, talk to him, Roger . . .'

She heard his sigh and then silence.

'You still there?' she asked sharply.

'Sure. I'll see you tomorrow.'

He had sounded stressed out. It would be work, and maybe the new woman was putting him through it now that the honeymoon period was over. Well, hard luck. He only had himself to blame.

There was Roger now. Sophie tapped on the window as she saw him getting out of the car, her heart – traitor that it was – leaping at the sight of him. Quickly, she popped Lily back in the pram. The baby, still tired, yawned and closed her eyes.

Endless sleep – that's all death was.

Another little flower in God's garden . . . wasn't that what they had put in the notice?

Sophie sat and stared at the baby as the memory she had nudged so far back in her mind began to nudge forward, dislodging like shifting sand now that she had seen Roger again.

Oh God, what had she done?

Fear gripped her like a vice. Made it difficult to breathe.

She would go down in a minute, when the panic had passed.

*

James had ordered mid-morning coffee and asked that it be brought to what he thought of as the cool corner off the reception area. Lemon and white striped sofas, glass-topped tables, white flowers. Sophie's Roger had a carrying voice and, quite clearly, James heard him as he enquired after Sophie, heard him ask for a message to be got through.

To James's consternation, he then headed his way, sitting opposite.

A waiter arrived with the coffee. James thanked him, tipped him and received a pleasant, 'Thank you, Mr Kendall' in return.

The man opposite looked up.

'So you are James Kendall?' he asked with a small smile, leaning forward and announcing himself as Roger Willis, Sophie's husband.

James nodded, uncomfortable. 'I met Sophie a few days ago,' he said, wondering how much of an explanation was needed, if any. 'We've had a few days out together.'

Roger nodded. He was older than James, older than he had imagined, with a good head of greying hair, worried eyes.

'How is she?' he asked. 'How does she seem to you? I would have gone up, but I thought it best we met here, with people present. Less likely to be a scene. I dread a scene.'

James told him she was all right, considering.

'Considering what?' Roger asked sharply.

James shrugged. 'The problem with the baby.'

Roger let out a huge sigh. 'What has she told you?'

'Look, I don't really think she meant . . .' James stopped, not knowing what to say. This was absolutely one hundred per cent none of his business. He had come to realize that he and Sophie were practically strangers.

'Do go on,' Roger said, finding difficulty with his smile. 'What has she been telling you? It matters.'

'Just that Lily . . .' James struggled then decided there was no further point to this hedging about. 'We, everybody in the hotel that is, we thought the baby was hers. She certainly never contradicted that impression and then she told me the whole story, about Lily being Mark's baby and everything. Having to give her up now. The commune.' He managed a small smile. 'That's going to be hard for her. She loves that baby.'

'I know. But you see—'

'Here she is,' James said, relieved as he saw Sophie and Lily approaching from the direction of the lift. She paused at the reception desk and, opposite him, Roger gave a little nervous cough as if composing himself.

'Thanks for helping her get through these last few days,' he said. 'She needed someone. You've no idea how worried I've been about her, how worried we've all been. She just shot off, you see, shortly after the funeral and we had no idea where she'd gone. She left a note telling us not to worry, but after all she's been through lately – well, it did cross my mind she might do something stupid. And then I got this phone call from some woman who'd met her down here and she said she had a baby with her and then the penny dropped. . . . Oh God, if you only knew.'

James gave a short sympathetic smile, waited.

At the desk, Sophie was messing about with keys, bills and so on, her bags now brought down by the porter and then, checkout completed, she stuffed receipts into her bag and turned, smiling as she saw Roger, leaning down to whisper to the baby, to point Roger's way.

James had an urgent need to melt into the background. No way was he going to be involved with this.

'Nice to have met you,' he said to Roger, clearly signalling his intention to leave. 'I hope all goes well. And give my . . . er, good wishes . . . to Sophie and Lily.'

'Thanks.' Roger took the proffered hand, clasped it firmly. 'Thanks again. And by the way . . .' – he leaned a little towards James, lowered his voice – 'it isn't Lily.'

Chapter Twenty-Two

ONCE Sophie and the baby were installed in Roger's car, James insisted on another word, shocked rigid by what Roger had said, checking on what Roger intended to do, before he let them out of his sight.

'Don't worry. The police have been notified. They're waiting just over there,' Roger told him grimly. 'And the baby's parents. They didn't want to come in here all guns blazing as it were. We had to be careful, you see, knowing her state of mind, that she didn't do anything stupid, harm the baby, although I don't believe she would ever have done that.'

'You're right. She would never have done that,' James said. 'Harmed herself perhaps.'

'Well, yes. Sophie couldn't cope, James. Not with losing Lily. She was convinced she made a mess of bringing up Mark, although I don't think we were any worse than a lot of parents are. Anyway, she thought of Lily as her baby and it was true that Mark wanted her back, just like she said, but then Lily died. Nobody to blame. Meningitis. Very quick. And she couldn't cope. I hope they'll be gentle with her.' He sighed, managed a smile. 'I've ditched the blonde, James, and I'll be looking after Sophie now. Time I did.'

Moved very nearly to tears himself, James waited, watching as Roger moved the car to just outside the hotel entrance, seeing a police car parking behind it and a great flurry as people exited it. Not able to bear to watch, he turned away.

'Hi, there. Isn't it a lovely morning?'

Amanda.

Emotions bubbling over as they were, he wanted nothing

more than to hold on to her. For her to hold him. But if they did
that, he might very well at this moment fall completely apart. He
had to get a grip. Fast.

'Has she checked out?' Amanda asked.

He would tell her later.

'Come with me,' he said briskly. 'I'm taking you to see something.'

'I'm sorry. I have other plans,' she said. 'I'm going to have my
hair done for the party tonight. Are you coming along?'

'Might as well. I have an invitation.' He glanced at her impatiently. 'What's the matter with your hair? It looks fine as it is.
Come on, we've got an appointment for ten thirty.'

'Where?' She frowned. 'This had better be important, James. If
I cancel my hair for nothing.'

He loved her when she was cross. Eyes flashing. Cheeks
flushed.

He loved her whatever.

Bea was taking a stroll along the promenade to try to clear a
quite dreadful headache, when she saw Mary at the water's
edge. Inappropriately clad, she looked as if she had wandered
there by mistake, standing getting her feet damp, staring out to
sea.

Sitting on a bench, wrapping a peach stole around her shoulders to keep out the worst of the sea breeze, Bea waited patiently,
hailing her as she slowly clambered back over the shingle.

'Oh, Ms Bell . . .' Mary hesitated, coming nearer. 'Nice
morning. A bit chilly by the water, but then it always is. Geoff
used to say the breeze off the water is just God breathing out. We
always went to church, me and Geoff; in fact I think I might start
going again,' she twittered on, eyes bright. 'After all, these
things are sent to try us, aren't they, and we mustn't start
blaming God for it. I'm going to ask the vicar if I can have a
memorial service. I know they're usually only for important
people, but I reckon that Geoff deserves one. He would like it.'

'Sit down, Mary,' Bea said, needing to shut her up.

'I shouldn't really. We're not supposed to fraternize with
guests outside the hotel, Mr Morrell says.'

'That dumb cheapskate. I don't care about him. Sit down. I

wish to talk to you further and you look exhausted, my dear.'

'You look a bit tired too, Ms Bell, if you don't mind me saying.'

'A headache. A humdinger.'

Mary looked at her anxiously. 'Have you taken anything? I might have some aspirins in my bag.'

'I've taken several already. They will kick in shortly. Now, you may tell me, Mary, what is the matter?'

'Matter? I don't know what you mean?'

Bea clicked her tongue. 'Come on, you have a very open face, Mary, and I know when you are lying to me. I repeat, what is the matter?'

'I don't like to bother you, talking about my troubles, not with you having a bad head and everything, but it's been such a shock this morning.' She sat down beside Bea, quite close, and fumbled in her bag. 'There! You'll have to have it back.'

It was the necklace, wrapped in tissue, stuffed in a small plastic supermarket bag.

'What's happened?'

'Well, it turns out . . .' Mary was having great difficulty. 'I don't know if you know about this, Ms Bell, about the way some men are. Geoff used to call them queer, but I don't think you're supposed to say that any more.'

'Gay, my dear. Appalling misuse of such a lovely word but there you are. Oscar had his own name for them. I think I see. You have discovered that your gentleman friend is gay?'

Mary nodded. 'I can't believe it. He took me to the pictures but then, looking back, I suppose I should have known. Geoff would have known, straight off, but then if he'd been around, I wouldn't have been bothering with Dennis. Would I? It was only because I was lonely.'

'I've been lonely for many years but not lonely enough for another man. Not after Oscar,' Bea said, thrusting the necklace Mary's way impatiently. 'Keep it. Or, if you would prefer, I can give you the money you would have got for it.'

'He cheated me,' Mary said quietly, 'didn't he, Ms Bell? He must have thought I was an easy touch. He must have laughed behind my back. Although, if I'm fair to him, he never promised me anything. It was me. I just assumed and I feel such a fool.'

'I sometimes wonder if we live on the same planet,' Bea said thoughtfully. 'Men and women I mean. It all boils down to sex. In whatever form. Now . . .' She reached for her handbag, a capacious one of dark brown leather, and slipped the necklace inside, withdrawing a chequebook and pen.

'I couldn't, Ms Bell,' Mary said, when she took it and read it. 'Goodness me, it's more than I know what to do with.'

'Take it as a tip,' Bea said casually. 'Set up that lovely daughter of yours in business. She listens very nicely when I go to the salon.'

'I didn't know you knew Lucy? But then she never talks much about her clients.'

'I know lots of people, Mary. I merely observe . . .' She glanced round. 'Did you know that Mr Morrell and that dark-haired young woman – well formed bosom – are together?'

'Fiona, you mean?'

'Yes. Fiona. Something's afoot there. Quite obvious to me, of course. He is after her body, she is after his money. It might well work out. Good reasons all round.'

Mary tucked the cheque away. 'Thank you,' she said. 'I don't know what to say.'

Bea touched her arm, before rising awkwardly, feeling her headache pound and pain, even more than before swallowing the wretched aspirins. She had suffered for months and all the other symptoms added up. It was just a matter of time now and sometimes she wished it would be sooner rather than later. As for consulting a doctor – well, she had no wish to have her own diagnosis confirmed and she managed to keep the pain under control, so that it was bearable.

She had things to do today. She was attending the VIP reception this evening and she was looking forward to it. She would rest now, so that she had energy left over. Champagne was promised and she adored champagne. Fireworks, she could do without.

On a practical level, she must make alternative arrangements about where to live, for she may be yet here on this earth for months to come. And she must alter her will, because it would be quite disastrous if that little pip-squeak Toby were now to inherit her fortune. A sad day when dear Mr Morrell senior retired. Gardening and so on . . . Bea sniffed. He ought to have

214

carried on here until he dropped. If he were still here, there would be none of this nonsense about refurbishment.

She swung through the glass doors into the foyer, heels tapping on the marbled floor, taking a moment for her eyes to adjust from the brightness outside.

'Bea . . . honeybee . . .'

She looked round, hearing Oscar's voice, that wonderful deep velvet voice, but there was nobody.

Feeling very odd, reactions suddenly very slow, she leaned against the glass table, happily breathing in the intoxicating scent of the fresh roses. Such a strong scent, it invaded her whole body, sweet and heavy. It took her back at once to the rose garden at the plantation house, the English rose garden she had painstakingly cultivated. The roses smelled strong like these after a shower of rain.

Closing her eyes, she could hear a mumble of voices, serene voices calling, Oscar's honey-glazed one predominant, whispering and calling her. He sounded young and strong. Thank God, he was not angry with her, not angry that he had had to wait so long for her. There was pain somewhere, everywhere yet nowhere, fading fast. She fluttered her eyes open one last time taking in the blur of the foyer but most of all seeing the roses, reaching out to touch them, before, very gracefully, her legs gave way and she folded into a peach-coloured heap, her hat slipping unkindly off her head as she did so to reveal the old scalp with its fuzz of white hair.

She was holding a pink rose.

'I think you should know, James,' Amanda told him, on the way to wherever it was they were going, 'I have been looking at cottages. I've made up my mind to move down here as soon as I can arrange things.'

'Big decision.'

'But the right one,' she went on firmly, sensing a disapproval, a humouring. 'I like the sound of a new start and Ellie will get used to my not being around.'

'So will Henry,' he said, crossing the boundary of a village and negotiating a bridge over a narrow river. 'This is it. This is as far as we go.'

215

The house at the edge of the village had a 'For Sale' board outside. It was bigger and grander than anything she had been looking at.

'What is this?' she said, turning to frown at him. 'Don't tell me you're househunting too?'

'I've bought it,' he said. 'Yesterday. Made an offer anyway, and it's been on the market for months so the owners are desperate to sell.'

'Bought it? Are you mad?'

A wild hope spun in her as she looked at him, a hope that perhaps after all he had come to his senses. This house was a family home, the sort with photogenic dogs sleeping in front of the hearth and smiling children, the kind of place that featured in those country house magazines, the ones she thumbed through at the hairdressers with the greatest irritation. It was absolutely bound to have an Aga.

He stepped out of the car and she followed him up the path. It was like a doll's house, double-fronted, pink-washed. Empty. It did not have roses round the door, just ivy, but there were plenty of unpruned roses in the garden and lots of wild grass. In an instant, she had the garden transformed in her mind, dismissing the fact that she had never so much as lifted a spade in her life.

James had a key and unlocked the door, ushered her inside.

'How can you live here?' Amanda asked him, once they were in a spacious hall, scarcely glancing at the rooms either side, the doors of which were open. As with empty houses, their voices echoed. 'What about Leeds? What about the business? Have you told Henry?'

'Stop panicking,' he told her calmly. 'It's going to be a while before I do move. I've got to sell my house first, remember, and I won't let him down. I need to get something started up here and Henry and Ellie need to reach a decision about their future, too. They might move down here. We can all of us relocate.'

For the first time, Amanda began to look properly at the interior, peering into the nearest room, only half listening to James's enthusiastic ideas for improvements. The views from the windows were of the village on one side, complete with old

216

squat stone church and village green, and rolling hills on the other.

'Like it?'

'I love it,' she said, smiling. 'Outside my price range, I suspect.'

'But not mine. Victoria left me money, and as well as the house back home, there'll be some left over for what I need to do to it.'

'I see . . .'

'Come and live here with me, Amanda,' he said, standing beside her and looking out of the window at the hills. 'Wouldn't it be great every morning to wake up and look out at this?'

'James . . . can you hear what you're saying? How can you ask me that after what's happened this week? It's been hell for me. You and Sophie all cosy. You've made it clear that I've been a nuisance to say the least.'

'Ssh. You don't think that. You can't really think that. Come here.' He reached for her, held her close, settled her against his chest. She could smell his nearness, feel the strength of his arms around her. It felt good. Right. 'Forget Sophie,' he said. 'She was a mistake. She is a very disturbed lady.'

'I thought so. There was something there that reminded me of Victoria, James. It worried me. Why should you have to go through it all again?'

'She's gone back to her husband.'

'And? What happened? You sound strange.'

'You'll find out soon enough,' he said.

Curious, madly curious, she let it go. What did it matter? He was holding her, not Sophie.

And at last, his whisper against her ear, a gentle brushing of his lips against her cheek, told her what she needed to know. That he loved her. He *loved* her.

Then, he was kissing her as she wanted to be kissed, as she had dreamed of being kissed by James. Sweet and urgent and promising so very much. Hands gently moving over her, cupping her bottom, pressing her nearer.

She kissed him back, holding back though because this was neither the time nor the place. He seemed to think that too, because he pushed her gently away, holding her there a moment, smiling at her, before letting her go and suggesting they see the rest of the house.

Quickly, they inspected the remainder, although she loved it already and it really wouldn't make any difference if the other rooms weren't up to scratch. Looking at it from the lane had already sold it for her.

'I'm glad you like it,' he said, waiting at the foot of the stairs, watching her every move, as she dallied a little before almost floating down towards him. She felt strangely light-headed as if slightly off balance. 'Victoria loved it too.'

Delight dissolved in an instant. Heavily, she thudded down the final couple of steps, heart pounding with annoyance.

'Victoria? For goodness' sake, James, don't tell me she's been here.'

'We came here on our honeymoon.'

'What? To this house?'

He nodded. 'It was a tea-room then. We had a cream tea.' He pointed to one of the living-rooms. 'In there. We sat by the window. A little round table with a pot of flowers on it and we had the best scones we tasted all week. We took a photograph just outside. I've still got it somewhere.'

'Victoria's been here,' she repeated, feeling she was a balloon pricked with a pin, her short-lived happiness simply oozing out.

If he was listening, he would have recognized the warning signs, but then so often he did not listen. She wandered into the kitchen which, complete with ancient rusty Aga, was in need of an urgent makeover. A bit like herself.

He followed her in, looking puzzled.

'What have I said?'

She let a whistle escape her pursed lips. 'Don't you ever think? I'm not living here. I'm not living anywhere that's got her stamp of approval on it. Sorry, but that's how I feel.'

'That's not how you feel,' he said, moving closer. 'That's not how it seemed a few minutes ago. I've not been kissed like that in a long time. In fact' – a smile hovered – 'I don't think I've ever been kissed quite like that.'

'That's as maybe,' she said, flustered by his look but standing her ground. 'But we have to face it, James, we can't get away from her, can we? She's always there, spoiling things for me.'

There was a silence, tight, uncomfortable.

218

'Oh, I see. In that case' – he dangled the house keys in his hand – 'Perhaps we'd better forget it. But *you* forget, Amanda' – for a moment, unusual for him, his eyes blazed with sudden anger – 'she was my wife. She was part of my life for a long time and I won't ever forget her. If you need some sort of promise from me about that, I can't give it. And, if you can't live with that, then that's just too bad.'

'I need time,' she said, knowing she was making too much of this, but unable to stop herself. It was as if Victoria was here with them, mocking her. . . .

'Time!' Exasperated, he pushed at his hair and sighed heavily. 'How much time? Haven't we wasted enough time already?'

'When I said I wanted a new start, I meant alone. My own place. It will be better that way.' She looked round. 'Sorry. I can't stop you if you decide to move, but I would prefer it if you'd just let me get on with it myself. I'll never shake myself free of you, will I, if you follow me around.'

'Shake yourself free?' There was a doubt now in his eyes which she made no effort to dispel. Serve him right for being so sure of her.

She wandered off outside, leaving him to lock up and follow, taking in the quiet stillness, knowing she would love it here, but hanged if she would settle for second best with him, hanged if she would live here with Victoria's ghost sitting there forever in the dining-room eating her eternal cream tea.

They spoke little on the return journey. She was not interested in whatever tangle he might have landed himself in. He had not yet signed anything so nothing was binding. It would cause annoyance if he backed out, nothing more.

'See you this evening,' she said curtly, when she escaped the car. 'And then I think it would be best if we went home and forgot all this.'

'Amanda.' He took hold of her arm. 'What do I have to do? What is it you want me to do?'

'I don't know,' she said miserably. 'I'm just mixed up, James. I'm insanely jealous of Victoria, and you don't have to tell me how ridiculous that is, but that's the way it is. I'd always be looking over my shoulder. Seeing her.'

'I love you,' he said.

'Do you? Or do you still love her?'

Back in the hotel, it had been utter pandemonium, the receptionist told Amanda, as she collected her room key.

'Ms Bell collapsed. Caused mayhem,' the receptionist went on. 'Right in front of the vase there.'

Amanda followed her gaze. Everything looked much the same as usual.

'You should have seen Mr Morrell. He was completely unfazed but then he is such an organizer. We had the ambulance here within minutes to take her away.'

'Is she all right?' Amanda asked, fearing the worst as she saw the look in the other woman's eyes.

'Sadly no. Dead before she hit the floor, we think.' She managed a shaky smile. 'Such a character, wasn't she? Swore like a drunken sailor. But she was so sweet and she would have hated all the fuss. Shame isn't it, to go like that, in full view. She was nearly bald too, bless her.' The receptionist blushed, lowered her voice. 'I got there first, so I put the hat back on before anyone saw. It didn't seem right.'

Amanda smiled. 'That was nice of you.'

As, chastened, she made her way towards the stairs, she was accosted by Mr Morrell himself.

'Dreadful news about our wonderful Ms Bell,' he murmured, almost sliding to a halt in front of her. 'Although, she was a very old lady of course, and her passing was swift and painless I'm sure.'

Amanda nodded. She needed time to collect her thoughts. She had not known Bea Bell at all, in the same time James had not known Sophie. It took years not days to know somebody. But, she had felt a fondness for all that. A lady of the old school. Mannered. Immensely loyal to her husband and that was no bad thing.

'Miss Lester.' Before her eyes, Mr Morrell appeared to grow several inches. 'May I say how grateful we are that your report was so complimentary? We are delighted to retain our place in *The Harlequin Guide* and let me assure you that we do not take our inclusion for granted. We will constantly strive to uphold our standards.'

Amanda hadn't a clue what he was talking about but she had neither the time nor inclination to find out. Let him think what he would.

'And I trust, madam, you will be at the champagne reception this evening?'

'Absolutely,' she told him. 'I wouldn't miss it for the world. I love fireworks.'

'Good.' He flashed a smile sideways at someone who had just entered. 'Excuse me, I see our celebrity has arrived.'

There was a sudden flurry of activity in the foyer, a number of people arriving and amongst them, a familiar face. Totally surprised, in the manner of most people when confronted by a television face, Amanda found herself gaping at the vision that was Sasha Rogers-Reed. Off duty. Skin-tight jeans, backless high-heeled mules, and just a white sports bra by the look of it. Surrounded by a couple of minders, who were pushing back photographers.

Smiling a little at the frenzy her arrival had stirred, Amanda escaped to her room, leaving them to it.

Chapter Twenty-Three

Chef was over his daily tantrum and in a relaxed mood when Toby dropped in. The kitchen staff were on full alert, but everything, Chef assured him, was under control.

Toby, tempted by the morsels, tasted one light as air pastry and nodded his approval. After the shamble of the morning, he hoped that the rest of the day would be filled with good news.

The weather was set clear.

Alice, hair piled up to give her yet more inches, was in her crisp decisive mood.

Sasha Rogers-Reed was looking fantastically good.

Local television had arrived and he was to record an interview presently. Sasha Rogers-Reed would, of course, steal his thunder but he did not mind. Publicity was publicity was publicity.

And, although it was much too soon to make enquiries – far too insensitive – he lived in hope that Beatrice Bell's fortune would come his way. All his problems solved at a stroke. Poor dear lady. But everyone had to go sometime and she had, in the event, managed to fit it in before things got altogether too hectic this evening. He was proud of the way they had dealt with the emergency, pleased that the emergency drill procedure he had initiated had been tried and tested.

Minimum fuss. Minimum disruption. Maximum discretion.

Mavis, horrified at Ms Bell's demise, had suggested they cancel the party as a mark of respect but he said no. Ms Bell was a trouper of the old school and she would have insisted the show go on. She was that sort. If she had still been alive, she would have been afloat on a sea of champagne bubbles by midnight, as shimmery as the fireworks themselves.

As for Fiona. . . .

He picked her up in the evening, his heart thumping as he caught the movement of her figure beneath a simple black gown. Glowing skin. Scarlet lipstick, silver fingernails and the most heavenly perfume.

'You are beautiful,' he told her, meaning it, helping her into the car.

'And you look very smart, Toby,' she said, giving a small satisfied nod. 'I shall be so proud to be beside you.'

Passing James's room on her way back from lunch, Amanda saw a man and woman with suitcases stepping inside. Furious that he should have gone without telling her, Amanda was tempted to forego the party and set off for home herself.

The big baby! If he did love her, as he said he did, then he had to work harder than that. All right, she knew she was being incredibly difficult about Victoria, but he couldn't just give up. Could he?

Later in the afternoon, bored out of her mind with party preparations such as painting her nails and other inconsequential things, she tried to ring Ellie.

'Oh, it's you,' Henry said, sounding as if he wished it wasn't.

'Hi. Everything OK?' she asked, hearing children's voices in the background. 'Are you managing without James?'

'No problems,' he said.

Amanda sighed. 'Henry, you sound a bundle of fun today. Is Ellie there?'

'She's not in,' Henry said.

'Where is she?'

'Shopping,' he said, sounding guilty and quite obviously lying. 'It wasn't important, was it? Are you still in Devon?'

'Yes, but James is on his way back. He's made an offer on a house down here. Did he tell you? Completely mad. He wanted me to go and live with him.'

'Did he?' Henry sounded very strange. 'That's good, isn't it? Why don't you?'

'Talk sense,' she said briskly. 'I admit I thought about moving down here but it's just not on. I have a good job in Leeds. And so do you, Henry. Don't let him uproot you and Ellie. All this,

Henry, after he spends all week chasing this other woman and leaving me stranded. If he thinks he can make it all right by proposing to me, he can think again.'

'Steady . . . has he proposed by the way?'

'Not exactly. Come and live with me, he said, which isn't quite the same.'

'I've proposed to Ellie,' he said quietly. 'Again. She said thanks but no thanks.'

'Ah well. You know Ellie.'

'Do you want to speak to Megan? She's tugging at my trousers.'

'Yes.' Amanda smiled into the phone as she heard the little voice. 'Hello, sweetheart. Is Daddy looking after you?'

'Mummy's gone to see Grandma Enid,' she said distinctly.

'What?' Amanda frowned, the phone whisked away at the other end before she could say goodbye to the little girl. 'What did Megan say?' she asked Henry. 'About Enid?'

'No idea,' he said. 'Wrong end of the stick I think. Look, Amanda, I'm going to have to go. Every bloody thing's boiling to buggery. Bye.'

She replaced the receiver. Taken aback.

Henry very rarely swore unless he was terribly terribly agitated about something.

Under the red dress, Amanda wore brand-new underwear in oyster silk. Tiny ridiculous knickers and a push-up bra. It made her laugh looking at it but it did the trick and the dress, shored up on its flimsy foundations, looked fabulous.

Although with James gone, the excitement was turned down a notch. Picking up a little clutch bag, she went downstairs, passing the room that had been occupied by Sophie and the baby. She wondered. James was being very secretive.

But she believed him when he said it was over. If only the other were over too, the one who mattered, the one who was still wrecking things for them. Trying to put it all aside just for this one evening, she made her way through the foyer towards The Clovelly Room.

Taking a glass of wine from a passing waiter, she backed herself into a corner for a minute so that she could take stock.

'Ah! The Inspector calls . . .' a voice at her side said.

'What?' She looked up. 'What do you mean?'

'Aren't you the lady inspector from *The Harlequin Guide*?' the man asked. He had a spiky haircut and very pale eyes. Not quite as awfully awful as the man in the flat below back home, but creepy enough for all that and just the sort of man she did not want to get landed with tonight.

'No, I am not,' she said testily. 'I know nothing about *The Harlequin Guide*. I'm a solicitor from Leeds, if you must know.'

'Honestly?' He peered at her, quite watery-eyed, and she stopped a shudder. 'You surprise me. Alice has got it into her head that you're the inspector.'

'Who are you?'

'Alice's guest,' he said with a grin, and she relaxed, knowing he belonged, thank goodness, to somebody else. 'She works here. Duty manager.'

'Right.'

They looked across the room to where Alice was otherwise engaged, organizing a line of very important people into a reception committee to greet the mayor and mayoress.

'Are you with somebody?' Alice's guest asked. 'You look like you're on your own. I'm only trying to cheer you up.'

'Thank you,' she said drily, as she thought of ways of getting rid of him. She wished she was more direct, like Ellie, but she found it difficult to be really rude to someone. Just thinking about how rude she had been to poor Ms Bell the other day now mortified her. She had apologized, an apology graciously accepted, but she still wished she could take that moment back.

The music was hotting up and the floor was filling up and before she knew it, she was dragged on to the floor by her not-to-be-dashed companion.

'Won't Alice mind?' she found herself asking, as she was clamped to him and they started a slow shuffle.

'God, no, she's my sister,' he said, and at that unwelcome news, Amanda felt her spirits deflate completely. How did she do it?

It was then, as they moved round the floor and she searched for an escape route that she saw James striding in.

At that moment, he looked like her knight in shining armour, or rather in a well-cut dinner suit.

It felt like a miracle.

It gave her the courage to dump Alice's guest and she caught up with James soon after.

'What are you doing here?' she asked in astonishment. 'Haven't you checked out?'

'No. I've moved rooms,' he said, taking her arm and steering her towards the buffet. 'Do you mind if I get something to eat? I've been driving for hours and I haven't had time to have a bite.'

'Where have you been?' she asked, watching as he helped himself from the gorgeous-looking buffet. 'You can't possibly have been home and back.'

'No.' With a slight smile, looking tired, he handed her a plate and she shrugged a couple of tiny morsels on to it before they retreated to a quieter spot. 'I met Ellie half way. She gave up her Saturday for me. Let me tell you, Amanda, that sister-in-law of yours is some woman.'

'You met Ellie half way?'

'Yes,' he said, patient with her as she struggled to understand. 'On the way, she picked up something for me. Something from Enid.'

'But they don't speak,' Amanda said, mystified. 'How did you get her to do that?'

'By telling her the truth. I told her I'd upset you, told her about the house, told her how you'd turned me down, wouldn't come to live with me and well, just everything really.'

'How could you?' she said, frowning. 'Honestly, you might as well announce it over the tannoy as tell Ellie. I don't know what I'm going to do with you, James.'

'Oh come on, this is supposed to be a grand gesture. Don't spoil it.' He started again. 'After all that happened this morning, I knew I had to do something to convince you. So, I rang Enid.'

'You rang Mother? But you hardly know her.'

'I do now. We spoke for ages. She likes me,' he told her with a sudden grin. 'She says it's about time you got yourself married.'

'She's been saying that for ages. You didn't say anything, I hope.'

A small fanfare heralding the arrival of the mayor and

mayoress interrupted them and they joined in the applause.

'She guessed,' he said. 'Although I was going to tell her anyway.'

'I shall never hear the last of it now,' Amanda said, anticipating a long interrogation when she got back.

'Did I tell you that you look stunning tonight?' James said.

'You've seen this dress before,' she said, ungracious she knew but powerless to stop, for he was being annoyingly enigmatic and she hated mysteries.

'You were wearing that dress at the dinner party at Henry's,' he said, surprising her by remembering. 'Just before we came here, the one with Jennifer, my friendly psychiatrist.'

'I know which one,' she said. 'As if I'd forget her in a hurry.'

He ignored her bad humour, smiled instead.

'I was pretty floored by it then, too. I think it was the first time I looked at you properly. The first time I saw you as a woman, Amanda.'

'Oh please, James,' she sighed. 'A lot's happened since then.'

'The fact is I've been denying my feelings for a very long time because, at first I was married to Victoria and then, afterwards, I thought you were just a friend. Can you forgive me?'

'I want to,' she said. 'I want to, James, but I need to be sure *you* are sure. I know it's silly but I want guarantees.'

'It's that job of yours,' he said. 'it makes you distrustful of relationships, doesn't it? Thinking of all that can go wrong.'

'Partly,' she admitted. 'I want to be like Henry and Ellie. Absolutely sure of each other.'

'Dance with me,' he said, leading her on to the floor as the music started up again. It was, Amanda realized with some surprise, the first time he had danced with her. Also, to her surprise, he was a better than average dancer.

'Henry can't dance.' she told him, for something to say, anything to control her feelings, as she was held in his arms. Sasha Rogers-Reed was already draped over her partner, the mischievously transparent side panel in her dress providing entertainment for the other men as she danced by.

'To hell with Henry,' James murmured, moving her closer and drawing in her scent appreciatively.

'What were you doing this afternoon?' she asked, trying to

keep sane, even as his hand trailed down the silky material of her dress to linger at her waist. 'You still haven't told me.'

'To answer that, I need to be alone with you,' he told her, whispering the words against her ear. 'Shall we abandon ship?'

'What do you mean?'

'Go up to my room.'

'But you've checked out of it,' she said stupidly.

'I told you I've changed rooms,' he explained with a smile. 'I'm in one of the promenade suites now.'

'A suite? How extravagant. Is it meant to win me over?' she asked, rebellion not quite dashed. 'I'm not easily swayed.'

'Aren't you? I've one or two other things in mind,' he said. 'Come on, let's go.'

Flushed, feeling that everybody knew, she allowed herself to be led, silently, up in the lift and taken to the suite with the four-poster bed in it, bottle of champagne and flowers, all the works.

'Well. . . ?' she said, deliberately not making any comment on the room's over abundance of luxury. 'Explain please.'

'I rang Enid,' he said. 'I told her who I was, although I have met her once or twice and luckily she remembered me. And' – he smiled a little – 'I didn't know what the hell to say, so I told her the truth. That I loved you and wanted to marry you but that, even though you loved me too, you seemed determined to make it very difficult.'

'Why did you ring her? I can't believe you rang Mother and told her that. You needn't ask her permission: I am thirty-three, James.'

'Her blessing then,' he said. 'I didn't want to do anything underhand, anything to upset her. I want to get on with Enid, it's important to me. We got chatting and I think I can safely say she knows all there is to know about me.' His voice took on a serious edge. 'I like her, Amanda, I think we'll get on.'

He reached into the pocket of his jacket, pulled out a tiny jewellery box. She knew what it was. It was Enid's ring, one she had inherited from Amanda's grandmother and Amanda had long admired it. Enid wore it often, particularly proud of it because it was part of her family, a cluster ring, the brilliant centre stone surrounded by ten smaller ones. An antique treasure. Priceless to Enid.

'She wants you to have it,' James said softly. 'She insisted when I told her I was going to ask you to marry me. "You must have a ring to give her", she said.'

Amanda took it from him, looked at it. 'Enid thinks the world of this ring,' she said. 'My mother ... my *real* mother ... her rings were never found,' she said, eyes blurring with tears for the woman she had never known, the mother whose life was ended somewhere over the Alps in a plane crash. 'She was never found either. Just ... you know ... bits.'

'I know, darling.' His voice was gentle, caring, and she loved him so much at this moment, her eyes telling him that, as she sniffed away the tears and managed a shaky smile. 'This is Enid's way of telling you what she can't say in words.'

She nodded, understanding.

'And you persuaded Ellie to go to see Enid and get this for you?' she asked. 'That can't have been easy.'

'No. But Ellie believes in us.'

'I know, but it was a pretty impressive thing to do. I hope Enid didn't give her a hard time.'

'An uneasy truce, I believe,' James said, taking her hand and slipping the ring on to her finger, looking at her all the while as he did so. 'You will marry me, won't you?'

'How can I refuse after all the trouble you've been to?'

'Then you will? Thank God for that. Enid will be so pleased.'

She laughed. 'And you, I hope. I love you. As if it matters what Enid thinks. What anyone thinks come to that.'

'It mattered to Victoria what people thought.'

'Oh James, don't let's talk about her tonight. Please.'

'One last time: let's just get this straight. I need to tell you this, Amanda, because if she was still alive, then we might still be together. . . .'

'I know. I wouldn't have split you up.'

'I know that, too. You're much too nice,' he said, his eyes warm with tenderness for her, 'but just look what we would have missed, you and me. This time, as of now, I have no doubts. I've never been so sure of anything in my life.'

She looked at the ring on her finger. 'It's lovely,' she said. 'And so are you,' she added, hugging him, too choked to say anything else.

'Champagne?' James lifted the bottle.

She looked out at the night sky, could hear the murmur of excited voices below.

The fireworks would be starting soon.

Downstairs, Sasha Rogers-Reed had launched prettily and competently into her speech and afterwards, the cake, the icing cinnamon dusted, was cut and tiny pieces distributed.

'I adore your hotel,' Sasha told Toby. 'Heaven.'

'Thank you. We do our best,' he said, disturbingly on a level with her breasts and not knowing quite where to look for decency's sake.

'And you may rest assured we will do you a good programme,' she said. 'A recommendation from us, Toby, and we will treble your bookings next year.'

'Thank you again,' he said, annoyed because she made him nervous and he hoped to God it didn't show.

'Time for you to give the signal, Mr Morrell. The fireworks people are ready,' Alice said, at his side. 'If I can drag you away from Miss Rogers-Reed. . . .'

The two women smiled broadly at each other.

If he didn't know Alice better, he suspected sarcasm.

He grabbed the microphone to announce that guests could now make their way on to the terrace where the champagne was being served, hovering afterwards in The Clovelly Room to make sure people had been herded out and there were no stragglers left behind.

Timing was crucial.

He noticed Fiona standing alone by the window, waiting for him, smiling as she saw him. Last night, during one of his usual tangle of dreams, he had dreamed of her. And she now looked so dreamy and wonderful, her plain dress so much sexier than Sasha Rogers-Reed's split-asunder statement. Up close, Sasha was a big disappointment. She didn't smile so much off camera, and up close, she had ropey skin and there was a hard edge to that smile and calculation in those ice-blue eyes. He had had enough of women like her to last a lifetime.

'Toby – they're starting,' Fiona told him as he drew near. 'The fireworks . . .'

The crowd, in the mood, chanted the countdown.

Eight, seven, six, five, four, three, two, one. . . .

As the church clock began its chimes, the sky lit up as the first flurry of fireworks shot and whooshed their way upwards. A moment's pause and then an explosion of myriads of white and silver twinkles of light failing like snowflakes to be carried away out to sea by the night air.

'Look.' Fiona, holding her glass of champagne, was like a little girl, quite thrilled by it all, pointing out this and that as the display gained spectacular momentum. Increasingly childish shrieks came from the assembled distinguished gathering as the colours changed from silver to blue to pink to gold, shimmering wildly down on them, as if the very stars were losing their grip on the heavens. 'Oh look, isn't it beautiful?' Fiona exclaimed, eyes shining, too. 'Everyone's saying how wonderful it all is. You're so clever, Toby, to have organized all this.'

'Marry me,' he said, before he could stop himself, heady as he was with success, catching her arm and looking into her eyes. 'I love you, Fiona. I know we've not known each other long,' he gabbled on, 'not in that sense. But I believe in fate and we have to grab happiness while we can.'

'Marry you?' She disentangled herself from his touch. 'Did you just ask me to marry you?'

'Yes.' Outside, green jewels dangled a moment in mid space then flooded the sky. Toby held his breath, regretting his impulse. Too soon. Too bloody soon. Cocked up again.

'Toby, it's very sweet of you . . .' she said after a pause. 'And I'm terribly flattered . . .'

He downed his champagne. Wait for it.

'Forget I mentioned it,' he said, intending to lead her out, so that they could mingle. More mingling was called for.

'Toby?'

'It's all right,' he said. 'Don't bother with excuses. I'll get over it.'

'You don't understand,' she said with a smile. 'You took me totally by surprise. I never thought in a million years that you would ask me. And you might give me a minute to think about it, but, of course, the answer is yes. Yes please.'

Temporarily out of sight of the crowd, she kissed him then,

properly, fitting snugly against him, smaller than he was, smelling of perfume with a touch of fresh mint, moulding herself to him, giving a little delighted murmur. She then patted his chest and straightened his tie and told him to go and chat to people. She would powder her nose and be with him presently.

The display was reaching a climax, the air sweet with smoke and heat of a thousand miniature explosions. Toby, newly engaged, drifted importantly out and, in a complete daze of happiness, started to circulate.

The light from the fireworks danced round the room, although they were far too busy making up for lost time and missed most of it.

The red dress lay in a disgracefully careless heap somewhere *en route* to the shower.

They shared that, then the bed, and afterwards yet more champagne.

And they never once mentioned Victoria.

Epilogue

TOBY Morrell walked through the foyer of The New Grand. He was wearing a light grey suit and a blue shirt. The silk tie, a little more garish than he would normally choose, was a gift from his bride-to-be.

He tweaked the yellow roses in the silver goblet, avoiding looking down at the floor where, a week ago, Bea Bell had expired. His patience was rewarded and the hot news from her solicitor was that her entire estate was to come to them. In her latter years, with no family to call her own, she had felt the hotel to be her home, the staff her family, Mr Morrell her dear friend and confidant.

Toby was not going to argue with that. He and Fiona had attended the funeral, Fiona wearing a new black suit, the engagement ring, a pea-sized diamond, sparkling on her finger. Mary Parker was also there with a couple of the receptionists, all looking genuinely upset. The vicar spoke movingly of Bea's love of Virginia and of her late beloved husband Oscar. It was then, as Toby scanned the faces in church, that he realized that perhaps after all they had been family to her.

They would have to do something in her memory. A rose garden maybe, although Alice suggested a small drinks bar off the library – The Bell Bar – a very private place to get seriously sozzled.

Toby sighed. He would come to a decision on that shortly. In the meantime, he had to deal with the small matter of finding a new secretary, as Mavis had resigned in a haughty huff that everything had gone so well – even without a list – and miffed beyond belief that he was to marry Fiona.

The sun blazed a trail across the foyer and, in the very highest of spirits, he almost danced his way to the reception desk, where the girls were eyeing him closely. He took a moment to have a brief word, giving them one of his warm employer-friendly smiles. When Fiona returned here, it would be as his bride and not before. Her wish. She had nothing to say to the reception staff.

She was refusing to move in with him, quite rightly, until they were married. In fact, she was refusing everything until then, except teenage-type kisses. He wasn't sure he could last out for another three months dreaming about her the whole time. No time for a honeymoon, but that was the price they had to pay for being in the business. And she had mentioned something about St Moritz later in the year. Skiing and shopping.

Thank God, the sun was out again. The foyer took on such a splendid look when the sun glinted through. He spotted today's duty manager doing his bit greeting new arrivals. The boy hovering ready to carry bags. The girls ready to welcome them, brightly lipsticked and pleasantly smiling. Everything sparkling.

For the moment, just this moment, everything was perfect.

Welcome indeed to The New Grand.

Toby stood silently off to one side, his sweeping glance taking in the whole scene.

Then, turning on his heels, he walked swiftly out.